Like the royals for whom t
      family have enemies and rivals of their own…

As a soldier for the Crown, Dominic is charged with locating the Young Pretender to the British throne so he can be tried as a traitor. But his mission is altered when he meets Claudia Shaw, an intriguing young woman who has inherited a house of ill repute. In an effort to protect Claudia from her own recklessness, Dominic finds himself allowing the Pretender to slip away…

Claudia is one of the Emperors of London, but her family despairs of her impetuous behavior. And try as he might, the disciplined Dominic cannot quite curb her excesses. In fact, she soon drags him into her adventures—and toward a passion neither can resist. But when a deadly secret comes to light that puts their lives, and their love, at risk, Claudia won't allow Dominic to sacrifice himself. She is determined to have him—even if it means getting the Young Pretender out of the way herself.

"Lynne Connolly writes Georgian romances with a deft touch. Her characters amuse, entertain and reach into your heart."
—Desiree Holt

Books by Lynne Connolly

Emperors of London
Temptation Has Green Eyes
Danger Wears White
Reckless In Pink

Published by Kensington Publishing Corporation

Reckless In Pink

An Emperors of London Novel

Lynne Connolly

LYRICAL PRESS
Kensington Publishing Corp.
www.kensingtonbooks.com

Lyrical Press books are published by
Kensington Publishing Corp. 119 West 40th Street New York, NY 10018

All Kensington titles, imprints, and distributed lines are available at special
quantity discounts for bulk purchases for sales promotion, premiums, fund-
raising, and educational or institutional use.

To the extent that the image or images on the cover of this book depict a
person or persons, such person or persons are merely models, and are not
intended to portray any character or characters featured in the book.

Special book excerpts or customized printings can also be created to fit
specific needs. For details, write or phone the office of the Kensington
Special Sales Manager:
Kensington Publishing Corp.
119 West 40th Street
New York, NY 10018
Attn. Special Sales Department. Phone: 1-800-221-2647.

First Electronic Edition: December 2015
eISBN-13: 978-1-61650-572-1
eISBN-10: 1-61650-572-9

First Print Edition: December 2015
ISBN-13: 978-1-61650-596-7
ISBN-10: 1-61650-596-6

Printed in the United States of America

Chapter 1

"Are you sure you do not wish to return, Major?" General Court asked. "Now your family business is concluded, I would have welcomed you back. Your conduct was exemplary on the Continent."

Dominic shook his head. "I would hardly say my family business is concluded. I am the only male left to continue the line."

The general brightened, his ruddy face glowing. "Then once you beget an heir or two, we may expect you back?"

"Once I marry, perhaps." Dominic could see that in his future—marrying a suitable woman, begetting an heir, and then leaving her in peace to continue his career.

The general harrumphed. "Then hurry up and do it. We need experienced officers like you."

Dominic recalled a number of times when his superior officers had intimated otherwise. He glanced around the splendidly appointed room, with its display of silver on the sideboard and fine spirits in the glittering crystal decanters. If he didn't know better, he'd assume the General lived in this luxury all the time. However, he'd seen the man thigh-deep in mud, bellowing instructions to his men, refusing to leave the field until they were all safe.

He was no longer one of the general's officers and hadn't been so for six months. Ever since his parents had begged him to come home and find a wife. He'd done the first part but had yet to achieve the second.

He blamed himself. His two male cousins had been the heirs to the title, after him. Now they had died, and he was the only hope for his house.

Restlessly, he got to his feet. "If that's all, General…"

"No. Sit down."

Sometimes the man forgot that Dominic was no longer under his command. He let it pass and sat back down on the hard wooden chair provided for visitors. The full skirts of his woolen coat padded his arse somewhat, but he'd known worse hardships than this. Not recently, though. "May I be of further service, sir?"

The General gave him a hard stare before picking up a piece of paper and tossing across the desk. "Take a look at that. Tell me what you see."

One side was travel-stained, obviously a letter, with a seal hanging off one side. The address was a house in the City, Spitalfields to be exact. He turned it over and read.

"This is from Charles Stuart? The Pretender?"

"It is. Rallying his supporters in England."

"Have you visited the address?"

The General grunted his assent. "I sent someone last week pretending to be a seller of pots and pans. All this damned sneaking about makes me itch. Army intelligence is one thing, but this cloak and dagger stuff isn't what a gentleman should occupy himself with."

If the world were well organized and everybody told the truth, a military man might prefer to see the enemy and engage with him rather than run around lying. However, the man's professed bluster hid a devious and intelligent mind, so while the General's speech amused Dominic, it did not fool him. A gentleman didn't skulk around and spy, but somebody had to.

"Nobody seemed suspicious," the general continued. "It was the premises of a silk weaver and his family. The man did business from the house, but he had no reason to side with the Stuarts. His family were Huguenots, and they believe in pursuing the Protestant cause."

"Stuart converted to the Anglican church a few years ago," Dominic felt obliged to point out.

The General nodded. "For all the good it did him." He finished the glass of port he'd poured for himself when Dominic had refused refreshment. "The house is owned by the Duke of Northwich."

Dominic sucked in a breath. The Duke, the head of the Dankworth family, had long been a thorn in the side of the Crown. Long-time supporters of the Stuarts, the Dankworths had nevertheless evaded serious charges. Dominic reminded himself frequently that intrigue was none of his business, anymore. However, he did find himself wondering what the devious family was up to now.

"Why should that be a surprise?" He took another look at the letter. It referred to mysterious events, full of phrases like "our business" and "the parcel." Nothing new.

"The parcel referred to in that letter is a person. The Young Pretender, no less. Are you interested now?"

Sunlight streamed in through the dusty windows across the desk. The air was redolent with lavender and spices used by the housekeeping staff no doubt to clean and add fragrance to the air.

The world was normal and continued the same way, except that it had shifted a little to one side. Dominic began to understand the general's intent, and he didn't like it. "Why would I be interested?" he said smoothly. He put the letter down gently. He had affairs of his own to deal with, much less government concerns.

"We would like you to look into the matter. The government would be extremely grateful to you."

"I'm sure they would." Because he had seen the Stuart pretender when he was still a serving officer, so he would know him again. Dominic hadn't been wearing his uniform at the time and had choked down his distaste of subterfuge long enough to discover what his superior had wanted to know. He obeyed orders, but he hated the work. Lying stuck in his throat. He had particular reason to dislike it.

The General indicated a neat pile of papers stacked on the desk. "You are in a position to help us now."

Dominic had had enough. He had better things to do than listen to the general sidle around the subject. "What do you want?"

None of his London acquaintances would have recognized the sharp tones, the decisiveness, but they hadn't known him in the army. He hadn't served in a fashionable regiment, nor had the public honors he'd received been any more remarkable than many others. When he returned to London, he became someone else. Not the officer, but the aristocrat and the man of fashion.

The General didn't appear surprised at Dominic's incisive tones, but then he was better acquainted with Dominic the officer. "I want you to locate him. It shouldn't be beyond your capabilities. This time we have had enough of his dancing around London. We want Stuart in custody, and if necessary we will bring him to trial."

Dominic sucked in a harsh breath. "If you will forgive me for saying so General, that is a mistake. He is flaunting himself in order to get arrested. It's just what he wants."

"If he had heirs, if his brother weren't a Cardinal in the Catholic Church, we might agree with you." The back of the General's comfortable leather padded chair creaked alarmingly when he leaned back. Since he'd returned to London, he'd gained quite a lot of weight. The sedentary life obviously didn't suit him. "However, the hope of the Stuart Cause rests on him. We would prefer to put an end to that. It works both ways, St. Just. The line effectively ends with him, so if we take him, we have the family."

That made alarming sense. But a trial would encourage the kind of support the country could well do without at a time like this. With an aging king and a young and inexperienced heir in thrall to an unpopular advisor, the time was ripe to tip the scales back in the Stuart family's favor, if a person had a mind to do it. "If I see him, I'll inform you. Will that do?"

The General regarded him in silence for a full minute. Dominic knew better than to interrupt him, and he hoped General Court knew better than to press him further. Both men understood what that meant. Dominic would go hunting, and he'd find his prey, but if anyone asked, he'd never met Stuart, not even heard of him.

Eventually, the man nodded. "Very well. I appreciate your help."

"I hope you do." He would not forget the favor. Dominic would make sure of it.

Dominic left the room. He hurried down the stairs, more than glad to put the dust of this building behind him.

Someone calling his name interrupted him. "St. Just!"

Damnation. Pinning an affable smile to his face, he turned, letting the skirts of his coat swing gently around him. "Why, Malton, what a pleasant surprise! Do you come here on a visit, or business?"

Lord Malton grimaced. "Business, but nothing vital, as it transpires. I was merely surprised to see you."

He waved carelessly in the direction of the stairs, taking care to keep the movement elegant. "A social call. A man I used to serve under has returned to London. Paying my respects, don't you know."

"Ah." To Dominic's relief, Malton appeared to accept his explanation. His visit here had become annoyingly clandestine. "Is your business concluded?"

Not at all. "Completely." Dominic offered a smile and paused at the stand by the door to collect his sword. This set of government offices didn't even allow gentlemen to carry the mostly decorative swords. Dominic's was more than decorative, made of fine flexible Spanish steel. "Are you heading into town?"

"To Bond Street. I have to collect my sisters from the drapers'."

Dominic had planned to walk to St. James's, but abruptly he changed his plans. "Your sisters are up from the country?" Malton belonged to a large and influential family. Known as 'The Emperors of London,' they were a force to be reckoned with. Especially with regards to the Dankworths, supporters of the Pretenders, young and old. The family feud was so old nobody recalled its origins. It had renewed itself in force when the Dankworths and the Emperors took opposite sides in the Jacobite conflict. The Emperors could prove useful to him in his current quest.

Dominic was acutely aware of his lack of supporters. In the army he'd had a complete network of allies. Here, if he were found on the wrong side, he had no doubt the authorities would arrest him and cart him off to prison. If they needed a scapegoat, he provided the perfect subject. Most definitely he needed friends. Someone who knew more about this civilian battle.

However, despite Malton's cordial greeting, he and Dominic were only socially acquainted. Dominic sheathed his sword and clapped his hat on his head, then glanced into the mirror by the desk to adjust it to his satisfaction. Malton dressed soberly and behaved responsibly. Dominic did what he liked. Released from army discipline, he'd enjoyed spreading his wings once he got to town. As the heir to a wealthy and influential title, he was in great demand.

He had no doubt that was why Malton had invited him to meet his sisters. Dominic was not a philanderer, more a card player and a man who enjoyed all forms of entertainment, respectable and decidedly otherwise. However, he never toyed with society ladies. They might expect more than he was prepared to give them.

Malton and Dominic walked out of the offices into glorious sunshine. Dominic glanced up. "A pretty day, is it not?"

Malton nodded curtly. "Indeed, sir. Spring is well advanced, although last month it seemed as if it would never arrive."

They walked down Horse Guards in the direction of Bond Street. Up St. James's Street, with its burgeoning clubs, and past the palace, where the Royal Standard fluttering from the gatehouse proclaimed the King was in residence. A rare event, since his majesty preferred the more modest comforts Kensington Palace had to offer.

Dominic remarked as such to Malton and received a nod in return.

"I believe his majesty wished to greet the Ambassador of France. He'll scuttle back to Kensington as soon as he can." Malton smiled. "I do not begrudge him his comforts. The longer we can keep him healthy the better, would you not agree?"

Sounding him out, no doubt. "Indeed." Dominic had no hesitation in concurring. "It gives the Prince of Wales more time to mature into his role. I fear a king still in his minority could cause problems for the government."

"He is a promising child, but I fear far too ready to listen to his mother's favorite." Malton hesitated delicately before the last word, intimating that the Princess of Wales and Lord Bute were more than royal patron and favorite. Most in London considered them lovers.

A political situation that would be coped with, unlike the advent of a different branch of the royal house. "I don't pretend to understand politics." Dominic waved his handkerchief to illustrate his point. A fine lace-edged piece of linen, it would probably be ruined if he put it to any practical use. "It is all far beyond me."

"I'm sure you would cope." Malton sounded so smug that Dominic spared him a glance. No, he wasn't mistaken. Clearly, Malton considered Dominic as the intellectual half-wit he preferred people to think him. A man more interested in fashion and gossip than anything serious. The pose was beginning to pall, but it had taken a year and a half for it to do so. It might prove useful for a little while longer. When people underestimated him, they were more likely to talk freely in his presence. Consequently he heard much more of the gossip before others did.

"I find other matters more interesting," he said, lengthening his vowels to a fashionable drawl. "Surely gossip about the Princess of Wales and her lover is old news. May we discuss Elizabeth Chudleigh's latest exploit?"

They did, Malton discussing the subject easily enough, until they reached Bond Street. At this time of day, the fashionable and the wealthy thronged the place, from the boxing saloon at the end to the florist's at the other. While Dominic would have preferred the fencing-master's studio, Malton took him straight past it to the drapers' shop two doors down.

The curved bay window with its bull's-eye glass panes revealed swaths of fabric, a few toys strewn across it. His gaze met fans, handkerchiefs, and a particularly pretty necessaire, the separate elements of pen, paper, scissors, spread for the admiration of the customer. Dominic spared it a glance on his way inside.

Three ladies sat at the broad counter to the left of the door. Another counter stood completely opposite, and at the end, bales of fabric were stacked.

Dominic groped for the ribbon tied at his waist and lifted the quizzing glass he kept at the end of it. Surely he was seeing things. "You said sisters," he murmured. "You did not say twins."

Or beauties, for that matter.

"I omitted that part, didn't I?"

If he didn't know better, Dominic would have detected laughter in Malton's voice. So far his acquaintance with the man hadn't revealed a sense of humor. Despite Malton's enjoyment of his surprise, Dominic considered himself a winner here.

The two young ladies seated in chairs before the counter were slender of figure. However, their breasts swelled invitingly above their bodices, and they possessed clear-complexions. Both were possessed of heavenly blue eyes. They had lively features, although one bore an air of serenity, and her gown was a little more subdued than her sister's.

The other, the one with the slight smile curling her lips, intrigued him. Something about this one drew him. She wore pink, which should not have suited her with that red-gold hair, but it did, enhancing her slender loveliness. Dominic would not call either lady a beauty, not in the accepted society sense, but they were lovely enough to create a sensation if they wished to. Their chins were slightly too pointed, their noses too large. He liked them; they added character.

While Malton performed the introductions, she watched him. He only looked away when his bow required it, and then glanced up and found her challenging gaze fixed on his. He flicked her a hard stare, before he recalled himself and allowed his lids to droop over his eyes in his usual society manner.

Her eyes widened. "I did not meet you in town last year, Lord St. Just. I would have thought you very hard to miss."

She scanned his red coat, matching waistcoat, and spotless white breeches. Gold buckles adorned his shoes, with the tiniest of diamonds and rubies, and his sword hilt was encrusted with jewels and engraving. The fact that good Spanish steel was sheathed beneath may have passed her scrutiny.

Showing no sign of insult, Dominic took her careful observation as a compliment. He flourished his hat, which he'd taken off when performing his bow. "You are too kind, Lady Claudia."

She made a sound in the back of her throat that could have been the start of a derisive snort. Except for that tiny sound, Dominic would never have known she was laughing at him from her gracious smile and nod. She'd was probably been taught from the cradle to hide her true emotions. "My lord, it would be difficult to miss such magnificence."

"The color is rather engrained in me, I fear." He straightened up. He, too, could don a public mask. After all, what was his whole appearance but a mask? "I was until recently taking the King's shilling."

Gratification swept through him in a warm tide when her eyes widened. He'd won an open, startled reaction from her, enough to make him want to see more. He wanted to get to know her better.

She was the first woman to affect him in this way since he returned to England.

"You were a soldier?"

"If your brother had introduced us formally, he'd have mentioned that I am Major Viscount St. Just." Ignoring Malton's muttered apology, he concentrated on her. "I am home now because my two cousins sadly perished last year, leaving me the sole hope of my house."

"The only male heir," she murmured. "Now you come to mention it, I do recall something about that. I beg your pardon, I should have paid more attention, and I am indeed sorry for your loss."

He hadn't meant to make her feel guilty. "I barely knew my cousins, I regret to say. I had a lot to arrange when I came home, so I decided not to come to town last season. My parents remain in the country."

Leaving him to hunt down a bride, something he resented. He hadn't meant to marry for years yet, and he was doing his best to deter them, but it was proving difficult. Society understood the value of the estate he stood to inherit and the necessity of marrying and begetting.

Once he'd done that, he could consider returning to the life he loved, in the army.

For the present, he had a delicious distraction. He could only consider her as such. Someone of her temperament would probably not agree to remain quietly in the country while he went back to war. He needed someone sweet, docile, and happy to rusticate. Not this handful of trouble. Even now her eyes danced with mischief.

Now she'd softened a little toward him, he saw that more clearly. "Were you in one of those pretty regiments, the ones that dance attendance on court and curry favor with foreign dignitaries?" she asked. "You would be a credit to them."

He almost laughed, but contrived to keep a straight face. "No." He would give her no guidance. Let her discover for herself. "Discussing the past can be tedious, can it not?" He gestured to the pretty display on the counter. "Have you made your decisions, or may I assist you in any way? My mother tells me I have an excellent eye for color."

The laughter disappeared, and her mouth flattened. Disappointment? Perhaps so. Perhaps he should not think of getting to know her at all. "Except for the green. I dislike it. It's so predictable to put a red-haired woman in green, don't you think?"

He picked up the fabric, a delicate silk in a shade of green he privately labelled puke-colored. "It slips through the fingers nicely."

As her hair would, did she ever let him near it. The notion came to his mind unbidden, as did the notion of stroking her skin to discover if it was as satiny as it looked.

A fine sheen smoothed over it when the sun came out from the clouds and streamed through the broad shop windows. It turned her hair into a ball of fire, and then the light went, disappeared behind its cover.

The shock numbed him. He dropped the fabric and reached out, touched her arm between her elbow-ruffles and her wrist.

She gasped and drew her arm back. Startled, wide eyes met his, but he said nothing. Just stared. That contact had changed everything for him, although if anyone had asked him what "everything" meant, he couldn't have answered.

"St. Just, are you feeling well?"

Malton's gentle query brought him back from wherever he'd gone.

With a short laugh, he shook his head to clear it of the odd emotion he had difficulty describing, even to himself. Exhilaration and a sense of rightness, of things falling into place was the nearest he got to it. Like at the end of a long military campaign.

"I'm sorry, a moment's inattention. That is all." He recalled the topic of conversation. "I think, madam, there are different shades of green. While I have no doubt you would appear charming in apple green or the green of beech leaves in springtime, this green is definitely to be avoided."

"Hmm." She touched the spot he had lately been, letting the material slip through her fingers.

Dominic braced himself against a threatened shudder. What if she touched him with such delicacy? A shiver racked him. He froze his features, fighting for control.

"I believe you are right, sir," she said softly. "This fabric is not for me."

She flipped the stuff back so it folded in on itself, revealing the ivory beneath. "Nor this one. Sallow skin and ivory do not make a good combination."

"Not sallow. Creamy," he said. Her skin reminded him of nothing more than a bowl of cream fresh from the dairy, whipped for a special dish, ready to enrobe and enrich a dish of fresh strawberries. It would taste best taken from her skin.

He took a hasty step back. This highborn lady was not one he should be dallying with. How could he let himself think such a dangerous notion?

Rebuking himself for a fool, he picked up a piece of fabric at random. The shopkeeper had created a brilliant display by tossing rolls of expensive fabric across the counter, so it lay in gorgeous disarray. The piece in his hand had cherry-red stripes. He pushed it aside and found the only one on the display that he considered worthy of her. "A green like this one." This was stiffer taffeta, a rich green that would flatter her, the color of mint leaves. It held a cool quality that would counter her fieriness.

"Why you are right. I hadn't considered this one." The minx gently removed the taffeta from his grasp and cradled it against her cheek. "It is a little rough."

He suppressed a sigh of longing, when he considered how soft that cheek would be.

She knew it, too. Her eyes flashed wickedly as she blatantly checked his response to her flirting.

He rallied. "Certainly not to be worn next to the skin, for sure," he agreed. "Though it would make a wonderful sacque. It would drape extraordinarily well."

To his relief, he rediscovered his society mask. The idea of her in that puke-green silk made him bilious. "I would love to make a gift of it to you, but I fear you would take such a personal token amiss."

One side of her mouth quirked up, and a dimple appeared. "Indeed I would not, sir. As you said, it would come nowhere near my skin."

The vixen handed the stuff to the avidly listening shopkeeper. "I'll take this. Send it to my mantua-maker, if you please. Madame Cerisot. Send the bill to Viscount St. Just. I beg your pardon. Send the account to Major Viscount St. Just."

He smiled. She was not trapping him into any more flirtation. From now on, he would do his best to avoid her until he'd thoroughly analyzed the odd feelings she evoked in him. The stirrings of lust, certainly, but anyone looking at these two would consider that. No, the more tender, gentle emotion with which he was entirely unfamiliar. Except with his parents, and that was an entirely different case. No similarities at all.

Chapter 2

This early in the morning very few people of fashion ventured out into Hyde Park, so Claudia considered herself safe for half an hour to follow her inclinations. At the moment, that included riding properly, not the sedate walk allowed by society.

The rough track extended before her like a challenge, and only one or two people were cantering along it. The morning mist, like steam from a kettle, drifted around the bare earth and the grass bordering it. Trees spread their sheltering boughs at a short distance. Behind her lay houses and civilization. In front, who knew?

Claudia walked her horse, urged him to trot, and then to canter. The breeze drifted past, ruffling her hair, even though she'd taken care to pin it firmly to her head, and her hat on top of that.

As she passed a man riding on a fine chestnut, she kicked her mount into a gallop and shrieked.

Such delight, to let herself go for just a few minutes! Here in town she had to think every moment of every day, work out what she should do and why, and behave like a proper lady.

Hooves thundered behind her in a pounding gallop. A race! Her heart quickened and she urged her horse faster, leaning over his neck to gain an extra spurt of speed.

Her hat flew off, but apart from a shot of annoyance she ignored it. The breeze accelerated to a wind, and some of her hairpins went, too. She shouted with laughter, glanced to the side, and then back again.

Grim determination delineated the features of the man galloping by her side. He returned her glance.

After a moment, she recognized him. He looked nothing like the exquisite she'd met in the company of her brother at the draper's.

This man wore plain riding-dress and rode with the skill of someone born in the saddle. No polite society smile graced his grim features. The hooded eyes and lazy regard were nowhere in evidence. In that one glance his sharp, fierce glare had almost stunned her.

Enough to make her lose her concentration for the second it took her horse to stumble. She had to stop.

Regaining her seat, she pulled on the reins, shortening them as her mount slowed his pace.

Lord St. Just did the unforgiveable. He rode close and tried to seize the reins. "What are you doing?" she demanded, snatching them out of the way.

"Dismount," he ordered. That was what it was—an order.

Although she usually responded badly to commands, Claudia obeyed this one. If she did not, who could tell what he would do? She didn't know him well enough to take the risk of defying him. If he told her brother what he'd just witnessed, Marcus could well make her early morning gallops impossible.

Sighing in exaggerated annoyance, she drew her horse to a halt by a couple of large elm trees. Before she could slide out of the saddle, he was off his horse and had his hands around her waist. His firm grasp and the way he held her as if she weighed nothing sent exhilaration flying through her. He settled her gently on the ground.

Then his annoyed expression brought her back to earth. "What were you thinking? I saw you and heard you cry for help."

Even his voice sounded sharper, harder. She preferred this no-nonsense viscount to the man of fashion she'd met yesterday. However, she couldn't allow him to get away with a blatant untruth. "I was shouting with pleasure, not crying for help. Don't you know the difference?"

An expression she could only describe as wolfish made his eyes brighter, gleaming with feral promise. "Sometimes they sound remarkably similar."

Dragging her close, he brought his lips down on hers.

When she gasped, he drove his tongue into her mouth. Was the man mad?

Mad or not, he kissed extremely well. Abandoning her reputation and her reason, Claudia flung her arm around his neck and returned his embrace with all the enthusiasm she could muster. Almost better than a dawn gallop.

He groaned, and the vibrations echoed deep in her throat. He liked this as much as she did. He slid his tongue around the interior of her mouth. She caressed it, the connection intimate enough to send a thrill right to the heart of her.

When he tried to pull away, she tightened her hold on him. She wasn't ready for this to stop.

Unfortunately his strength was superior to hers, and on his second attempt he pulled away. But she didn't let go.

"Lady Claudia, you are a flirt."

She smiled wickedly. "Oh, I'd say this was a bit more than flirting, wouldn't you?"

Shaking his head slightly, he removed her hand from his neck. "A reaction to thinking you were in danger, that's all. I thought your horse had gone out of control. It's a large beast for a small woman."

She huffed her displeasure, but she didn't move away. That would be to give ground to this man. "He might be a gelding, but Storm still prefers to be referred to as 'he.' I've known him since a foal. He's as gentle as a kitten."

As if to prove her point, Storm nudged her in the back and sent her off balance. Laughing, she fell into Lord St. Just's arms. "Truly, there was no need for you to be concerned." He was much stronger than she'd imagined, his fashionable clothes serving to disguise his strength. Today he wore a comfortable country coat in dark green, with a brown waistcoat and breeches. Nothing like his scarlet finery of the day before.

"And how exactly was I expected to know that?" He spoke incisively, each word snapped off, totally unlike his fashionable self's lazy drawl.

He had a point. He didn't know her well enough to know her prowess on a horse. "You'll know next time. If you don't recognize me, you'll know my horse."

"Society would condemn you for a hoyden if they saw you like this." Amusement lurked at the back of his voice.

So Lord St. Just lost his temper, but it was quick as a flash, because he wasn't angry now. Unless kisses dissipated his anger. Perhaps, having been a soldier, he was used to controlling his moods. But for that moment, he'd been angry. And she'd loved it.

He released her and bowed slightly. "I should leave you alone if I see you in distress again, is that it?"

"Certainly." She put up her chin, but inside she was glowing, the effects of the kiss still radiating within her. She wanted him to repeat his action, but she doubted he'd do it just because she asked him.

This tedious season was growing far more interesting. A challenge would liven it up nicely. "I appreciate your concern, but there was no need. Except that—" She broke off, because the hint was better than saying aloud that she would claim another kiss if she could. He could infer what he wanted.

She bobbed a curtsey, but due to her riding habit, it was not as elegant as it otherwise might be. "Thank you for rescuing me, sir. Now if you could help me back into the saddle, I promise to go home at a sedate pace."

"Madam, I live to serve."

His deep voice and the heat in his eyes promised more, but she would not claim it now. Like a good wine, men improved if they were made to wait. Being a member of a large family had taught her much, not least that pearl of wisdom.

He threw her into the saddle with little seeming effort and then mounted his own steed. Lifting her leg over the pommel, she settled her left foot in the stirrup and took the reins, which he'd looped over the horse's neck for her.

"Storm and I thank you."

"Can he take a man's saddle?" He wheeled his horse, ready to turn back.

"He's my horse so he's been trained for a side saddle. I daresay it wouldn't take much to retrain him. Not that it's likely to happen." She gave Storm a consoling pat and set off at the pace she'd promised, a sedate walk. She didn't go above a trot all the way home. He kept by her side the whole way, despite the groom she'd left at the gate falling in behind them as they left the park.

His conversation was unremarkable but clever. As her attention drifted from one subject, he moved swiftly to another, keeping her amused until they reached the mews behind her house. After she assured him she could get down by herself on the mounting block, he touched her gloved hand and told her to behave herself and remember her promise.

He left, his seat on his horse immaculate. Not at all like the man she'd met before. This man intrigued her.

She climbed down and went in the house to change for breakfast.

* * * *

Some families ate breakfast in their rooms, privately and in silence. Others ate in formal splendor, fully dressed and receiving guests. The cacophony filtering down the hall as Claudia made her way to the breakfast-parlor of the Strenshall London house sounded reassuringly familiar. She plunged in without hesitation. She needed some distraction to help her forget this morning's disturbing but exhilarating meeting with Lord St. Just.

The sheer noise gave some people pause. Her cousin Julius, the grand Earl of Winterton, had visibly winced when he visited them last week. He had not been back for breakfast since.

They ate at noon, making the meal a feast. Most, like Claudia, had been out or at least up and dressed for hours. Not her brother Valentinian.

Val was dressed in a glorious red banyan embroidered with dragons breathing fire and sported the matching cap on his unwigged head. In defiance to his mother's edict about keeping elbows off the table, Val had his firmly in place and his chin resting on his hand. Claudia sat next to him and deliberately knocked the offending joint away.

Val's chin nearly hit the white linen cloth. He pulled his head clear with a whisker to spare.

Unrepentant, Claudia clapped her hands and shrieked with laughter, and she wasn't the only one. Her twin, Livia, grinned, as did their sister, Drusilla. Val's twin, Darius, positively howled.

Claudia's mother had the ability to speak above the hubbub without actually shouting. "Claudia, you will apologize at once! I will not have such behavior at the breakfast table!"

"Or anywhere else," her husband murmured, sparing a glance at his daughter before returning to his newspaper.

Claudia offered her apology, to have Val grudgingly accept it. The scold was worth it.

"Did you know that the Young Pretender could be in London?" her father said.

His heir, Claudia's oldest brother, Marcus, scoffed. "That was four years ago, Papa!"

The marquess shrugged and turned a page. "I have no idea why it took The London Mirror so long to discover it, but it's here now. Perhaps he's returned."

At least three conversations were going on while that small exchange took place. Each member of the family had its own pitch, the better to communicate. Claudia tended to converse just above her twin and Dru. Now she busied herself getting a plateful of hot food from the sideboard instead of taking part in the talk or responding to her brother. Val was currently grumbling about sisters and pouring himself a fresh cup of coffee.

Claudia took her seat and grinned at him. "Out late last night, Val?"

Val grimaced. If the women who flocked around him in company could see that face, they wouldn't call him handsome. "Early, you might say. Nevertheless, I came out the winner. A thousand to the good."

"Damn, Val, what are you doing? Robbing the tyros fresh off the stage coach?" Marcus demanded. Tricksters and madams thronged the coach yards in search of pigeons ready for the plucking.

Val waved a dismissive hand. "I play games of skill and make sure I practice. Most of the game is watching your opponents. It's tiring."

"Oh, I'm so sorry for you!" Claudia said. "You only won a thousand? That's more than a workman earns in his whole life."

Val grunted and drank his coffee in one gulp. Dark hair peeked out from under his cap, and his chin was covered with black stubble.

Claudia loved this part of the day. With the sound of fork and knife scraping against china and the clicking of tea-dishes and coffee-cups, together with the scent of her mother's chocolate drifting over the aroma of freshly fried bacon, this meant more to her than any society dinner.

It meant home. Wherever they were, the family gathered for this meal. Her mother declared it was what kept the family together, although all were aware they would soon inevitably separate.

All the girls were of marriageable age. Soon they would leave home to form families of their own. Considering the family they came from, they would make a formidable generation. If they ever left home.

Unlike many families, their parents were not over-eager to push the three girls out of the door. They had money and influence enough. Time to find out who they were and what kind of husband they wanted, their mother told them, but not too loudly.

Claudia thought she would keep them all at home if she could. But by coming to London every year and keeping the house in the country full during the summer, her mama was providing every opportunity for them to find someone they would partner in life.

Her brother Val had recently become betrothed to Lady Charlotte Engles, the cherished only daughter of the Duke of Rochfort. Although everyone was pleased for him, nobody was quite sure how it had happened, even Val himself. He appeared content with his bargain, his mother expressing the forlorn hope that Lady Charlotte would settle him down somewhat.

Privately Claudia and her twin considered the ultimate outcome would be the other way about. When Val had announced his news, at breakfast of course, they'd run off to their bedroom as fast as they dared to discuss the development.

While Livia and Claudia were very different in temperament, their features were as similar as identical twins tended to be. For all their differences outside the confines of their bedroom, within it they frequently saw developments in a similar way. Indeed, Claudia had no idea how people without a twin managed to get through life. Even her own sister and brother, the singles in a family blessed by two sets of twins, seemed strangely isolated sometimes. She had no doubt that Darius had been the first to know of his twin's betrothal.

Val had been uncharacteristically silent on the subject.

Today, though—the heat that swept through her, the shivers that tingled her skin when Lord St. Just had touched it—they were all hers. She refused to share that, even with her sister. What she'd done was forbidden and sinful. But the other sensations, the loosening and moistening of her most secret parts, had excited her and made her want more. Just by touching a man?

Now she knew it was possible, she wanted more and as soon as she could find it.

A footman carrying a salver full of correspondence followed a knock on the door. After moving the marchioness's plate, he placed the post reverentially in front of her.

Lady Strenshall glanced through the pile, dividing it up. When her oldest son had the temerity to protest that he wasn't a child anymore and didn't need his post sorted for him, his mother had fixed him with one of her stony glares and said, mildly, "This is my house, my dear. My rules."

As usual, her husband had grunted his assent. The marquess was never very communicative at breakfast. Although the public often repeated that his wife henpecked him, that was far from the case. He had a formidable presence in the Lords, was a stalwart member of the most exclusive clubs, and never missed an opening night of Garrick's. When Lord Strenshall wanted to have his way, he usually got it.

Claudia's mother put the letters into piles, and when she handed them out, commented on each. "Malton, you should let a little enjoyment into your life. Every one of your letters is on white linen-laid papers, the addresses are perfect copperplate, and most are hand delivered. From the City, I presume. For goodness's sake, boy, I will exchange your letters for Valentinian's one day." She handed over the thick stack of business correspondence. Unless Marcus's mistress cleverly disguised her presence by using perfect copperplate.

"Val, you should be ashamed of yourself." His mama handed him three notes.

Claudia caught the pungent scent of violets from one mingled with the other's attar of roses. The third was a bill. "Perhaps you will pay your tailor from your winnings. I caught one lurking by the doorstep the other day. It is most disconcerting to discover a man of that nature at one's entrance."

Lady Strenshall glanced up sharply, catching Claudia in the act of sniggering as silently as she could manage. She handed Claudia a letter that looked remarkably like one of Marcus's. "If I didn't know better I'd say this was something official. If it is, you should tell your father without delay."

Lady Strenshall was of the opinion that the man of the house should handle official business. This was because, her daughters readily believed, that mortgages, court cases, and contracts of any kind bored her. She told the lawyer what she wanted and left him to take care of it, she said, and her husband served the same purpose. She got on with the important things in life, such as who their children should marry and where they should live.

Claudia had never shared that opinion, but she was woefully inexperienced in legal matters. She read through the letter, scripted in a hand she didn't recognize, three times before she looked up from the paper in total shock. "It appears I've inherited a house."

Chapter 3

Even Val opened his bloodshot eyes wider when Claudia came out with her news. "How daring," he murmured and subsided back into his pained silence as he continued to drink his way through a pot of coffee.

"You must have it wrong, dear," her mother said. "Give the letter to your father. Let him deal with the matter."

Stubbornly, Claudia shook her head. "I want to deal with it. It's only a small establishment. It must be, because it's in London." She would keep the address to herself for now. "It's from Great-Aunt Dorelia, the one who died at Christmas."

"Why has it taken so long for the news to reach you?" her mother demanded. "Does the letter say?"

"Yes, it's because she appointed a new lawyer to deal with her will. He did not hear of her death, because the old one took charge. She has an heir, her husband's cousin, and he has taken control of the estate. That is unchanged. The lawyer informs me that the heir doesn't object to the legacy. There's a letter from Great-Aunt Dorelia, which he encloses."

"Read it, then, girl!" her father snapped impatiently.

She glanced at him. The marquess id not usually become agitated, especially at the breakfast table. The hubbub of breakfast with the Strenshalls eased to a murmur. She broke the seal on the letter the lawyer had enclosed.

She pored over the spidery script for a full minute before she could interpret it. "It says that every woman should have at least one house of her own as a retreat from a demanding family."

Her mother gave an exaggerated sigh. "If only that were possible!"

"When you marry, it will go to your husband," Livia said.

"No it won't, because if there's any danger of that happening, it will revert to the estate," Claudia said. "It's in trust for me, with the solicitor, so that my husband can't touch it."

"Where is this house?" her father demanded. "Out with it, girl! You've been havering around that point for the last ten minutes. Every time you come to mention it, you talk about something else. Where?"

She sighed. She'd enjoyed the dream while it lasted. "Hart Street." After folding the letters, she placed them on the table but kept her hand over them. She might still make something of this. Over the noise that had erupted over the address, she shouted, "It's mine and I'm keeping it!"

Silence fell again, stony and complete, until her father broke it.

"You can't, Claudia. You know that. A house in that neighborhood is not eligible."

Before she could censor her words, she burst out, "They're not all brothels!"

Dru's shocked laughter echoed around the silent walls. Nobody else spoke.

Ah, well, in for a penny. "It could be a coffee house or a shop selling something quite innocuous."

Her mother took a hand. "Claudia, you have already garnered a reputation for wildness. You cannot afford more gossip, so in this case you must hold yourself at a distance. I daresay Lady Dorelia has lived long enough away from London that she does not know the reputation of that area. Did not know," she corrected herself hastily. "If you sell the house, the money may be added to your portion. Who knows, that might have been the intent of the legacy."

Claudia shook her head. "Not according to the letter." When Marcus reached across the table for them, she snatched the papers away. "If I sell the house immediately, the money will go to the estate. I must keep it for at least a year."

"I always said the woman was mad," her mother said. "Living on her own, with that odd companion."

"She loved Violet," Darius said quietly. "When she died, Great-Aunt Dorelia lost the will to live. The light went out of her life."

Darius spoke with deep understanding and sympathy. Everyone stared at him instead of at Claudia.

Claudia sent him a grateful smile. Darius had the full support of his family, even after society chattered about his relationship with a young man of good family. Only they knew the truth, and they were telling nobody. It didn't make any of the people in this room love him any the less.

Of course everyone in the family understood Lady Dorelia had peculiar tastes, but again, nobody discussed the matter. Of all her relatives, Dorelia would be the one to give her a very interesting legacy.

Hart Street might have been a fashionable part of town once, but it was decidedly not so now. The knowledge made Claudia even more determined to see the property, but on her own terms.

She was to visit Vauxhall Gardens tonight with Marcus, Val, and his betrothed. The perfect chance to slip away.

* * * *

Claudia wasn't sure if her new pink gown suited her, but she wore it anyway, and when her maid produced the powder pot, waved it away. Her gown should clash horribly with her red hair, but for some reason it did not. In any case, she wasn't so much red as a kind of gold with strong red hints.

Her mother despaired of her twin daughters, their coloring far too flamboyant for fashionable taste, which preferred ethereal blondes and dark, sultry brunettes. Perhaps Claudia's hair had flung her into more trouble than it might have done had she been born with a more serene coloring, but she doubted it. The devil had been in her from the moment she took her first breath, her mother said. She said it with a smile, unlike the more censorious of society's matrons.

Having second thoughts, she had her maid apply a layer of powder to her hair. That would help with her disguise later.

Claudia had always longed for somewhere of her own, a place she could retreat to. Nobody would burst into a room she was in or insist she join in something when she wanted a quiet hour to herself. Even she wanted that sometimes.

She could insist that this house remain hers. She had no intention of selling it. Ever, whatever it turned out to be.

She took care to take her thickest most enveloping cloak, secreting a couple of items in the pockets. She'd engaged the services of a pair of chairmen she'd met in the Exchange that very day. No family retainer would report her adventure back to her mother. If she planned this right, she could slip away, view the house, and then return before anyone was any the wiser.

Accordingly, halfway through the tedious concert her staid brother, Val, and his betrothed listened to with avid interest, she begged to be excused. "I will attend Lady Colm's. Mama is there. The carriage is outside."

Her maid waited for her in the carriage, and of course two of the sturdy footmen her father employed, so she would not be alone. If she took the carriage, that was. She would say that she felt ill and went home instead and took the chair rather than the carriage so that Marcus and Val could take it. That was likely to earn her a rebuke, but she'd had enough of those to cope with another with equanimity.

Having gathered the cloak around her and put on her hat, she scurried out of the gardens, contriving to lose the footman accompanying her. That proved easier than she'd imagined. As a firework exploded overhead, she took one of the side paths. She scurried straight for one of the side exits, the one where she'd arranged to meet the chairmen.

She breathed a sigh of relief when she saw two shadowy figures standing by a battered sedan chair covered in dark leather. As she approached, one swung open the door and she climbed in, ensuring none of the gown showed for anyone to recognize her. The color was rather too bright. She should have worn the blue, but the pink made her feel light-hearted. She wanted this adventure to be an enjoyable one.

The time was barely half past eight. If the house proved to be one she should certainly not visit, she could go home or even to Lady Colm's. Too bad that her ladyship would not be glad to see her. She had set her heart on grabbing Livia for her second son, and Claudia and he had never rubbed along.

She planned to have the men pause outside the house so she could just look at it.

They took her through Covent Garden, an adventure in itself, since at night ladies only travelled this way to visit the theater. Respectable women often passed through with the blinds down on the carriage, lest they damage their delicate sensibilities.

Claudia didn't consider her sensibilities delicate in the least. She enjoyed the sight of London's demimonde, already out in force and angling for custom. Brightly clad women wore gowns cut a tiny bit too low and perhaps a little worn and démodé. They'd bought them from the second-hand shops that thronged the large space of the Garden.

Hastily, she fastened on the black half mask she'd brought with her, the plain kind that ladies sometimes wore in the street.

Many of the well-built red brick houses ringing the Piazza were devoted to the life of the demimonde. But at ground level they were shops, coffeehouses, and a few other businesses. Perhaps her house was a respectable one. If she didn't discover it for herself, she never would. They would sell it and put the money to her portion and that would be that.

"We're 'ere ma'am," one of the chairmen said after they dumped the chair down on the pavement.

The jolt made her gasp, but she peered out of the window and took stock. The house was part of a row, of reasonable size but not as large as the ones ringing the piazza. The shutters were up on the single window by the front door, which opened off the street, instead of set back and up a shallow flight of steps like her parents' London residence.

Trepidation made her throat tighten, but after taking a few deep breaths, she pulled her hood over her head and marched to the front door.

It opened at her knock to reveal a huge man who looked as if a baker had kneaded his face into a new shape. He glared at her from baby blue eyes. "Are you the new girl?"

Blinking at his abrupt question, she nodded. "That's me."

Her parents would kill her, but they would do it later. After this man had his turn. She had made a hasty copy of the documents that afternoon. She could show them and prove this house belonged to her.

The door was a smaller, narrower copy of the one she used every day. The black paint was duller but not peeling or old, which she took as a good sign.

A roar of merrymaking rocked the house as she entered. Men's voices, interrupted by the higher pitch of female, burst from the room upstairs. Down here relative quiet reigned, and she could just make out shapes covered by canvas and covers. A shop, probably. Shop by day, brothel by night.

The man jerked his head to the staircase at the end of the room. "Up there. What's your name?"

She'd prepared one. "Ellie Franks." The combined names of two servants at the London house.

"Go and serve some drinks. If a gentleman takes a fancy to you, you can stay. Usual rates."

She dared not ask what they were. Once she showed her papers to whoever was in charge, she wouldn't be collecting any drinks or money.

Up the stairs, she found one large room, the narrow supporting arch barely holding up the roof. That would have to be shored up to be safe. The floor was bare boards, well polished but worn, dipping in places where it was most frequently walked on. She could barely see it, because most of the space was taken up. Two long tables stretched widthways with a jumble of chairs, none matching, gathered around them. All were occupied, some of them double.

Men were engaged in drinking, laughing, and fondling. On one corner of the table, two men were engaged in what appeared to be a game of piquet. Their cards were in neat piles, together with tokens that would presumably be converted into money at the end of their play. They were oblivious to the goings-on in the rest of the room. The room was ill-lit, probably on purpose, dark corners providing useful corners for more intimate play.

Claudia had never seen anything like it in her life, and it fascinated her.

The women were in various stages of undress. A man dragged a bodice down and sucked on the girl's breasts. Claudia stood close enough to hear the growls he made and the giggles from the girl. How could she allow anyone to maul her like that? The bitter flavor of distaste filled her mouth. Even for money, that was taking matters much further than Claudia wanted to go. She couldn't imagine doing that with anyone, even Lord St. Just.

She dismissed him from her mind. This was most certainly not the time to think of him.

An older lady, wrinkled breasts on full display, approached her. "Yes?" she said. "Did Harold let you in?"

Claudia moistened her lips. "Yes, he did. I have to show you something."

The lady had shaved her brows, but the penciled ones demonstrated her surprise as well as the originals would have. "You're not showing enough as it is. If you want to get some customers, you'll have to tempt them more than that."

In response, she drew out the copies of her letters that she'd hastily made that afternoon and handed them over.

Claudia had pushed her bodice as low as she'd dared, but she wouldn't dream of exposing her nipples, as this lady did. Even less talking rationally while having them on blatant display. The more Claudia tried not to look, the more she wanted to, although it was far from a savory sight.

The lady carried an odor with her, a mixture of camphor, lavender, and stale sweat. What wreathed around her nose most was a heavy, thick, unpleasant scent, spiked with a sharper smell not unlike two-day-old fish. Her stomach roiled and she pressed her hand to it. Maybe the lamps in the hall outside were using cheap fish oil.

No, it wasn't that. She knew what it was, and she hated to admit that she did. Unwashed female. The heavier smell must be the men in the room, although she had no knowledge of what men's private parts smelled like. If this was a sample, she wanted none of it.

She couldn't imagine Lord St. Just carried that scent under his pristine, expensive clothes. When he'd kissed her, all she'd smelled was a faint citrus aroma and warm, clean male. She was accustomed to that scent in her brothers, but not the heat and the muskiness. The memory helped to block out the unpleasant ones assaulting her now.

The woman sniffed and wiped her nose on the back of her hand before returning the papers to Claudia. She took them and folded them, taking care not to touch the spot the woman had smeared with her snot. She'd as lief throw them in the fire, but this evening had proved mild and there was none. Besides, it would look decidedly strange. She'd tear them up when she got home. They were only copies.

"You're the new owner. What do you plan to do with the place?" the woman demanded.

"Nothing," she said. "I only wanted to see it."

"What, you couldn't make an appointment like any normal gentry-mort?"

Fascinated, Claudia tilted her head and wondered what a gentry-mort was. Whatever the meaning, it appeared she was one. "I wanted to see it during...working hours."

The woman cackled. "Well, here we are. Do you like what you see?"

She moved closer and Claudia was hard put not to step back.

"Some ladies come 'ere of an evening to join in. Are you of that mind?"

Claudia shook her head. Waves of nausea swept over her, and she had to fight to keep her dinner in her stomach. "May I watch? Please, don't tell anyone who I am." She could put up with a little stink.

The woman shook her head, the lappets of her cap grazing her bare shoulders. "You shouldn't be here. I wouldn't let any of my little 'uns see me in working hours. Whatever is your mother thinking?" She clicked her tongue. "You could get robbed, or worse. Still, Mother Finch'll take care of you. If anybody asks, tell them you're reserved and your gentleman isn't here yet. He's paid a lot for you, and he wants you to wait. We gets all sorts 'ere. Some like to watch and most gentlemen have their favorites. I'll send you some wine over. There, in the corner near the fireplace. Don't sit there like the specter at the feast. Smile and laugh and look like you're having a good time."

After a nod, Claudia made her way down the side of the room to the seat the lady—Mother Finch—indicated. A big man who could have been the twin of the one outside, except that the pattern of battering was different, handed her a grubby glass of red liquid. She thanked him and sniffed the contents of the goblet. Wine, for sure, but she had no idea what else was in there. It could be vinegar from the way it smelled. She wet her lips with it and her tongue shrank from the acrid taste.

The sound in the room had continued unabated. A fat, florid man stared at her, his gaze roaming lasciviously over her figure. She wished now she'd worn a less vivid color, for the pink gown seemed almost gaudy in this place. She had a double ruffle of lace at her elbows, not her finest lace to be sure, but too fine for this room. Lace was expensive, so dear that smugglers gained a good price from it. As well she hadn't worn her gown with the laced petticoat. The people here might have ripped it off her or even killed her for it.

She shuddered and took a delicate sip of the wine.

The man was still watching. His face was red, from wine or the heat of the small room crammed with unwashed, excited people, she didn't know. He wore relatively grand clothes. Blue and mustard in color, the waistcoat was a little too long for current taste, the sleeves of his shirt even fuller than her brothers had. No, not unfashionable. Foreign. The style was French, or maybe Italian.

She didn't care. The man had a bulbous nose, no doubt from over imbibing over a period of time, and his pale blue eyes were unpleasantly prominent. His lips were full, almost like a girl's. He smiled, revealing white teeth, though she wasn't close enough to ascertain whether they were his own or artificial.

She didn't care. Looking away, she was just in time to catch the rush of a dark green coat as its owner sat next to her. He smelled of citrus and warm, clean male.

"What…"

With a laugh, Lord St. Just caught her in his arms and pressed a kiss to her mouth, stifling whatever she was about to say.

Chapter 4

When he'd stepped into the brothel, Dominic's first urge was instinctive. He wanted to shake her until the teeth rattled in her head and then hold her close so that nobody would see her or know her. What the hell was she doing here? From his vantage point across the street, he'd seen her arrive, but hadn't recognized her. He did now she'd thrown her hood back. She was sitting wide-eyed, watching his quarry.

A half mask and powder did not disguise that straight nose and those sensual lips. He'd know them anywhere. The curl of red-gold hair missed when her maid had powdered the rest of her locks only confirmed his firm belief. Lady Claudia Shaw had once more ventured to a place she had no right to occupy.

If anyone else recognized her, she was done for. Didn't she realize that men she might have met in a ballroom earlier in the evening might come here to carouse before the night was over? The idiotic woman didn't have the sense she was born with.

He sent away the chairmen who'd brought her, swearing he'd take care of her. How she managed to charm two ruffians like that he'd never know, but he hoped it wasn't the same way she'd charmed him.

When she opened her mouth, he let his instincts take control. A kiss was just what he needed, but it served the purpose of hiding her face from view.

Their lips touched and he almost lost his mind. He'd been dreaming of that warm, soft mouth since he'd kissed it before. Her pink lips moistened, her mouth open—it had been too much.

The tang of cheap wine nudged his taste buds and then was gone, replaced by her heat and her special flavor. He wanted to sample every part of her. The delicate skin at the back of her knees would taste different than her navel. He badly wanted to claim the sweet, dark heart of her for himself.

His cock rose to her command, even though she would not know it. He'd had the forethought to sit next to her and not haul her into his lap, as he longed to do.

Most of the doxies were thus occupied, even the two fawning over his quarry sitting on the other side of the fire.

Hell and damnation, what was he thinking? He wasn't here to kiss a woman, however tempting she happened to be, but to watch the man he'd been following all night. Although he hadn't planned to enter the house, but wait until the man emerged, when Lady Claudia entered he'd followed her in. Spies and traitors came in both sexes.

He couldn't believe Claudia was a traitor. For one thing, she belonged to a family adamantly and publicly opposed to the Cause. For another, she wasn't. He didn't believe it.

Her lips tasted sweet, of wine and raspberries, or some sharp fruit. Delicious, but leaving him wanting more. With an effort of will he pulled away, but not too far. "What the hell are you doing here?" he murmured next to her mouth. Lovers' talk of a very different nature, but he kept smiling.

"I could ask you the same thing," she mumbled breathlessly.

He'd done that to her, made her bosom heave and the heat rise to her face. The notion made him absurdly proud. "I am on business."

She pulled away sharply, almost tumbling off the end of the short bench they sat on. Automatically he reached out and pulled her back, keeping hold of her arm. When she tried to shake it off, he kept hold. He was hard-put not to bruise her because she made a concerted effort to get away.

"Sir, can I 'elp you?"

The bawd stood over them, glaring at him.

"We're quite all right, madam." He narrowed his eyes, assessing her. Yes, she knew who Claudia was. Didn't the girl have any sense of self-preservation? The madam had extortion material for the rest of the season, if not longer. "I've come to retrieve her. I'm her…betrothed."

"I see. Well, call if you want anything."

He had to get Claudia out of this room before someone recognized her. He'd been so close, too. His plan thrown completely awry, he accepted he'd have to wait until another night to trap the man. Damn the woman.

Yet he couldn't blame Claudia as wholeheartedly as he perhaps should. She'd created a pile of trouble he'd have difficulty recovering from. It would take time he didn't want to spend on the problem. When he'd tracked the Pretender down, he hadn't quite believed his luck until he realized the damned man had the intention of flaunting himself over half London. If he'd stood in front of Kensington Palace waving his arms and yelling, "Arrest me!" he could hardly have been more obvious.

When Claudia tried to speak he kissed her again and then stood, dragging her to her feet. "Come with me, sweeting. We'll find somewhere a little more private." He flashed her a message with his eyes, opening them wide and then shaking his head slightly.

She looked a little stunned, but put her hand in his and let him draw her to her feet. He glanced at the table and took her wineglass too.

Madam Finch showed them the way to the stairs. "Any door that's open upstairs, sir." She nodded when he handed her a few gold coins. She bit every one before she handed him a candlestick and allowed them to climb the rickety flight of stairs.

Every tread was an adventure, wobbling underfoot or uneven enough to throw a man off his balance. He trod carefully, memorizing the characteristics of each stair. Very few failed to make some kind of sound.

Upstairs, three doors out of the five were wide open. He kept going until he reached the one at the end, away from the two closed ones. He put the candlestick and wine glass on the table set just inside.

The door slammed behind him, probably the result of the worn nature of the timbers making it tilt. She jumped and then stumbled, and he was forced to catch her before she fell. Not that it was a hardship. Warm and ripe, she filled his arms beautifully and he would have had to be made of stone not to kiss her.

Part of him did feel as if it were made of stone. His low groan vibrated against her impossibly soft skin, and she opened her lips on a sigh.

Taking advantage, he tasted her, but took care, afraid she would pull away if he thrust his tongue deep, as he wanted to do. Instead, he touched her lips gently. Exaltation surged through him when she responded by opening her mouth wider. He slid the tip of his tongue along her teeth, and then deeper, caressing her tongue with his. He held her as tightly as possible, but not tightly enough. His instincts drove him to grind his erection against her warm body, but he couldn't get close enough. Yards and yards of fabric were sandwiched between them, cushioning his reaction to her.

She'd granted him access to her mouth. He shouldn't be so greedy. Avid possession swept through him. A primitive rhythm began deep inside him, a beat as old as time, his pulse drumming in his ears and around his body. Tearing at the strings of her mask, he got it off her and tossed it aside. She didn't protest, and he didn't stop kissing her.

He delved deep, working hard to keep his kiss within civilized levels. When she leaned into him, as if trusting him to hold her steady, he lost his mind.

This woman would be the death of him. How he could react so strongly beat his understanding, but he did, and he responded to the lust roaring through him.

Supporting the back of her head with his hand, he feasted.

He lifted his mouth to adjust their position and seal their mouths together more securely. She spluttered a word against his mouth, but he was too far into this to stop now. With one hand around her waist cinching her tightly he held her, directed her as he wanted her.

She went limp and moaned against his mouth. He kissed her mouth, her cheeks, and then down her neck. All the places he'd wondered about. He wanted the rest, but a soupçon of sense remained, nagging at the back of his mind. He dismissed it because he wanted one more thing, just one, with a desperation he couldn't control.

He touched the upper slopes of her breast, grazed his fingertips along the wonderfully silky, soft skin. Her delicate shiver gave him tacit permission to carry on. Only a few seconds to ease her breast from the deep décolletage of her gown, and then it was in his hand.

"Beautiful," he said, his voice barely above a breath.

Her nipple crinkled and the tip grew more prominent, changing from its original rose pink to a duskier shade. He wanted to taste it more than he wanted to take another breath. He sucked it into his mouth. Claudia followed her choked-off cry with pressure on the back of his head as she pressed him closer. She smelled of sweet, hot femininity, her delicate taste a compliment to her lovely skin.

Letting her nipple go, he closed his eyes, breathing deeply.

"You are bad for my self-control, my lady," he murmured, his lips touching her skin with every word. "We cannot continue, or I will take you further than either of us wish to go."

"What you're doing… It feels so good."

Her soft, dreamy tones gave him a jolt, and brought him back to reality.

Tugging at his head, she murmured, "There's a bed over there."

That brought him right back down to earth. Lifting his head, he took one last lingering look at the bounty exposed to his touch and kiss, and then tucked it away. "We don't want to go anywhere near that bed," he murmured. "They don't change the sheets between clients, you know."

Her face flushed as she stared at the bed. "I-I can't believe I did this…"

"Hush." He stroked her cheek.

She pulled away. "What am I doing? What on earth have I done?"

Needing to reassure her, he said the first thing that came to his mind. "Nothing anyone need know about. I'm as much at fault as you. You're intoxicating, my lady. The moment I saw you I wanted you, and had you been different, I'd have made you an offer then and there. A disreputable one, I'm afraid."

"Oh!" She clapped her hand to her mouth. "I don't know whether to laugh or be offended."

Backing off hastily, she tugged at the folds of her fichu and covered the upper slopes of her bosom.

"Be complimented, at least in the confines of this room." Shoving his hands in his pockets, he strode toward the door and back again. "We must keep our voices low. This is not a house of friends."

Stilling, her hand to her bosom, Claudia stared at him, eyes wide. "What do you mean?" Groping in her pocket, she found a couple of folded papers. She stepped forward, her shoes on the boards the only sound in the room. Raucous carousing came from below but here all was quiet.

Dominic scanned them the papers she gave him. She owned this place. This house had belonged to a relative, recently deceased, and now it had come to her. Bequeathed rather than inherited. Interesting.

His lips compressed tightly together, he lifted his head and silently handed back the papers. "You have the originals safe?"

She nodded. "I wanted to see the place for myself before my brothers sold it. It's mine, in trust. Nobody can touch it."

"If they sell it, that will cast aspersions on you. Your family is famous for its loyalty to the Crown. You have fought against the Jacobites, one family in particular, have you not?"

A frown creased her brow. "The Dankworths, yes. The feud started with a stupid boundary dispute centuries ago. At least, that's what I was always told. Then, after the death of the last Stuart monarch, something mysterious happened."

He lifted a brow.

"I don't know what it was!" she said, with more than a touch of exasperation. "I'm a woman. They don't tell me delicate matters, and this one seems to have been hushed up. The Dankworths went abroad in support of the Stuarts, and my family took the opposing camp. Ever since, society assumes our main disputes are political." She shook her head. "Sometimes it seems to get very personal."

She glanced up, into his eyes. The jolt of blue fascinated him. Nothing could prepare him for that candid regard.

"I see." He spread his hands. "Did you notice anyone downstairs? In particular, I mean?"

She bit her lower lip and frowned. "A fat man with two women dancing attendance on him kept staring at me."

"God in heaven, give me strength! Don't you know who that was?" After what she'd told him, surely she knew?

She shook her head.

"Your brothers are right. They should not have allowed you out of the house without an escort. That, my dear, is your family's avowed enemy. Charles Edward Stuart, otherwise known as the Young Pretender. He prefers people to address him as 'Your Highness.'"

* * * *

Claudia heard his words in a state of dull acceptance. Of course it was. What else could go wrong with her inheritance? Perhaps she'd discover that they sold smuggled goods here, too. Or counterfeit coins, or something else equally disreputable. "Why would I know him? The pictures of him show a slim, handsome man, beautifully dressed."

"After the 'forty-five he turned to drink," Lord St. Just said. "And women. He has a regular mistress, and he beats her. He has not yet married. Some of us believe it's because he has not given up hope of the throne. In that case, he will marry a princess. Perhaps one of the King's daughters or grandchildren to unite the two branches of the houses."

"Who are you discussing when you say, 'us'?" She picked that out of his words as worth further information. Clubs and secret societies abounded, and he might be with one of those. "What are you doing here in any case? Did you follow me?"

He spoke so quietly she could hardly hear him. Was it to make her move closer? Stubbornly, she planted her feet to the floor.

"To answer both of your questions, when I was in the army, I rendered some few services to the intelligence unit. Therefore I have some experience in the field, and my superior officer requested that I visit someone in Horse Guards." He waved his hand dismissively. "I am working for the British government. I am only to follow Stuart. That's why I'm here tonight. I was watching. I only came in when I saw you. I wanted to know where he was so I could take him quietly. Some factions would prefer that he be arrested and brought to trial for treason. Others wish him to leave, so they can forget him."

"Yet others want him to be king," she said quietly. That was the part she was familiar with. "What does this house have to do with it, apart from having him in it?"

Instead of answering her directly, he said, "Pick up your wine and hold it to the candle."

Suspicious of his meaning, she nevertheless did as he asked and held up the glass. It was engraved, as many were, but she hadn't explored it properly. Now she did.

The design was of a thistle and a rose twined together, with a crown over the whole, blatantly a Jacobite drinking glass. Some of his supporters had a bowl of water to hand. They'd pass the glass over it before drinking to symbolize the king over the water.

If this house had these glasses, had they bought them to please their new customer, or was it a known house? "This is a traitor house?" Distastefully, she put the glass down as if it held poison. "The wine is sour. That seems appropriate."

"Yes, it's a traitor house. They call themselves loyalists, so take care what you say here." He stepped closer.

Claudia clutched the folds of her skirt, ready for another onslaught. She could not resist him. He could do whatever he wanted to her. For the first time she wanted someone safe with her, instead of chafing at the bit to get away.

This powerful man presented a potential danger to her. She'd never resist him if he pressed her to give him more than a kiss.

When he laid a finger over his lips, she nodded and swallowed. Now she stood away from him, she could see him properly.

This man appeared more like the man in the park than the one at the draper's. He wore his own dark hair tightly tied back. His hat, which had tumbled off his head in their previous bout of passion, was undecorated. He wore no rings, had no embellishments at all on his person. His clothes were sober and respectable but not made of expensive material. Fancy lace didn't decorate the sleeves, only a small ruffle of linen.

He'd been a soldier, and not in an ornamental regiment, and now he looked every inch the man of action. This man understood danger, had probably seen death, and she was more than half afraid of him.

"Don't raise your voice," he murmured, his tone far too intimate. "In this house, no room is safe, not even the ones with closed doors."

Taking her hand, he led her to the other side of the small space, to a spot by the begrimed window. "Please, don't fear me, ever. I will never offer you violence. I swear it."

She believed him. "I was startled because you look so different."

He gave that lazy half smile that remained a constant, however he looked. "I'm the same person."

"Is this who you are? Not the man of fashion?"

"I am both," he said. "I find great amusement in my other appearance, but I have to confess to you that I allow my valet to select most of my clothes. I begin, and then I grow bored."

He touched her chin, so softly she hardly registered it.

"I wanted to retire completely from the service, but I had the skills and they knew where to find me. Once I have done with the task, that life is over for me. My parents are aging and they worry about me. I left the army for them, and I will leave this, too."

No one showing that degree of consideration to his parents could be as severe as this man appeared. Moreover, he kissed like an angel. Or a devil. Already tingles rose up her arms, in the secret places of her body and he drew her so that she found herself leaning in to him. "What do we do now?"

"We leave," he said simply. "I'll continue this another time. I know where he goes now, and I am learning more than we imagined about his habits. He's visited London before, you know."

"In fifty-one." It was supposed to be clandestine, but word had got out.

"And after. He's made quite a habit of it."

She stared at him, wide-eyed. "How does he get away with it?"

He smiled, and then bent and kissed her, so swiftly she had no way of stopping him, even if he had wanted to.

"I'm sorry. Don't look at me that way," he murmured against her lips.

She smiled, her mouth caressing his. "Why not?"

"Because it makes you irresistible. You are adorable like that."

She bridled. "Like a kitten?"

"Exactly like," he said, unabashed. "Not at all like the wild Lady Claudia Shaw"

"People condemn where they don't know. If I have done something slightly wrong, they exaggerate."

Leaning forward, he placed his hand on the wall behind her head. "They wouldn't have to exaggerate this escapade. What were you thinking?" He frowned. "How did you do it?"

"I went to the pleasure gardens, and then I told my brother I was joining my mother at Lady Colm's."

He rolled his eyes. "You run rings around them all."

Before she could think of her actions, she reached out and grabbed his arm. She couldn't get her hand half way around it, but she didn't let that give her pause. "You won't tell them, will you?"

After regarding her for a fraught moment in silence, he said, "I have to. Because you're here, in this house, at the same time as he is. The Pretender."

His words brushed her face, like an invisible caress. She arched up without conscious volition. "Kiss me again." She could think of nothing else when he was this close.

With a groan of surrender, he complied, but he did not embrace her as he had before. He kept one hand propped above her head and the other at her side, caging her in delicious captivity. This time he kept his kiss tender, and when she opened her mouth for him, he barely dipped his tongue inside, delicately teasing her.

Eagerly, she chased him with her own tongue and found him waiting for her. Dominic sucked gently, as she touched the tip of her tongue to the roof of his mouth. Then she nuzzled his teeth, sharp and predatory. He did not scare her. He aroused her.

He was far more dangerous like this, tempting her to explore and discover for herself what these wonders were like. Oh, she'd been kissed before, but never with such care, such attention, as if she were the only woman in the world.

That was it. He made her feel special. As if she really mattered. At home she was loved but as one of a family of six, not as a whole, for herself. As a twin, one of a pair. Society loved them for that, but she did not. She wanted to be herself.

She opened her eyes. He was watching her, his dark, stormy eyes fixed hungrily on her features. The contact sent a new sense of awareness through her, and she moved back, although she had nowhere to go. Her back rested against the wall behind her, and as she stared at him, the chilly damp of the plaster seeped through her clothes. "I should go," she said.

"I will take you."

Turning her head, she glanced out the window and turned back to him in alarm. "My chair, it's gone!"

"I sent them away. We'll get a hackney," he said. "You may say you were taken ill and you never went into Lady Colm's."

She nodded. "I want more kisses."

With a sudden powerful push, he moved away from her. "Then you'll have to want. You'll get no more here." He spoke in firm, loud tones now. "Come. I'll pay the madam and we'll move on."

His sultry smile reminded her of the part she was playing here. Claudia should feel dirty, but the notion excited her, sent passion burning deep inside her.

"You like the idea, don't you?"

She put up her chin and shook out her skirts. "What idea?"

"Customer and whore."

The words sent a shaft of heat to her center, that spot between her legs that dampened when arousal struck her. She should deny it, be indignant and protest that she didn't know what he meant. Maybe flounce to make her point.

She did none of these things, but stared back, meeting his eyes boldly. "Yes."

Silence ticked between them until he smiled lazily.

"Good," he said. "Lovers play games, do they not?"

"We're not lovers."

"We are nearly lovers."

She couldn't deny that. Nearly was very different to actuality. The idea of lying in that bed with him, completely naked, turned her insides to fire, but she would not let him know. He had that admission, and that was all he was getting.

"The idea is amusing, you must admit."

To her relief he played the game. "Very amusing. Madam, shall we go?"

When he stepped forward, she lifted her face, already prepared of his kiss, but he merely bent and swept the mask up from the floor.

"Turn around."

When she obeyed, he fastened the ties deftly. Then he pulled her cloak back around her and tugged her hood back over her head. He caught a lock of hair, sending a shot of pain through her. When she lifted her hand to free the curl, she found him there. "You should ensure your maid covers all your hair next time. That color is singular."

"My sister has the same. Our father used to, before he turned grey. My cousins on his side of the family have it." She didn't like to think she was so easily identified.

"It's yours alone," he murmured, tucking the offending curl into her hood. "There. Keep your head down and we'll scrape through this."

Her adventure was ending and she regretted it. "This is still my house."

"That is what concerns me."

He opened the door for her and took her downstairs. After handing the landlady the extortionate sum of a guinea—it would hire a room for a year if this house was not engaged in nefarious activities—they were allowed to leave.

Outside, he threw back his head and took some deep breaths, as if the very atmosphere in the house were tainted. It did stink of wine, tobacco, and other smells but she'd known worse. Pigsties, for instance, if they were not cleared out.

"Do you want to close this house?" she said. If he did that, maybe she could have it renovated. People of fashion lived around here. Cheek by jowl with less reputable houses, to be sure, but it could be achieved.

He glanced down at her. "Not immediately. Pretend we are lady of the night and her man for the next hour. We'll draw less attention that way, and you may escape notice."

He drew her to his side by curving his hand around her waist. She didn't resist. She felt safer with him this close, anyway, and it worked as their disguise of whore and client. She rested her head on his shoulder. He must be six inches or even more taller than she was, so his shoulder was at a convenient level for her. Very convenient.

His chuckle vibrated her body pleasantly, rousing her senses.

"If the house remains open, I know where to find him. He has regular places he likes to visit. I was unaware of this one until tonight, although it does not try to hide itself. Those glasses are not easily concealed. Other subterfuges are more clandestine and easily denied. It speaks of overconfidence, or…something else."

She glanced at him. He was frowning. Just then they walked into the brighter light of the Piazza and his features became better delineated.

She liked his face like this, without that society frivolity and lazy droop of his eyelids. Alert and strong, the lines carved with care by some celestial builder, this man appealed to her.

"Do nothing," he said. "I'll visit you tomorrow. Will your family be in?"

"I do not know."

"I'll send a message and ensure I can obtain an interview."

Alarm streaked through her. She liked him, she was attracted to him, but that sounded far too much like he wanted to pay his addresses. She'd only met him twice! "What kind of interview?"

His glance at her face held amusement but also tenderness. "To discuss this situation. Not me and you—we'll brush through this if you do not make a habit of running off to brothels—but the house and its contents. Your involvement in the affair."

Affair. That word meant more than politics, threats to the Crown. She could see the knowledge in his eyes. He meant it.

He had kissed her like he meant it, after all.

"You mean that I own the property. My great aunt left it to me and she hadn't visited London in years. I just wanted to see it." She sighed. "I want somewhere of my own, a place I can close the door and know that nobody will come in. I love my family, of course I do, but just once—"

"If you keep sighing like that your bodice will give way," he said. "While I would much appreciate another view of your lovely body, I don't think this is quite the place."

Aware she'd pushed her bodice down as far as she dared and consequently was not as securely laced in as usual, she drew her cloak closer around her. "You've seen that already."

"I have. Only a taste. I want more, Claudia. You're a respectable woman, so I'm going to have to wait."

He gave her such a look of deep melancholy that she burst out laughing, her embarrassment forgotten. At the time, embarrassment had been the last thing on her mind, but now, brought back to a sense of reality, it could have suffused her. It should have, except he was right.

She wanted more, too.

Chapter 5

Aware of her family's exaggerated need to protect her and the other women, Claudia refused to go out with her mother the next morning, pleading a stomachache. She'd used the same excuse the night before, when she'd arrived home on her own. Dominic had left her at the end of the square until she knocked and went in. He made her feel safe, but that could be an entirely false premise.

When he arrived, he was in full society mode. Blue today, not a dark shade, but a vivid ultramarine tone. His breeches were as white as snow and his waistcoat embroidered in gold. She was too far away to see the design. As he handed his hat and the ridiculous cane as tall as he was to the footman, bright gold caught the sun and dazzled her.

When she blinked the light out of her eyes, he was looking up at her. She must have made a sudden move and alerted his attention. No point hiding now.

Claudia hurried down the stairs, trailing her hand lightly on the banister. "Did you think to find me away from home?" she said brightly. "Strange how insistent my mother was that I attend her this morning. That was just after my father let slip that you were visiting to discuss the house on Hart Street. I suspect my brother asked her to ensure I was out of the way." She smiled saucily. "Well, as you can see, I am not."

"You're appearing to great advantage," he said.

He didn't mean her clothes. She could tell by the way he looked over her, taking in her bosom, today respectably covered with a linen fichu. He'd seen it uncovered, or part of it at any rate. The knowledge made her heat up.

"I love that blush," he murmured.

She turned away, employing her fan to cool her complexion. She thought she'd controlled her reprehensible habit of blushing at the least provocation. The easy capacity to blush came with her coloring and that damned pale skin. "We should go to the study. They're all waiting."

She led the way but refused to take his arm.

The study was rather crowded, containing as it did, not only her oldest brother Marcus, Lord Malton, but her father, Val, and Darius. None of them were smiling.

Marcus glared at her. "You're not supposed to be here."

"I have a right to know what you're discussing." Claudia worked hard not to push her lower lip out as she had as a child. As soon as she said it, she felt like a child. How else to assert her rights? She tried again. "Let me make this clear. I have the last word on what happens to that house. My great-aunt said so when she made her will. Anything else would go against her desires."

"How about if we discuss the matter and then inform you of the best path to take?"

She shook her head. "I want to hear the options."

Glumly, Marcus got to his feet and brought his chair to her side of the desk. Putting up her chin, she thanked him and sat. It put her at a disadvantage, having to look up to the others in the room, but she had no choice.

To her shock, Dominic stepped up to stand by her side. "It seems reasonable that the owner is involved in any decision taken."

Val glanced up from the papers strewn across Marcus's desk. "She's been anything but reasonable recently."

"Maybe because you insist on treating me like a witless female."

Dominic's support had affected her more than she realized. Tears threatened, but they would prove her father and brothers' opinion of her. She had behaved badly recently, last night the culmination of a series of escapades, but her aunt's legacy had helped her decide what she really wanted. To be her own woman, to have men regard her as a sensible person and not a featherheaded fool.

Not to be bored any more. Her sister enjoyed reading and study—that was her escape. Livia spent as much time with her nose in a book as she spent begrudgingly attending balls and society events.

While Claudia was reasonably well-read, her passion didn't lie there. Sensing the man at her side, she feared "passion" might describe what she wanted exactly. Which was a shame. As a well-born protected young woman, she was unlikely to find that this side of marriage. She wasn't nearly ready to marry anyone yet.

While her brothers voiced their protests, her father held up his hand. When that didn't work, he yelled, "Quiet!" in a tone so stentorian it would have stopped the whole of the House of Lords in its tracks.

It took her brothers a minute to wind down, but eventually silence fell.

"Since she's here, Claudia may as well have a say. You are feeling well enough, my dear?"

His solicitous smile fooled nobody, least of all Claudia. She had not been ill, and her stomach pains of last night mere fabrication. She prayed he wouldn't discover where she'd really been.

Tension tightened her stomach. Would Dominic tell them about her escapade? She glanced at him. He sent her a reassuring smile that told her nothing. She was in his hands, if not literally, figuratively. He could ruin her chances of being treated as an adult.

"I had the carriage drive past the house yesterday," she said. "It's a modest establishment." She sighed. "I fear I couldn't live there. I could rent it out."

Her father shoved some papers across the scarred surface of the desk. "Read those while I ascertain why Lord St. Just saw fit to visit us this morning."

"It's about the house," he said, "or I wouldn't have intruded."

Claudia picked up the first paper. Her hand trembled. Would he tell them? "I wouldn't have thought such a modest establishment would interest you, my lord."

If he detected the warning in her tone, he ignored it. "I think the information you have will explain my presence here."

It would. Silently she handed him the first paper while she read the next one. The note informed Lord Strenshall that the suspicious activity concerning the house in Hart Street was confirmed. That was all. The second sheet was damning. It recorded the activities of one CJES, who could be none other than Charles James Edward Stuart on his visit to London two years ago. The address in Hart Street featured three times.

"Explain." Lord Strenshall leaned back in the chair.

Marcus leaned against the bookcase behind him, while Val and Darius stood to one side.

Sometimes she hated that her family members were all so damned intelligent. She could never slip any subterfuge past them, although she'd tried often enough.

Dominic still stood close to her. He took the second document when she gave it to him.

Claudia took her time reading all six documents. They told a similar story. The house was a place where known Jacobites met. The authorities were leaving it alone because it was a useful fount of knowledge. They had not tried to infiltrate it or let the occupants know that they knew about it. But it had been a hotbed of sedition for at least five years.

Now it belonged to Claudia.

Dominic dropped the papers back on the desk. "I'm working for the government," he said.

"Does that mean you'll report anything we decide back to your masters?" Val shoved a hand into the pocket of his dark brown coat.

Dominic showed no alarm, even though Val could have his hand wrapped around a weapon. He put one hand on the back of her chair, as if protecting her. The gesture made her feel absurdly safe.

Today Dominic was all dandy, but she didn't assume his foppishness was anything but faked. Perhaps he was a little less primped than he'd been the other day, his clothes less gaudy, maroon rather than crimson, buff rather than blinding white. He smelled the same, of citrus and clean male virility, reminding her vividly of what must lie beneath the clothes. He was all powerful male. She wanted him with a rawness that shocked her.

He took his time answering Val. "Not necessarily. I don't obey orders blindly. I never have."

Lord Strenshall grunted. "That must have made you an interesting soldier."

"At times an army needs an officer who can think for himself."

The pressure on her chair increased, tilting her slightly toward him. She would have gone to him, but the notion of a room full of angry males did not appeal.

"Why are you working for the government?" Marcus snapped.

Dominic turned his head to address Marcus directly. "Because I worked for them before, and this method keeps me informed. I prefer to have a say in what happens in my country. I believe we are in a state of flux, and if we're not careful, we could find ourselves plunged back into civil war. The present monarch believes in consultation. We have taught him the value of it, and once Pandora's Box is opened, it cannot be sealed again. Even if the Stuarts return, they would not be an absolute monarchy." Even to say that much was treason, but nobody in the room appeared surprised at the statement. Dominic even garnered a few nods. "I believe that, for all their talk of sharing, that is what they want."

Silence fell, but not for long. That pause was telling, allowing everyone to think over what he said, although Claudia had heard similar discussions over the breakfast table. Only *en famille*, though. They probably went to White's and discussed everything, but she doubted it.

"Maybe I should start an exclusive club for ladies in Hart Street."

She hadn't realized she'd spoken aloud until Dominic snorted with laughter.

"If anyone could do it, Lady Claudia, I believe you could."

She warmed to him even more, as the men in the room hooted. Claudia let them have their fun. She'd have the last laugh. When they had cleared the nest of traitors from her house, she'd put serious thought to her idea. A club for ladies sounded like the kind of establishment she would enjoy. They would thumb their noses at the men who thought they ruled the world.

In the meantime she'd see what they wanted to do with the house that she owned.

"We should clean the place out," Val said. "Get rid of the seditious bastards." He glanced at Claudia and mouthed "sorry," presumably for using the curse word.

She shrugged and smiled. She'd heard worse words, and she had asked to be involved in this business. Forced her presence on them. She could hardly blame them for speaking freely.

"Then what?" she asked.

"Then in the fullness of time, you may sell it and add to your portion," Val continued. "You said you could not live in it."

She nodded. "I want to think about it. It might be more profitable to rent it out."

"As long as you ensure the tenants are loyalists," Marcus shook his lace ruffles free of his wide coat cuffs and picked up one of the papers. "You know where we obtained many of these?"

She nodded again.

Marcus glanced up at Dominic. "You?"

Dominic shook his head. "Tell me."

Even if he did know, that was a smart move. He might learn more. He probably thought they got them from the authorities, but if they had, it was by another's hand.

"Julius," she said.

Her father nodded. "Indeed. My wife's older brother is the Duke of Kirkburton. His son and heir, Julius, Lord Winterton, is particularly interested in the incursions of the Jacobites into London. You know of our family's long rivalry with the Dankworths I presume?" He never took his attention from Dominic's face the whole time he was speaking.

Claudia could only imagine how Dominic was feeling now, with the attention of her father and his three sons fixed on him. They were a formidable bunch. But then, Dominic was a formidable man.

Her father continued, "Our families have been at odds for some time, and now it comes down to the political divide between Jacobite and loyalist. I am not a foolish man, and I would not be speaking to you so frankly if I weren't sure you were on our side. I have friends in Whitehall."

"General Court," Dominic said with a twisted smile.

Lord Strenshall inclined his head. "As you say."

Dominic continued, "Then you should know that I am the only heir to my father's title now. I intend to take my responsibilities seriously. I am a Whig by persuasion and a loyalist by inclination. I have never met the Stuarts—formally—but I have seen them, and I know what they want. I cannot see their aims being good for the country as it is now. Besides which, the current monarch rules at our wish. The will of the people."

"You're getting close to republicanism there." Darius pressed the side of his thumbnail to his bottom lip.

"Do you object?" Dominic asked quietly, but menace growled low in his tones.

"Not in the least. A man is entitled to his opinions, but he doesn't necessarily have the right to impose it on others."

"Agreed."

What, had she set her sights on a republican? What did that mean? What did she want from him? Showing no sign of her agitation, Claudia forced her attention back to the present. At the moment she wanted to help decide what would happen with her house.

"I'd hardly say the Pretenders have republicanism at heart," she said, reminding them what they were here for. Increasingly she was getting the feeling that they wanted more than they said. They were interviewing Dominic, dammit. Yet again, matters were spiraling out of her control. She hated that, almost more than she hated anything else.

"They do not." Dominic shifted position and his hand grazed the side of her neck.

The touch hardly there, shivers went through Claudia. He hadn't done that by accident.

Her oldest brother cleared his throat, stood, and flicked his coat skirts. Habitually, he played with his clothes when he wanted to distract attention from something else. He'd seen that touch and detected her reaction to it.

"I do not want that house disturbed for the time being," Dominic said.

Darius, who had been staring at his fingernails as if detecting a flaw there, looked up. "The devil you say. Why not?"

"Because I want to observe what goes on there." Dominic paused before he spoke again. "I should not be telling you this, you understand?"

The men in the room grunted or nodded their assent, because they must have known he would say nothing if they did.

"The government has had enough. The prime minister wants Stuart arrested and brought to trial."

Darius and Val hissed through their teeth, Marcus muttered a word that he should not have used in mixed company.

Her father merely nodded. "I expected as much. Newcastle does not have the subtlety of mind of his brother."

The late Henry Pelham-Holles had died two years ago, much to the general lamentation of the Whigs. Yet another reason for striking now, if the Jacobites were attending, while politics was in a state of flux. Where the Duke of Newcastle was intelligent, his brother Henry had been brilliant. Now Henry had gone, everything worked a little less well.

"I believe you're right." Dominic's hand tightened on the top rail of Claudia's chair. "I came today to inform you of the government's intention."

Marcus laughed roughly. "You always meant to tell us, did you not?"

"I considered it," Dominic said. "May I be frank?"

The men either nodded or agreed verbally.

"I don't think a public trial for Stuart is the best course. I still think the Cause is better dying a slow death."

"I agree," her father said without hesitation.

"You want him in my house?" she demanded. "Is that it?"

"I want him where I can find him," Dominic said steadily, but this time he addressed her. Their eyes met. His crinkled very slightly at the corners in the beginning of a smile that did not reach his lips. "I want to know what he is doing in London and who his associates are."

"We know that," Darius growled. He kicked away from the wall, heedless of the scuffmark he made on the paneling.

Their mother would not appreciate the extra work he'd made for the servants, and she would no doubt speak to him later about it. Claudia looked forward to it. The men got away with far too much in this house.

"I say we take him and send him back to France," Darius said.

"Italy," his twin corrected him.

"I care not, as long as he's out of this country."

"To plot again?" Dominic looked away from Claudia and addressed her brother. "To send messages to his partners in crime in London?"

Val sighed. "He's right. The more we know, the better we can deal with the situation."

Still tracing a line on the desk with his forefinger, Marcus lifted his head. "What concerns me is the coincidence. How did Claudia come into possession of one of the most notorious houses of sedition in the city? In the country, for that matter?"

"Oh, I think we know the answer to that," her father said steadily. The chair creaked as he leaned forward, resting his arms on the wood. "It screams 'Dankworth' from every pore."

Chapter 6

Jacobites lived by schemes and plots. Dominic studied the occupants of the room. As enemies, the Emperors would prove formidable, if this were any sample of what he had to deal with. But if he had to, he'd take them on.

Ironic that of all people, he was dealing with spies and conspiracies. A lie had chased him abroad, and it remained with him still. One day he'd speak to his parents about the deception they perpetuated that sent him into the army. Then his life could change for good.

However, at the moment, they were in agreement. At least they understood the sense of his plan.

How could anyone think that holding a public trial would help anyone except the Stuarts? It would end nothing, just give the deluded fools who considered they had the right to claim the throne more fodder to stir up unrest.

When General Court had outlined his plans, he'd known he wouldn't be obeying his erstwhile superior to the letter. He would watch Stuart, but he would have no part in his capture.

Aware of every movement he made, he lifted his hand from Claudia's chair, brushing her silky hair as he walked away. He could not make his preference too obvious, could allow no weaknesses to show. Not yet, or the men here would take advantage.

"What you do with the Dankworths is your affair," he said. "It is none of mine, unless they are directly involved in this business. What makes you think they are involved in the house in Hart Street?"

"Instinct," Lord Strenshall said.

In this confined space, the Shaws could be formidable. So could he. Strenshall was a formidable patriarch, and with his sons around him, he appeared like nothing so much as one of the leaders of a rookery gang. Except the Shaws had even more power, and the ears of the most influential people in the land.

Although a viscount and the heir to an earl, Dominic had fewer than they did. He had spent most of his adult life abroad serving with the army. Although he'd met men from these families, he'd had no opportunity to form connections such as they had done. They would prove useful allies.

"However, I may be able to help," he said.

"In what way?" Strenshall asked. The lines around his mouth tightened.

"By letting you know what I see or hear," he said easily.

Was it his imagination or had the atmosphere in the room snapped taut? No, he had staked his life on sensing such subtleties before. He was not wrong. They knew something they were not telling him. A secret that could help him. "In return, I want your complete confidence."

Darius Shaw laughed, a sharp bark of laughter that echoed off the walls. "What makes you insist on that?"

"It isn't as if you're family," Valentinian put in.

Dominic glanced down at Claudia. "I could be," he said. The notion shot through him in an instant. "Shall we make a match of it, Lady Claudia? What do you say?"

Her eyes widened and her jaw dropped. She closed her mouth with a snap before getting to her feet in a swirl of silk. "I will not be spoken to in such a way! I may have—" She flushed. "That is, I wish to choose my husband carefully. Not take a man because of convenience!"

"You are four-and-twenty," her father said mildly. "We have been extremely lenient with you and your sisters, but perhaps it is time we thought of betrothals. However"—he turned his hard gaze to Dominic—"my daughter has the right of it. Her marriage will not be the result of subterfuge or a cold arrangement."

"She may wish to jilt me at the end of the season," Dominic drawled, meeting his lordship's gaze. "I would not object if she discovered we did not suit. However, as her betrothed husband, I would have a right to examine her properties, would I not?"

They could think that was the reason for his seemingly sudden proposal, but he wanted more. He wanted Claudia. Not necessarily for life, but he wanted to discover what fascinated him, why she drew him with such certainty. If he entered a room, he knew she was there, even if he couldn't see her. When he'd entered this house this morning and when he'd entered the other. Truthfully, he hadn't been sure it was she who'd entered the Hart Street house. Instinct had driven him, and he hadn't needed to see her face or that wayward golden curl to know he was right. He'd felt her.

"Lady Claudia is a lovely, intelligent woman of good family. My parents wish me to marry soon. I have seen nobody who attracts me as much as she does." He met her fulminating glare and smiled. "I do mean that."

"That's preposterous!" Claudia said. "I will not stay."

He had to admire her magnificence as she stormed from the room, her skirts swishing as if to emphasize her fury. She didn't even slam the door behind her.

With her gone, he could speak more frankly. "Sir, you need someone to watch her. I believe she could be in danger because of...events she witnessed."

If he'd recognized her so easily last night, someone else might well have. That house held any number of dangerous men. He was infuriated that she had blindly walked into it, but he didn't blame her brothers for the lapse in care. At least not entirely, although he'd have probably put a sturdy footman with her. She was willful, even wild, and her reputation in society or so he'd learned, was a woman on the edge of disgracing herself.

She needed better care. She needed him.

Strenshall put his head in his hands, but with a deep breath, lifted it again. "I know it, but she is resourceful and unafraid."

Marcus sighed. "A lethal combination. Her twin has no such urge. I have spoken to her, and so has our father."

Dominic would wager his best diamond neckcloth pin that they'd exacerbated the problem. Claudia was restless and bored, any fool could see that. Except her family could not. They merely saw a willful child.

"Even now I worry where she's gone," Strenshall said. "One day..."

Val moved first, dragging a gold pocket-watch from his waistcoat and flipping open the lid. "I have to go, I'm afraid. I have an appointment."

His twin tilted a brow. "With a lady, no doubt."

"At this time of day?" Val laughed. "I doubt any lady I'm so intimately acquainted with is even conscious at this time of day. No, a meeting in a coffeehouse, and then to White's. I'm meeting our redoubtable cousin Max." He nodded to Dominic. "The Marquis of Devereux. Maximilian."

"I am aware of the connection. A large family with such unusual names tends to stand out," Dominic said. Not to mention that Devereux, despite his title, was one of the most powerful men in the City. In fact, that was why the Emperors of London were so dangerous. They extended into most arenas of power, and they worked together. The combination could be lethal to their enemies.

Unfortunately, their enemies had similar influence, although in slightly different circles. That made for an uncomfortable situation in the country.

One day they might recall the initial reason for their dispute—argument over a piece of land didn't sound right to Dominic— and then they might combine. He repressed his shudder.

"If we are of the same mind, I have no objection to sharing my thoughts and information with you. As long as you do the same." Dominic lifted one shoulder in a shrug. "I know you're hiding something. I caught those looks. I have other matters to pursue, and no doubt you will want to consult other parties before confiding in me."

He strolled to the door, and then paused with his hand on the knob and turned back, as if on an afterthought. "I will find out what you're hiding, one way or the other. Make no mistake about that."

His parting shot delivered, he had no reason to stay. He opened the door and walked into the bright expanse of the hall with its crisp black and white tiles.

As the footman left to fetch his outerwear, the door to the room opposite opened. Claudia rushed out and grabbed his hand. Without stopping to speak to him, she dragged him back to the room.

"Close the door."

"Won't your duenna object?" Her mother or someone. For heaven's sake, the men of her immediate family were in the room opposite. They'd run him through, given half a chance. "Shouldn't we leave the door open?"

She snorted. "Do you see a duenna? I have no need of any such thing. Besides, you all but proposed to me in my father's study. Whatever got into you?"

He would show her exactly what. He pulled her into his arms and to the echo of her shocked squeak, he crushed his mouth to hers.

No gentle salute this, but a passionate kiss of desire. Exactly what he'd fantasized about while he was standing in front of her father. Her proximity there had tortured him, especially the saucy little looks she kept shooting him. Teasing him.

He lifted his mouth from her gratifyingly kiss-reddened one. "Did you think I didn't notice the way you looked at me? You are playing with fire, madam. Do not flirt if you have no intention of continuing."

"Oh, I have every intention of continuing." She sighed and reached around his neck, tugging him down to her and this time initiating the kiss.

With a groan, he surrendered. She tasted of honey, and Claudia. When he drove his tongue deep into her mouth he detected a touch of the coffee she must have drunk at breakfast.

He caressed her, holding her tightly to him. Today her hoops were modest and he could draw her closer, but frustratingly not close enough.

He badly wanted to treat her like the most experienced of doxies, but for all her eagerness, she was untried, even innocent in physical matters.

When he lifted his head, her lips were slick with his caresses. He didn't release her and she didn't try to pull away.

Her eyes danced. "Do you mean to do that every time we find ourselves alone?"

"Yes." Why equivocate? He couldn't keep his hands off her, and as long as he kept his baser desires strongly leashed, he could at least have this.

"Then I'll have to find more excuses to be alone with you." She touched his nose with her finger, tapped it as if in rebuke. "Mind you, that doesn't mean that I will fall in with your outrageous suggestion. Kissing you is a little different to a betrothal."

"We'd have more time alone together." That in itself was a good reason as far as he was concerned. He worried about her. He wanted to keep her in view, in case she took some idiotic idea into her head to run off and infiltrate another house of ill repute. How on earth could he let her do that again? The very thought made his stomach churn.

"We could be pressured into doing something neither of us wants." Pressing her hand on his chest, she stretched up on her toes for another kiss.

"Yet you've reached the grand old age of twenty-four without marriage."

Although she wore a lawn fichu over her breasts today, he could still taste them. He wanted that satiny bounty he'd touched last night again. That was not the reason for his sudden proposal, though. He needed to keep her safe. He very much feared that without him, she'd hoodwink her family again. This time she could find herself in the kind of trouble she couldn't escape from.

"I have." She flashed a saucy grin, and those enchanting dimples peeped out.

He could not think of one reason why he should resist. He kissed them, dotting his mouth first on one, then the other. "I daresay you're expert at evading unwanted suitors."

"I am. Any number of fortune hunters have tried to lure me into their carriages."

"That sounds ominous." It did. "What made you think you were safe with me last night?" Unexpectedly, anger surged up to burn him. He never allowed anger to control him, but he had to remind himself of that fact. "You went into a house of ill repute that just happened to be full of traitors who would have killed you if they discovered your identity. You went into a private room with me."

She moved closer. "I think I was safest there."

He groaned as her body heat seeped through to him. "It depends what you regard as safe. Do you really think I'd have held off for much longer?" Holding her firmly, he refused to let her squirm against him. The minx knew full well what she was doing. "If you tease men in this fashion, you'll not remain a virgin past another day."

She went absolutely still and her lovely face turned solemn. "Would it be so important if I were not a virgin?"

Now his anger ratcheted up to fury. Who had done this to her? "Why? Has someone hurt you?"

She shook her head. "No. I have every reason to believe I retain the precious commodity. It's just not right, Dominic. Why should I keep myself pure when it's highly likely that my husband, whoever he turns out to be, will not?"

"Ah." Clearing his throat, he gave his emotions a moment to subside. Not, unfortunately, his erection, which strained against his breeches. As well she couldn't sense that. What was it about this woman? She aroused him, angered him, and amused him, all at the same time. He never knew where he was with her and he'd always preferred certainty in his life.

No, she couldn't be for him, not for a lifetime. He'd do his job, ensure her safety and move on. If she agreed to a temporary betrothal, he could keep her close while he worked. Either that or she'd drive him crazy while he abandoned the work of getting Stuart out of the country. Then there'd be hell to pay because he'd wager he wasn't the only man working on this task.

"Claudia, will you accept a temporary betrothal? You know we would not suit in the long term."

She broke out of his arms, lifted her skirts, strode across the room in a most unladylike manner, and then turned and came back to him. "Do I truly? Indeed, I have discovered no one with whom I could imagine staying for a lifetime. Is everything temporary? Do I have to console myself with mild friendship or a business partnership? Or maybe I'll find some luck. My parents are devoted to each other, yet they barely knew each other when they became betrothed. I want something more." She spread her hands. "I want love."

"You deserve it." He meant that. Whatever other labels he stuck on this woman, one remained with him. She was passionate. He'd hate to see that fire dimmed. "I fear I am not the man who can give it to you." All his life he'd spent alone, as if somehow he wasn't a part of what was going on around him. That feeling had only increased when he discovered his parents were keeping a secret from him.

Claudia made him feel alive, truly in the present for the first time in forever. She deserved better than what he could give her. How long would that elusive feeling remain once he knew her better?

"Then I won't marry you and I won't agree to a false betrothal."

He would persuade her. He had never yet failed, but he set himself to a longer campaign than he would have liked. "In that case, I will court you. Every ball, rout, performance at the theater. I'll call on you to take you riding in the park, and I'll invite you to music recitals and displays of soldiering skill at Horse Guards. You will not rid yourself of me."

"I'll have my own duenna, is that it?" She made a face. "A male one."

Taking the step that separated them, he hauled her back into his arms for a kiss. This time he thrust his tongue into her mouth without preliminaries, desperate to taste that recklessness that he had never unlocked in himself. Everything he did was calculated, analyzed, and worked out. This woman showed him a touch of danger, true danger, the kind that came of plunging in with her heart instead of her head. It invigorated him while it terrified him, and he couldn't let her do it alone.

She pressed against him and threw herself into whatever he wanted to do with her as recklessly as she did everything else.

When they separated their lips, they were both panting. Her bosom enticed him, its fine covering of lawn the most tempting sight he'd witnessed for a long time.

"Very well," he said, "I agree, for now. I'll court you. If society shows any sign of creating a scandal, we will be betrothed."

"I'll be even worse off when I jilt you," she pointed out. "Then they'll have another name to add to the list of the things they call me."

He gave her a wolfish smile. "Then I'll have to make your reasons for doing it very good, won't I? Shall I have a mistress and flaunt her before you? Or swear that I'll never let you out of my sight, that I'll be locking you up in my house in the country for your own good?"

"Or I was mistaken about you," she murmured against his chest. "You're not the man I took you for. Maybe you're a changeling, swapped by the fairies at birth for one of their own. It would certainly explain the flamboyant clothing. Are those buttons real gold?" She toyed with a waistcoat button right over his chest.

If wishes came true, he'd be naked and she'd be stroking his skin, but there was a saying about wishes and horses.

Good lord, he'd have to tell his parents! How on earth would they take the news that he meant to court one of the most notorious women in London? He could hardly tell them the truth even if he knew it himself. He was beginning to think he understood nothing about this affair, and for the first time in his life, he was truly out of his depth.

Nevertheless, when he kissed her again, he stopped worrying.

* * * *

After a week, Claudia was no nearer getting to know the man so assiduously courting her as she'd been when she first met him. He charmed her, bestowed glorious kisses on her when nobody was watching, and ensured people saw him in public wherever she was.

She didn't trust this man. He confused her. All his previous confidences and truths were gone, disappeared after that meeting in her father's office as if they had never existed. Every time she tried to get close to him, he evaded her. He brought her into the company of people they could discuss nothing with, or kissed her. Every time he kissed her, he took her resolve away completely.

She wanted him so badly, but she wanted the man she'd seen glimpses of, not this society fribble. The man exasperated her.

On the Monday after his declaration that he would court her, she met him in a thankfully abandoned corridor in a house she happened to know well on the evening of a ball at her grandfather's house. Her grandparents lived in a grand mansion near Piccadilly, one of the few still standing after the building craze had razed many of them to the ground.

Slapping her hands on his chest, she pushed. It proved an effective way of moving him, impelling him back into a small chamber, one used by the family. Smiling, he put his hands over hers and backed off, even being so obliging as to open the door.

Then he made her breathless by swinging her around and claiming a kiss. He'd taken control of the situation as easily as if he'd initiated it. She responded, as always, with eagerness and pleasure, giving a small moan when he slid his tongue into her mouth. She loved the way he did that. Intimately, as if he were making love to her in truth. Now she had her doubts and that was what she wanted to talk about.

He drew away reluctantly, their mouths making a sweet, wet sound when they separated. "You taste so good, Claudia. You bewitch me completely."

This time she was determined not to allow him to seduce her away from her purpose with tender words. "What is happening, Dominic? You agreed that you would not shut me out. Why, then, have you done so?"

He closed his eyes and dropped his head, so his forehead touched hers. "There is nothing to tell, dear one. Truly. I have discovered nothing. It's as if they were waiting for something to happen, but I have no idea what that is."

At last, the first words on the subject she'd persuaded out of him in a week! "What are you doing?"

"I'm following you, and so far it's proved the most rewarding part of this investigation."

"What is he doing?"

"You know you are adorable when you're like this," he mused.

"Like what?" She could have bitten her tongue out, because all she was doing was giving him a chance to distract her. Which he did, skillfully.

He swept his palm up her back and touched the bare skin above her bodice, which, since this was a ball, was cut lower than usual. Then he smiled and kissed her. "When you're excited or angry about something, your eyes sparkle and you get the most becoming flush here." He traced a gentle line on her cheekbones and then down her throat. He skated it over the place where a frill of lace peeped over the top of her stiffly corseted gown. "It's immensely attractive to feel and see such soft, enticing flesh above a rigidly laced-in body. I can hardly feel you through your gown, what with all the boning and undergarments, but I know it's there and I want more of it."

She would have given it to him, except she had not lost sight of her goal. "What have you been doing?"

His sigh was theatrical. "Nothing, sweetheart. At least nothing of import. I swear it. I've been watching the house, and I've seen him a time or two, it's true. But he's gone out, come back and so far he's done nothing. He's kept to his usual haunts and his usual cronies."

"Did he visit the Dankworths?"

"Not directly, but he went to places they also attended." He smiled wryly. "I took you to that tedious concert at Ranelagh because he was there."

"That was why you left me in the company of my family for a half hour?" She pulled away.

But he drew her back "Yes it was." He kissed her forehead. "I learned nothing and saw nothing, other than a man who should not have been there talking a gentle walk with companions I already knew about. A waste of time I would much rather spend with you."

With more than a little exasperation, she pulled out of his arms. "Then what's to be done? Is this a private visit and he'll go back with no harm done?"

"We can hope so." He held out his arm. "Let's go back before they miss us. People are watching us for just such incidents as this. If we spend too much time out of the view of interested parties, they will assume our betrothal is done and dusted."

With a snarl and a growl, she pushed past him, aware as she did so that she couldn't have done it had he wished her not to. That infuriated her, too. What wasn't he telling her?

* * * *

With a smile he ensured she didn't see, Dominic followed Claudia back to the ballroom. This house had several large reception rooms, and they'd opened them all. They stretched in enfilade on the first floor, up the staircase that swept up in graceful curves from the ground floor. An elegant residence. It amazed him that at one time London had many more. They'd all gone now, replaced with the long streets and wide squares of Mayfair with houses that appeared the same from the outside at least. Like the one he lived in.

All the doors were open. The spectator could see straight through from the large room at the end, currently designated the ballroom, to a closed door four rooms away. Everyone in that line of sight was on display, part of the way society worked. This was one of the "must" balls of the season, one that everyone would try to attend. If they weren't seen there, it would be assumed that they were not invited.

Dominic strode into the first room, pursuing his quarry, and then the second, a smaller room where people chatted and took refreshments. Farther on was a smaller room and after that, the card room. He'd already seen it and wistfully thought of a quiet evening with a few friends, several bottles of wine and some packs of cards. He hadn't had a convivial evening like that for a long time.

This would most definitely not be one of them.

Her lavender gown swept the ground before him, but he didn't try to catch up with her until they reached the second room. Then, before any other of her suitors could do so, he quickened his pace. He appeared by her side, courteously offering him the support of her arm. She'd just opened her mouth to speak when another voice sounded form behind them.

"There you are!"

A perfumed elegant man in a pink as delicate as any woman wore glided up to them with all the elegance of a swan. He bowed, all sinuous grace, and took her hand. "Claudia, I declare you are finer than any other woman present!"

"I'll wager you said that to my mother, too," she said with a grin.

Dominic and the newcomer bowed to each other. "My lord," the man said, and "My lord," he replied. Lord Winterton, son and heir of the Duke of Kirkburton, who owned this house, gave him a considering smile.

Dominic wore eau-de-nil, but he'd tempered the delicate green of his coat by having it made up in a twilled silk. Winterton had no such qualms. His pink coat gleamed with a surface so glossy it was almost reflective. If Dominic was considered a dandy, Winterton took the art to atmospheric levels.

He wore a patch in the shape of a heart next to one eye. Dominic noted the paint on his face with a jaded lift of one brow. Winterton smiled blandly as if he hadn't seen Dominic's unspoken comment. This man missed nothing.

"I am delighted to see you here, St. Just. It means I may destroy the note I had written to you."

"You have news?" Claudia asked.

Dominic held back. Winterton was waiting for his response, watching him carefully. "I have no idea why you would wish to see me, but of course a summons from you is always an honor."

Instead of taking offence, Winterton's mouth moved in an infinitesimal way as he bowed. "You're very kind. I wished to discuss certain matters that we have in common. A person I employed to fulfill a particular task happened to notice your presence in a place I was not aware you knew of."

Dominic followed the convoluted explanation without difficulty. He was used to discussing private matters in public too. "I saw nobody." Since he was used to spotting spies, Winterton's employees had to be skillful. "I thought I stood there a little too long," he commented. "No doubt you know what I was doing there."

"Probably." Winterton smiled broadly, but his voice held no amusement. "I would appreciate you leaving the place to me. It is, after all, a family matter."

"I beg to differ."

"I don't pretend to know what you are talking about." Claudia sniffed. "I will find out. I can guess enough."

This time, Winterton's smile was genuine. "You're an intelligent woman, Claudia, but a mite too inquisitive at times."

Had he seen Claudia at that house? Apprehension tensed Dominic's muscles, but he kept his stance carefully relaxed, praying Winterton hadn't seen the light twitch of his little finger.

Winterton's cold blue gaze switched from Dominic's face to his hand. Of course he had seen. He said nothing about it. He would have noted Dominic's reaction, though. Dominic had never met Winterton for more than an exchange of courtesies. Now he wished he'd kept that up, because close up the man was as formidable as his reputation.

Not that most people knew it. To them he was a wealthy fop, one of many in society, who did nothing while spending much. However, in certain circles, such as the ones Dominic had frequented from time to time, he'd heard rumors. The man was powerful, intelligent, and curious. Dangerous, in other words.

Winterton was a loyalist, so at least on the surface he should be Dominic's ally, but the earl put his family first. Everybody knew that—"everybody" being the shadowy people behind the people ostensibly in power.

Far Dominic didn't trust him. "Sir, you should know of my interest in your cousin," he said. "I have certainly made no secret of it."

"Indeed, we wait daily upon an announcement." He said it without inflection, as a bored man about town. "Was your recent absence an advance in that sphere?"

"Alas, no." Their absence had been noted. This was Winterton's way of telling him. "I attempted the question, but the lady is too clever for me." He heaved a theatrical sigh. "She would not answer, and fearing the gods of propriety would follow us, I escorted her back here."

Her *cicisbei* could breathe sighs of relief. Claudia had quite a court.

"The last time you saw us, Julius, you were convinced you could not tell Livia and me apart," Claudia said. "I'm surprised you find you can do it with such ease."

Winterton turned a bland smile on her. "Indeed, I have learned the way. Tonight you're wearing lavender, and your lovely sister is in pale blue. She is in the ballroom, enjoying the company." He addressed Dominic next. "I wonder you can tell them apart, sir. How do you do it?"

"I have no difficulty," he said. It was true. He would know her anywhere, could pick her out unhesitatingly had she been one of three or four. He had no idea how he knew, but he did. He would never confuse the sisters. "Were you ever taken as each other?"

She laughed, a bright unshadowed sound that he immediately wanted to hear again.

"We used to play at it. Mama would put us in different gowns so that the company would have no difficulty telling us apart, and we would slip away and exchange them. Even my studious sister has her lighter side."

"I suspect you coerced her into it," Winterton said with a smile that was decidedly fond. "You never tricked me."

"No, I don't suppose we did, Julius, but you were good enough to pretend sometimes."

His smile broadened. "Yes, I did." He blinked, and if melancholy shadowed the earl's eyes, it was gone when Winterton turned his attention back to him. "You will not bring any member of my family into your games." He spoke quietly, steadily, always with that damned smile on his face, but his voice held a menacing note. Winterton's words held no threat. They were a promise, the "or else" unspoken but understood.

"That is the last thing I wish for. Sir, I believe we have business to discuss. I will call on you tomorrow, if you have the time."

Winterton nodded. "Unfortunately, I am engaged for the whole of tomorrow, but I agree, we need to discuss various matters. However, I would suggest the day after, at eleven, if you please. Do not come to my house for our meeting. I will speak to Strenshall, my uncle, and we may meet at his house."

"Agreed." Their mutual enemy could get to hear of Dominic visiting Winterton and become alarmed. However, he was already courting Claudia, so visiting her house would be considered unexceptional. He bestowed a smile on the earl as pleasant as the ones Winterton had given him. "I look forward to it."

Winterton bowed and moved away, after soliciting a dance from Claudia later. To the casual viewer, this was less the sight of two male stags locking antlers for the first time than two fops assessing each other's costumes and manners.

Dominic preferred to keep it that way for now, although already he was tiring of the pose.

When he glanced away, to ensure nobody was paying them particular attention, he met the gaze of a fat man with protuberant blue eyes.

At the same time as he made the connection, Claudia gasped. "That's him!"

Dominic's smile changed to a rictus. He didn't have to turn to know that Winterton had returned and was standing behind him. "Leave this to me, if you please. I'll have him removed, and it will be as if he were never here."

This was Winterton's parents' house, so he had the right.

Lynne Connolly

He stared at the Pretender and the Pretender stared back. If matters had turned out differently, he'd be bowing to the man and calling him "Your Highness." Charles Stuart had wrecked his chances of that nearly ten years ago. The years had not been kind to him, or he had not been kind to the years. Nobody had actually poured the wine down his throat and forced him to eat too much rich food and take too little exercise.

Dominic did not bow. Instead, he offered Claudia his arm. The men were too far away to speak, but that was as well, since fury simmered through him. He took her through to the smaller room away from the Pretender while Winterton dealt with the intruder. He didn't hear a sound, but he didn't turn to watch the way the ejection was accomplished.

He was sure it was done with the greatest respect.

Chapter 7

Since sleep eluded him for much of the night, Dominic rose early and went for an invigorating ride in the Park. Unfortunately, Hyde Park contained a number of fashionable carriages and riders, even at this hour. So he couldn't undertake the flat-out gallop both he and his restless mount would have preferred. But he did break into a reckless canter once or twice, so they made do with that.

On returning to his house, he discovered he had not been the only person up early that day. Instead of having the family house opened for him, he'd hired a smaller place that suited him better in the fashionable area of town. So it shocked him when he spotted a hat he knew well on the stand in the hall.

His heart lighter, despite the complications the arrival brought, he glanced at his butler.

"I put them in the drawing room, sir, and gave orders for breakfast to be brought forward."

"Thank you, Gibbs." He'd hired new servants, too, rather than bringing anyone except his valet to town. He liked the notion that they owed him nothing except ordinary service. They hadn't known him as a child, and they hadn't followed him into the army.

He took the stairs two at a time, but he was still in riding dress. So he continued to his bedroom. His valet was waiting with one of his less flamboyant coats. He shrugged into brown breeches, green waistcoat and darker green coat before shoving his handkerchief, watch, and purse in his pockets and racing back downstairs.

The tantalizing smell of bacon wafted around him. The servants must be bringing up breakfast. He went straight to the breakfast parlor, where he threw his arms wide. "Mama!"

She flew into his arms and hugged him tightly, her head barely reaching half way up his chest. "Dear boy, I am so pleased to see you! It seems an age since I saw you last!"

Without disentangling himself from her scented embrace, he held his hand out to his father. "Sir, welcome."

His father shook his hand.

"Why did you not use the Grosvenor Square house?" his mother demanded.

He laughed. "And rattle around there like a pea in a drum? No, I thank you."

"Well we are having it opened so you may come home," she said. She stepped back and smoothed a curl under her cap.

"Don't let your tea get cold." He drew back a chair for his mother and took the one next to her.

His father sat on his other side. His craggy, timeworn face beamed, but soon relaxed into its customary folds. Even when he was younger, Lord Brampton had a face his contemporaries referred to as "lived in." Now, in his sixties, it had settled into a gun-dog lugubriousness. It belied his character, which was generally sanguine. A smile looked out of place, but Dominic loved the incongruity.

"Papa, what has brought you to town? Estate business?" He was clutching at straws.

His father gave him a lowering glare from under bushy brows. "You are fully aware of the reason. We have heard from various acquaintances that you are seriously courting a young lady."

He sighed. "I am, but it isn't for the reasons you're probably suspecting."

"That's a shame." His mother poured herself a dish of tea. "It's time son. We thought you were in town for that purpose. To find a bride and then to make an heir."

"It's imperative that you do so," his father said sadly. "I know you didn't know your cousins well, but they were good men. They gave you a freedom of choice that you do not have any more."

He nodded and glanced at the footman standing impassively by the door. "That will be all, Selkirk. I'll call if we need anything."

Getting to his feet, he proceeded to fill a plate for his mother from the viands on the sideboard and then prepared one for himself. His father had joined him.

Dominic might as well eat while he still had an appetite, because despite his early morning exercise, he doubted it would last for long. He tucked in to the succulent bacon, following it with a swallow of tea. He began on the chop.

Then his father spoke. "Son, we expected a letter before now informing us of your good news."

"Lady Claudia has not agreed to marry me, sir."

"Have you asked?"

"I have." He should probably have sent them a letter at that point. Definitely, because although his pursuit of Claudia was not for the reasons everyone supposed, it appeared that way. "She has refused me once, but gave me indications that I should persevere. However, she says it is a matter of wanting to know me better."

His father grunted. "In my opinion, young people should have no interest in an arranged marriage, other than liking each other well enough."

Lady Brampton smiled. "You would have thought he had not fallen head over heels for me the moment he saw me and proposed two days later. Without telling his parents. What, my dear, are you telling me that you regret your rash action?"

Her husband's mouth twitched. "Not for a minute. Not a second, my love."

Such displays of emotion might embarrass a family less close, but Dominic was used to it. His father's actions often belied his words. Usually Dominic took little notice of the edicts that issued from time to time. Instead he paid more attention to the excellent example his father set.

This was no different. "I was not sure. I wanted to write to you with different news." No, it would not do. He couldn't keep his parents at arms' length. He never had, and he wouldn't start now. Right on cue, his appetite disappeared as his stomach tightened with nerves. He'd felt better before going into battle leading a hundred men or more to possible death.

Dominic pushed his plate away. "No, it's not that. It's something else."

Starting at the beginning, he related finding Claudia in that house. "You know I was not always engaged in straightforward military actions." His father nodded. "This is an example. The Young Pretender is in London again, and this time the government seems determined to make an example of him. I'm not so sure, but I will do my duty. He appeared at the Kirkburton ball last night."

His mother gasped. "Why on earth would he do that?"

"To throw himself at the country's mercy. Kirkburton's son got rid of him discreetly."

"I would have done the same. Who wants a scandal of that nature in their house?" His mother had an acute sense of social rightness. She rarely came to town these days, but once she'd been an accredited beauty and wealthy heiress. She knew societal requirements better than anyone. "Is he in custody?"

"No." He had heard nothing. If it had happened, by this time town would be abuzz. "For all I know, Kirkburton has returned him from whence he came. In which case our problems are over and Lady Claudia and I do not have to meet so often."

He wasn't aware he'd spoken with any melancholy, but his mother covered his hand with her own and squeezed before getting on with her breakfast.

"That doesn't mean you have to stop seeing her, dear. You're attracted to her, are you not?"

He could never hide anything from his mother and he'd given up trying years ago. "Yes, I am. I don't know if it is any more than that."

"Give yourself a chance to find out," his mother said. "We don't want to see you married if the result is unhappiness. If the business with the Pretender is concluded, it means you have more time to get to know her."

That made sense, so why did it sound hollow to him? A flash of totally inappropriate heat to his groin told him why. Because of that unexplainable attraction, the desperate need to get her into bed. Lust was only part of it. He had no idea how to explain the rest of it. A need to protect, but that was natural. But that feeling that he wanted her to look after him? He couldn't explain that. Bliss would be relaxing into her arms, and letting her take his head on her breasts.

Completely idiotic. He was tired. That was all.

Matters had come to a head, and he could defer discussing the topic no longer. The letter that had haunted him for years, the one that had proved the final straw and sent him abroad.

He pushed back his chair. "If you will excuse me, Mama, Papa. I would appreciate a private word with you when you have the time."

His mother spread her hands and looked up at him, smiling. "What's wrong with here?"

To spoil their appetite too? No, he would not do that. "Perhaps, when you are done, you can come upstairs to the drawing room." He forced a smile. "You have not seen the rest of the house."

"No, indeed. Although now we are here you may prefer to come to our own house."

Once he'd opened his heart to them, they would probably prefer not to be under the same roof with him.

He left the room, his pulse drumming in his ears. He had never been so apprehensive, never so much in need of a stiff brandy. He didn't have one, but went upstairs and collected the folder that was his constant companion. Even touching it made his throat tighten. He rested both hands against the dresser and leaned forward, forcing a series of deep breaths. He'd found himself in terrible situations before. He could get through this. After all, wasn't it better to know for sure than to live with more years of speculation?

He didn't know, but he feared he was about to find out. Unless, of course, his parents refused to tell him, but he had his own sources now. He would use them if he had to.

When he went downstairs to the drawing room, feeling more like a child going to accept punishment than an adult man of thirty-one, he approached the problem as he approached everything—head-on, without equivocation. Once he'd made up his mind, he would not go back. He never did.

His parents sat together on the sofa. His mother wore that faint smile that always gave her the air of interest in whatever the person confronting her was saying. Her patient endurance had infuriated her son more than once, but he refused to let it steer him from his purpose now.

She raised a brow at the sight of the folder. "That has been in the wars, has it not?"

She would probably expect him to find something elegant to put it in but the contents deserved only what he'd bestowed on them. Not even that, although the collection of them had cost him a lot.

He took the chair opposite to them and flipped the folder open, revealing its secrets. He was close enough to hand them the documents, but first he would tell them what he'd discovered.

"When I was seventeen, just before I left home to join the army, I discovered something by accident," he began. "Father was teaching me the management of the estate, so I was in the muniments room." He'd never set foot in it since, although he supposed he must one day. "If you recall, Papa, you told me to make free of the place. I don't know if you knew this was in it."

He picked up a nondescript sheet of notepaper, with a faded address on the back. He knew it by heart. "It comes from the Palazzo Muti, and it is addressed to my father. Shall I read it?"

Lynne Connolly

His father's face had turned white and he was gripping the sofa's armrest so tightly his knuckles were bone-pale. His mother's pallor owed nothing to the powder on her face.

"Please remind me of the contents," his father said. At least he didn't pretend he knew nothing of the document.

Dominic began to read, though in truth he could have recited it from memory.

"My dear Brampton," he began in a low, steady tone. As he had so often in the past, he cut his emotions away and refused to allow them to take hold of him any more than they had already.

"I have become aware of a favor you are considering bestowing on a young subject of mine. The lady is of good family and she has reason to wish for the item to be cared for in the most tender way. You will not regret your actions, and I will ensure you are rewarded as soon as we return to our rightful place in St. James's Palace, London.

"Until then, I remain, yours etcetera."

He looked up. "He only uses his initials, but it is enough. He placed his seal on the letter, too. James Edward Francis Stuart. He has the audacity to use a royal seal."

Dominic handed the paper over. He would prefer it destroyed, but when he'd discovered it, he already believed that whatever secrets it contained would change his life forever.

"You did the Old Pretender a favor. You never even told me you had visited Rome. How many times have you gone back?"

"Never," his father said in a thready voice.

"Did you know of this, Mother?" He refrained from using the more familiar "Mama." The word stuck in his throat.

"Of course I did," she replied. "What else do you have in that thing?" Disdainfully she indicated the file.

"Only a little slim evidence. When I found that, I determined to discover more."

"Why did you not ask us outright?" his mother demanded wrathfully. Her pale eyes sparkled. Lady Brampton did not lose her temper often, but when she did, the world knew.

"I did. I asked Father, but he refused to answer. Said it was nonsense, and it was merely a note from an old friend thanking me for transporting a large portrait home to his parents."

He stared at his father, who met his gaze steadily at first. Then he looked away.

Dominic returned his attention to the file. "You constantly taught me the value of love and honor, but you refused to honor me or my request. It was a lie. The Palazzo Muti was in the newspapers, and that seal? It's a royal seal. You should have said the Old Pretender sent this to you, and then I might have believed you. As far as you were concerned, the subject was closed."

He picked up another sheet. "I was lost, wondering what other secrets you'd hidden from me. I had long had the ambition to serve in the army, and despite your protests and mother's tears, I went. If I had not discovered this letter, I might have relented and stayed at home. I needed to get away."

He handed over the second document as if it meant nothing. "You know I was sometimes engaged in less-than-straightforward business. I came upon other evidence that you had helped the Pretender in some way. I kept the letters. You may burn them if you wish. I have no further use for them." The evidence was scarce, but he'd collected what he could find. A handful of mentions of his father, and then nothing more.

Abruptly he got to his feet, strode to the sideboard, and then changed his mind and walked to the window.

Life went on outside. At times the normality of existence soothed him, but today he resented it. How many people walking in the street outside suffered such disillusionment?

"You taught me honor and truth. You said that a man should always tell the truth and shame the devil. He should stand by his words and never act the traitor to his heart or his King."

Remembering the lessons he still tried to live by, Dominic wondered yet again why he had continued to stick by them. After all, a liar and a traitor had taught them to him.

"What do you mean to do?" his father asked quietly.

The sound of rustling paper showed him that they were going through the contents of the file. Ridding himself of it gave him some relief. He could breathe more freely now.

It was done and the secret was out. One thing remained. "What have you done?" he asked quietly.

"Who knows about this?" his father demanded.

"Only me, and of course, you. However, if you continue to act the spy and traitor, I will take steps to ensure you do it no more."

He had planned what he meant to do. Declaring his father a traitor in public would mean utter disgrace, probably the loss of the land and title. Not that he cared for those, but the people who worked on the estate deserved better. They depended on his father for a living. Society would totally destroy Lord Brampton, and for all this lapse of judgment his father had achieved some things in his life. "Are you still working for the Pretender?"

He leaned his forehead against the cool glass. A chair mender made his raucous way down the street. Occasionally, the sound of his voice raised up even here, and the chairs, the knives, and old chair-legs proclaimed his profession. Did he have an easier life? A man with a trade would never starve, or so his father had told him. A fallacy. A lie, like so much his father had told him. How could he trust anything his father said?

That was why he had left. To find his own truth. He had contacted his parents, visited them when he came home, but until now had never the courage to face them with what he knew. This state of affairs could go on no longer.

With a rustle of silk, his mother got to her feet. "This folder is missing one or two documents," she said, and when her husband protested, she continued, "I will fetch them. Like you, I carry some things with me always. I have a folder of my own."

In the five minutes she was gone, Dominic stayed by the window, his heart pounding again. Another folder? He'd expected them to deny it, perhaps lose their tempers and pretend not to know what he was talking about. They wouldn't have realized he'd become an adept at interrogation as part of his work. Since he'd been planning for a longer campaign, his mother's capitulation took him aback.

His mother returned, a pretty embroidered folder in her hand. "Unlike you, I adorned my portfolio. It's the most important possession I have, but I will trust you with it." She unfastened the red ribbons holding the folder closed. "You may do what you wish with the contents."

From precious to waste. Wondering at her attitude, he could yet read nothing in her face. His mother could have defied him for hours, had she wished. He could hardly employ some of the methods he had used in the past with his parents.

However, one decision remained firm. If they continued to lie to him and to refuse to tell him the truth, he'd walk away. They would be nothing but his parents, and he would no longer owe them his love. Only duty.

The folder only held two papers. One was another letter, one he'd never seen before. He knew the handwriting and the signature; the royal seal, although this one was small and cracked.

My dear sir,

I am pleased to hear that you are finally back in England. I would I were with you, but I fear that will not happen for some time to come. While I understand your decision, it grieves me to know that you will not help me in my quest. However, I will trust you with the enclosed document, on the understanding that you show it to nobody else. Then all will be at an end between us. My dear Maria sends her best wishes, but she understands the necessity of the action we take and she will not tell anyone of our bargain.

"About as clear as the one I have." Relief flooded through him. If his father had betrayed his King and country at one time, he had thought better of it later and refused to help further. That spoke for something, after all. He glanced at his father. Lord Brampton's left hand still clutched the armrest as if his life depended on it.

Dominic picked up the second paper, and everything he'd known before in his life changed. Nothing was the same, nor would it ever be so again.

Chapter 8

Claudia had not expected to see Dominic that morning. He'd quite clearly told her he intended to spend the day at his club, collecting gossip. She had teased him, telling him the club members sounded like a lot of old women and he'd be much better off at her mother's literary salon.

Just before they'd parted, he'd taken advantage of a nearby darkened doorway to pull her in and snatch a brief breathless kiss. He teased her with the possibility of more but never allowed it. "That is for your insults about my club," he murmured as he took her back to her coach. "You can wait for another, and I shall probably make you ask for it."

Today, she was emerging from a toy-shop in the Royal Exchange when he swept up to her. He grabbed her arm in a grip she could only describe as vise-like, since she didn't have time to think of anything more original. He dragged her to the end of the row, where narrow stairs led down to the ground level.

In the scant shelter offered, he dragged her close and kissed her in a way she had never known. His recklessness thrilled her to her marrow. He took her brutally, forcing her mouth open with his tongue, possessing rather than tasting and exploring. Desperation transmitted itself to her in the tense muscles under his unusually plain coat and his arousing kiss.

The dandy had turned into a savage. He heated her fast, her senses rising to respond to his demands.

Groaning, he finished the kiss but before he could do so again, she spoke. "My mother and sister will be more than shocked by your behavior. While I am flattered, didn't you say you'd be at White's today?"

He shook his head. "I needed to see you. You said you were shopping. I walked the length and breadth of Bond Street, and then I recalled this place."

While the Exchange was mainly for commerce, it also had a number of charming shops. A stroll around the upper floors, open to the fresh air, made the most of the pleasant weather.

"Bond Street is always crowded. Besides, I wanted to find a new fan, and the best maker in London trades from here." She spoke by rote, calmly.

He was agitated, his voice holding his distress.

"I'm sorry." He sighed and then turned, holding out his arm. "I just wanted to see you, that was all. One last time."

"What do you mean? Where are you going?" Now it was her turn to feel alarmed.

"Nowhere." He grimaced. "I have to talk to you. I will not—never mind, I cannot speak to you rationally here. I barely know what rational is any more. I fear what I have to say may involve your father and brothers. I must ask to see them." He paused. "They are at least men of honor."

"You are a man of honor."

He took her face between her hands. "I have cheated and lied for my country. I have caused people suffering when I wanted to learn the truth or reveal a secret."

He'd hurt them? He could mean nothing else. While she'd vaguely imagined his clandestine work had not been completely above board, she'd assured herself that he'd done it for his country. That made whatever he did expedient. She could not believe that he had prolonged suffering.

"You wouldn't have hurt them unnecessarily." She spoke firmly. A breeze swept past them, ruffling the folds of her light shawl and disturbing the curls brushing her neck.

With a slight wistful smile, he brushed a curl back and lingered to caress her neck softly. "You are utterly charming," he said, "I suspect your pragmatism outdoes mine. I cannot say I did cause anyone to suffer unnecessarily, but what is necessity?"

"Philosophy, here?" She glanced around. "I told you that you'd be better at my mother's salon. She's holding it in an hour. Will you come?"

He shook his head. "After what I have to tell you, you will not wish to be in my company. I will call on you as soon as I may and explain myself. I owe you that, at least. I will request that at least some of your family be present at that time. I cannot tell you more, my sweet, because I can't bear to say it more than once. Have no hopes in me. Whatever we thought was growing between us is at an end. We cannot continue with anything. I have plans to rejoin the army abroad, although my…parents… are against it."

"But you're the only heir!" How could he walk away from that? He would make his parents unhappy and deny everything they had worked for.

He only pressed another hard, feverish kiss to her lips, and then he was gone. He clattered down the stairs as her mother and sister rounded the corner and caught up to her.

Lady Strenshall gazed down the stairs. "That young man has a bee in his bonnet, and that's for sure. I'm not sure he'd be entirely comfortable as a husband."

To her mild surprise, Claudia found she could still smile at the vision of Dominic wearing a bonnet.

* * * *

"Have you not seen your favorite admirer recently?"

Claudia glanced sharply at her sister, who was placidly seated at the dressing-table mirror hooking in a pair of amethyst earrings. "Which one would that be?"

"You know fine well. St. Just." She finished and sat back to admire the result, shrugged, and got up to make way for her sister.

"Why do you do that?" Claudia demanded, eager to get the conversation away from her erstwhile courtier.

"What?" Livia twitched at her gown. Their maid had just left, dismissed by Livia before she'd quite finished. Livia picked up her spectacles and popped them on her nose before examining her appearance in the mirror and turning away.

"You are quite lovely, you know."

"Considering we are identical, that's rather vain of you."

Claudia smiled. "Some people can tell us apart, even when you're not wearing those horrible things."

Livia took off the glasses. "These horrible things save me from headaches when I'm studying. Twenty years ago, I would not be able to see so well close-up. Did you know that the expert in optics who developed these lenses lives in London?"

It was Claudia's turn to shrug. She took her place before the mirror and picked up the haresfoot. "I'm glad he's proved of use to you."

Prepared to continue the discussion, even accept one of her sister's lectures, she attended to her cheeks. She added some of the blush that had unaccountably disappeared over the last few days. She'd appeared almost lackluster when she looked at herself in the mirror in the mornings.

"Come on, Claudia, you've been tossing and turning all night. You can't hide it from me. Everyone else may think you're the same as always, but you've fallen out with him, haven't you?"

It wasn't like Livia to recall the original topic of discussion, especially when given permission to impart a nugget of knowledge. She must have really made her mind up to confront Claudia. That meant she wouldn't let up until Claudia said something.

Claudia racked her brains. "We do not suit, that's all. Our...association was exciting and interesting, but we tired of each other. Ran out of conversation."

"No you did not." Livia spoke so calmly, as if she'd been there. "It was after that day at the Exchange when he rushed you off and then ran away."

"He did not run away!" Claudia had no idea why he hadn't paid her special attention recently, except for that day. Except the possibility that had been nagging at her mind. Perhaps it was time to share it.

"That day he said he was going to talk to Papa. That was the day we heard from Haxby about Gates."

On hearing of the injury to his land steward, her father and oldest brother had set out for the family country seat in Yorkshire that very day. That had been two days ago. They should be there tomorrow. It would take them a while to resolve the matter, and then another three days to journey back to town. That was unless they chose to deal with other business or pay a visit to someone on the way back. Or unless the injury to Gates proved even worse than they imagined.

After Gates had fallen from his horse, the butler sent her father a letter immediately. Gates wasn't just a servant. His family had worked for her family for generations, and their children played together in the grounds of Haxby Hall. A bad fall could mean a broken neck. Not everyone died from that, but sometimes people wished they had.

"Do you think he's given up? I distinctly saw St. Just walk away from you when he saw us last night. He didn't cut us, it's true. Would he have done so?"

"No!" The idea made her feel slightly sick. "He is merely observing proprieties."

"Rubbish!" Livia rarely spoke her mind so firmly in matters of everyday life. Ask her the difference between translations of Virgil and she would have a decisive opinion ready. But ask her if she meant to wear the blue or the lavender, and she'd go into a tizzy of indecision. "He could not keep away from you before. When you were not looking, he gave you such a look of heartbreak. I swear, he appeared like nothing so much as a heartsick Paolo!"

She frowned. "Paolo?"

"Paolo and Francesca, silly. The people Shakespeare used as his models for Romeo and Juliet."

Claudia rounded on her sister. "I certainly have no intention of stabbing myself. Or of pretending to be dead, for that matter."

"Francesca did not have a chance to do that." That was better. Livia was speaking of academic subjects. Claudia should be safe now.

She stood and posed briefly, ensuring the big pleats at the back of her gown were straight. The topaz pendant on her pearl necklace was hanging perfectly, just touching the top of the cleft between her breasts. She would do, although the one she wanted to do most for, would most likely avoid her.

Even if he made an appearance at Lady Marbury's tonight, he would not stay long and he wouldn't speak to her.

This couldn't go on. She'd caught his burning eyes on her when she moved quickly or let him pretend she wasn't looking. He seemed to think that something had happened that made him unworthy of her. That was what he'd intimated to her when he'd confronted her at the Exchange.

Claudia wanted his kisses again, wanted to feel herself in his arms, experience his passion. Was he lavishing it on someone else? Surely not—not after three days. Even the idea of him doing with someone else what he did with her turned her stomach. One day, if she didn't make a push for her, he would move on. Find someone else. He was a passionate man. Even a paid mistress would distress her. Did he have one already?

Enough. With Livia prattling by her side about people long dead, Claudia went down to the hall where her brothers Valentinian and Darius stood waiting. They would go in twin strength tonight. Although neither set of twins made a habit of dressing alike, it would take more than different clothes to disguise their similarity to each other. As children both had great enjoyment hoodwinking their nurses and servants.

Those times were done, at least for Claudia and Livia.

Val whipped off Livia's spectacles, which she'd donned to find a book in the small shelf of volumes in their room and gave the offending objects back to her. Livia made a face at her brother and shoved them in her pocket. "How anyone can consider you handsome I have no idea. All I recall was your ability to get muddy on a summer day."

"Then they shouldn't have dressed us in white smalls." Val grinned. He wore white breeches tonight, but not a speck of dust or lint marred the pristine surface. Unlike when he was a child.

They went out to the carriage, chattering about Renaissance lovers and the state of affairs in London. Darius took great delight in recounting the latest murder trial at the Old Bailey, in which he had an unnatural interest. It kept them guiltily amused for the ten minutes it took for them to reach Lady Marbury's.

The torchères set outside the front door of the white-stuccoed house illuminated the usual morass of carriages disgorging passengers and servants attending to their masters and mistresses. Livia and Claudia generally saw to themselves. The evening was too mild to require more than a light wrap. As she handed it to the waiting footman in the hall, Claudia caught sight of someone rounding the corner at the top of the stairs.

She gave chase. He would not ignore her tonight. He would tell her what was troubling him, and she would make him, if they were the last words she ever had with him. She could not wait for this much longer, especially as her father and brother would be away for the next four days at the very least.

The inside of the house blazed with candles, making a warm evening even warmer. The great chandelier in the hall and the wall-sconces all contained lit candles, of the finest beeswax. Her mother, a thrifty individual, or so she always claimed, said wax candles were a shocking expense and something had to be done.

Or she might very well go mad.

She was not sure if he'd seen her, but he certainly set a punishing pace for a woman in the panoply of full ball dress. Claudia had learned to handle hooped skirts from her childhood. Now she was hard put not to send it swaying unforgivably as she pursued him determinedly across the rooms set aside for tonight's gathering.

A group of people gathered around the huge Van Dyck family portrait that was the pride and joy of this house. Claudia spared it barely a glance, merely curtseying to the matrons when she couldn't avoid doing so and watching in despair as her quarry disappeared out of sight.

If not tonight, tomorrow. She'd make him confront her, instead of disappearing like a damned will-o-the-wisp. She couldn't wait another four days. Or even longer.

Eventually she had to admit that she'd lost him, and settled to discussing some poet or other Lady Marbury introduced her to.

The poor young poet stood by helplessly as she burbled on. "Dear Lady Olivia"—it infuriated Livia when people called her that, as they did all too often. She would not disabuse the lady. Let Lady Marbury continue to believe Claudia was Livia.

Claudia didn't care what people called her. Had her ladyship been a noticing person she'd have spotted that at once. She was not, so she saw nothing.

The poet was handsome, tall and very slim, making Claudia wonder how much of his body weight was due to the heavy coat he wore. She didn't want to pursue the connection when he wouldn't meet her eyes and utterly refused to smile when she offered him one. Instead, he looked down his considerable nose at her and declared her "A positive beauty, I declare! You should pose for a portrait of Venus, that you should!"

Because she was fair-haired, or because he really thought it? The facile comparison should be under the notice of a decent poet. Mr. Pope would have twisted it into something different, making analogies until the ground under her feet became uncertain. Perhaps that was why women flocked around the diminutive poet. He'd been a favorite of her mother's, but when she recalled that to the poet, whose name eluded her, he sneered. "I could not possibly comment. He is far too obvious for my taste. I prefer the natural style."

"The rustic is charming, and it has a number of profound meanings." She wished she'd listened more to Livia when her passion for poetry was at its height a few years ago. Livia had read every volume she could get her hands on and memorized much of it before moving on to novels.

"Indeed so." The poet proved as loquacious as her ladyship.

Claudia was hard put to get away. But after at least ten minutes, she extricated herself by accepting an invitation to dance from a half-inebriated Lord Withermore, a loose-lipped man she usually did her best to avoid. She'd have accepted a dance from the devil if it meant she got away from the most tedious poet in London.

She would be sure to tell her mother about him when she got home, except she still couldn't remember the man's name. After she'd taken the floor with Lord Withermore for a country-dance, she feared her quarry was long gone.

Except she caught sight of him. Resplendent in emerald green, he was chatting to Lady Marbury, or at least, her ladyship was chatting to him. Spying Livia across the room, she exchanged a grin. Her sister jerked her head slightly in the direction of the card room. So that was where her brothers had decamped to. Picking up her skirts, she made a determined advance on her prey. He would not get away this time.

Lady Marbury had the great felicity of introducing them. She curtseyed as he bowed, but this time when he took her hand, he didn't kiss it, merely the air above it in the accepted manner. He behaved as if they'd never met before, so she pushed the acquaintance on a little.

"I believe we know each other already, sir."

He smiled, but it was a bland society smile that barely changed his expression. "I believe we do, ma'am. May I escort you to your mother?"

"She isn't here tonight. I'm with my sister and two of my brothers."

The orchestra chose that moment to strike up a fresh air.

"Oh, a minuet!" Lady Marbury exclaimed. "How delightful!"

Thus giving him a choice. If he asked Lady Marbury to dance, Claudia would find it hard to forgive him.

He held out his arm. "Lady Claudia, will you do me the honor?"

"I would be delighted, sir."

A minuet meant the couples remained together for much of the measure, but not all. In a country-dance they changed partners and met again at the end of the set, but a minuet was a courtship dance.

He led her on to the floor and they joined the other couples. "You shouldn't have avoided me," she murmured. "Why are you doing that?" Flicking out her fan with a snap, she waved it before her face three times as she curtseyed in the dance and then closed it sharply.

"I thought it better to remain apart," he replied. "No good can come of your acquaintance with me."

"Don't you think you should do me the courtesy of letting me decide that?"

"Or your esteemed parents. Believe me, they will bar me from the house once I've told them what I know. I was not aware of it when I first met you."

She didn't care. Why should she? The dance took them into a complex section, and she had to concentrate on the steps and keeping the shapes she made with her body graceful. At least he couldn't run, not without creating a scandal. He would once the dance was complete if she didn't say something. What could she possibly say?

Only the truth. "I have missed you. You hurt me by pushing me away."

"I'm sorry for that." He turned around her, keeping his gaze fixed on her, as the dance demanded. "I wouldn't have hurt you for the world. Believe me, had I known then what I do now—"

"What? You wouldn't have made love to me?"

"Keep your voice down!" Although he kept it low, his voice held a note of command. "Do you want a scandal?"

"I don't care." Her family had weathered worse in its time. Very few people could countermand the combined forces of the Emperors of London. "If you abandon me, I shall tell my brothers. My cousins. You can't walk away with no explanation. I do not want that. Society is already sneering at me." It wasn't, but she'd use every tool at her command.

By her reckoning, she had five minutes to change his mind. Otherwise he'd walk away and he wouldn't come back this time. The determination lay in his eyes. He didn't have to tell her.

"Society will recover. There is no scandal. I've been careful to ensure that."

She had a brainwave. "That day you kissed me? At the Royal Exchange? Somebody saw us."

"Who?"

"Lady Compton." At random she chose one of the biggest gossips in society. "Once she speaks to our hostess, our secret will be out. What price your clandestine habits then?"

"Quiet!" They were so close his breath heated her ear. "Wait until your father returns. I have to tell him first."

"Why?" she demanded through grimly smiling teeth. "Why can't you tell me?"

"Because it destroys everything I've believed in. Everything I fought for."

His voice was entirely without emphasis this time, so cold that she shivered from the chill. "I want to help."

"There is no help."

Turning his back, he walked off the floor, leaving her partnerless and stranded.

* * * *

Blindly, Dominic walked out of the room and down the stairs, heedless of the gossip that surged around him. He couldn't touch her, look at her, without wanting her, and he couldn't have her. Not anymore. His dreams of marrying one of the most highborn women from one of the untouchable families of London were at an end.

He strode out of the house, sucking in air tangy with soot from the torchères still burning outside the house. It seemed an age since he'd walked through them, determined to make an appearance and leave. The hostess was an old friend of his mother's—he smiled wryly—and he'd promised to put in an appearance. Well he had. Duty done.

Claudia danced exquisitely. The minuet was a dance of courtship. He could hardly bear it. People watched them, smiling indulgently. Their match was one many people had already made. He couldn't allow that.

He was nobody, brought up by liars, traitors even. How could he hold up his head with that kind of history behind him? One day it would come to light. Secrets always did, and then he'd drag her down with him.

Having recovered some of his composure, he turned to leave and only then recalled he'd forgotten his hat. People would stare. Let them. They'd stare even more soon.

"Dominic?"

"No." He spun around to confront her.

She stood there, watching him. She wasn't wearing a hat, either, only a froth of lace on her head. Her hair shone in the torchlight, its red highlights blazing. She was all fire, his Claudia.

Except she wasn't *his* Claudia, was she?

When she approached him, he held out his hands as if to ward her off and took hasty steps back. He turned and walked quickly to the end of the street. The sound of determined steps followed him. He spun around. "Claudia…"

A deafening report split the air, a crack and a whistle he knew well. He only had time to leap forward, wrap his arms around her, and drag her to the ground before the bullet struck.

Chapter 9

She jerked forward into his arms as the bullet hit her.

Never before had Dominic panicked, but he did now. Tears stung his eyes as he rolled her to her back on the dusty pavement. "Claudia, oh my God!"

Blinking, she met his eyes, her own dazed, her pupils wide. "What was that? What happened?"

He had time to get her away. A yell from the road attracted his attention. "'Ere, guvnor, in 'ere!"

Where the hell were her brothers? He had no time. Blood seeped through the sleeve of her gown, soaking the fine silk, turning the pale blue to gory red. Getting to his feet, he picked her up. He didn't think he was hurt. Certainly he was hale enough to carry her the short distance to the hackney. As long as his arms and legs were working, he'd carry her.

He climbed into the vehicle, leaping over the iron step. "Whip up the horses!"

"Aye, aye, my lord."

The hackney rocked into motion, its worn suspension making the carriage rock and sway, but Dominic was too busy stripping off his coat to bother. Grabbing the heavy stiffened skirt of the garment, he used it to press against her arm, where the blood was deepest. He wasn't sure where she'd been hit, but she was bleeding copiously. Raising his voice, he bellowed his address to the carriage driver. One person could help him now. Nothing else mattered except getting her to help straight away. "Claudia, don't leave me. Talk to me. Give me that wonderful smile." Desperation drew him now. He'd do anything to keep her with him.

"I thought my smile bored you."

He forced a smile of his own, although he feared it was more of a grimace. "How could it ever do that? I swear I've never said it, because it's not true. I would do anything for a smile from you."

The corner of her mouth moved. "Don't press so hard. It hurts when you do that."

"It would hurt more if I did not." He felt like a villain, but he had to do something to staunch the flow of blood. "Please, Claudia, talk to me. Tell me anything."

"I liked your coat tonight."

That was better. Anything to keep those lovely eyes open and hear her voice. If she lapsed into unconsciousness, they might not get her back.

The carriage turned a corner on one wheel and carried on at the same breakneck pace. Dominic held on to her arm, circling it with part of the skirt of his coat and pulling tightly. Anything to stop the bleeding. It had soaked through his coat now. Four layers of fabric plus a heavy buckram lining. Forcing himself to think, he tried to recall when he'd seen someone bleed this much and live.

Where the hell were they?

As if he had shouted the words, the driver yelled to the horse and stopped it. "We're 'ere, sir."

Dominic climbed out of the hackney carefully, never letting go of Claudia and keeping his gaze fixed on hers, willing her to stay awake. He would risk everything to save her now. A servant flung open the door to his house. "Pay the man whatever he asks for," he said tersely. "Double it. Don't stint him. He could have saved this lady's life."

Striding indoors, he bellowed the name of his servant. Not his valet, but his factotum, the man who'd served by his side in the war. Binney came up from below stairs promptly, wiping his hands on a towel. The sound of his feet hesitated on the hard floor, just once, and then they quickened as he approached the couple in the hall. "Can you get her up to a bedroom, sir? I'll get what I need. What happened?"

"She was shot."

"How about you, sir?"

He must be covered with blood. "Not at all or very slightly. I don't know. She's lost a lot of blood."

Binney, already half way up the stairs, tutted. "Now, sir, we've seen much worse than this and the man got up and walked away once I'd seen to him. Just take her into your room and I'll be there directly."

Within a minute of Dominic laying Claudia tenderly on his bed, Binney had returned. He carried an armful of towels and his bag, the one that went everywhere with him. Binney was a surgeon, a skilled doctor. Having seen the worst war could inflict on a person, he gave it up for a few years. Dominic would trust Binney with his own life, and he could think of nobody better to ask for help when he needed it most.

"Help her, Binney."

"Pass me a sharp knife. I'm going to cut off her clothing."

Dominic found one in the bag and handed it over. Binney took it without thanks, setting to slicing the gown off Claudia's body. She watched, but said nothing. When Binney jerked his head, Dominic climbed on the bed to sit on her other side and keep her attention. They'd done this before, but with all his heart, Dominic prayed the outcome would not be the same as ones he'd undergone in the past. Never had the survival of one of Binney's patients meant so much to him.

"You were charming tonight. I could not resist you, although I should have."

"Why should you have?" She gazed at him trustfully. He wished she would not. He didn't have all the answers.

He hesitated. He had sworn not to tell anyone, not until he'd informed her family, but he had little choice now. That was his best chance to stop her eyelids drooping. Give her something to think about

He met her gaze again. Binney peeled the sleeve of her gown away and began to slice her bodice off. The man had received so many confidences that he was more trustworthy than a priest, but this secret was so dire, he paused before vouchsafing it. He would not willingly put that burden on anyone else.

Binney glanced at him. "If it helps, I won't remember anything. Tell her. Keep her thinking and awake."

Dominic had little choice. "I have seen the record of my birth. My mother and father were on the Continent, travelling through Europe, when I was born. My father undertook some diplomatic tasks. My mother always attributed my conception and birth to the change of scenery, and she was right."

Her free hand twitched. He grasped it firmly. Paradoxically, having her little hand clasped in his gave him strength instead of the other way about. "They said I was born in Paris while my father was attending King Louis in Versailles, but according to the record, they were actually in Rome. I was born the child of an Italian woman. My parents bought me from her."

That was what had stung. The deception. Tears pricked his eyes, but not for himself. For her. She deserved better. He wouldn't vouchsafe the rest of his secret, not yet.

He glanced at Binney.

When she shook her head, her curls gleamed in the candlelight. It didn't seem fair that her hair seemed so full of life, when her skin was so pale and she was in so much pain. Binney had reached bare skin now and was busy swabbing away blood so he could find the site of the wound.

She winced, but kept perfectly still. "I don't care." She barely finished the last part. Her body twisted violently on the bed and Dominic grasped her waist to help to keep her steady. He climbed on to the bed, the better to help her.

"I want her lifted," Binney said. As always, he forgot social niceties, or disregarded them, when he was employing his professional skills. "I need to see the other side of her shoulder."

As gently as he could, Dominic slid his hand underneath her and rolled her toward him. She needed no conversation to keep her awake now. The pain did that more effectively than he could.

Downstairs, his doorbell clanged. Dominic groaned. It could only be one person, or a set of people. Shouts came from downstairs while Binney smoothed her clothes away and attended to the wound.

While Dominic was holding Claudia close, murmuring reassurance to her, the door to his bedroom burst open. In any other circumstances, her brothers would probably have run him through. Now, one soft exclamation and a curse told him they'd taken in the situation.

"She was shot outside Lady Marbury's house." He made up some innocuous excuse for her being outside with him, and then dismissed it. What was the point? "This man is in my employ. He was in the army with me as a surgeon and physician. Your sister couldn't be in better hands."

The brothers raced across the room and bracketed the bed, the one in claret, Valentinian, standing by Binney and Darius behind Dominic. "Let me take her," Darius said to Dominic.

He would give her up to nobody. "I need to hold her steady." He was lying on the bed, the better to provide support to her. The sight must be disturbingly intimate, at least if the onlooker discounted the blood.

Binney sighed and moved, rocking the bed.

Claudia whimpered. "No. I want you."

Foolish woman. He wouldn't let her go if that was what she wanted. He was her servant in every sense of the word.

The surgeon rummaged in his bag and pulled out a bundle of bandages. "It's a graze. Quite a deep one, but it hasn't touched any of the major blood vessels."

Sighing in relief, Dominic closed his eyes. "Thank God."

"Does that mean I won't die?"

She had her head half-muffled in his shoulder, and her breath warmed his neck. The notion of that stopping forever made his chest tighten. He would not allow it. As long as he lived, she would have a protector in him.

"That means you won't die." He had no right promising her that. She could still get an infection or other complications.

"Did she break anything?" he asked Binney.

"No, she has been very fortunate. I suggest that I clean and dress the wound and then put on new dressing twice a day."

"We'll have our own physician attend to her," Val said from Binney's side of the bed.

Behind him, Darius was busy lighting candles, casting more light on the scene.

Alarm streaked through him at the idea of her family taking her away from him, a primitive need to care for her taking hold. "I do not know of anyone who can care for her better than Binney," he said.

That was true enough. While in the field Binney had developed unusual techniques and developed potions and lotions of his own that helped to prevent wound infection and healed breaks cleanly.

"I want to keep her here to be cared for. Is there any way it can be achieved without her reputation being compromised?"

"There's one simple method," Darius said. "We can obtain a special license tomorrow."

"No." His response was instinctive. He couldn't help murmuring, "You know why," and touching her forehead in a brief kiss. He wanted to cherish her and to deny the possibility made his heart ache. While he was under this cloud, he could not do it.

"We all do," the twin in claret ribbed silk said. "It doesn't matter to us. We'll have the matter arranged in a trice."

Groaning, Claudia lowered her head, and leaned against him.

Val shook his head. "We don't know how many people saw us. Servants at the ball, your servant downstairs, the man who brought you here, there are any number of people. Who knows she was shot?"

"I don't know." Dominic frantically forced his mind back to when she'd fallen. "I'd walked away from Lady Marbury's, and she was running to catch up to me. I did not mean for her to do that."

"If she marries, that will give her a chance to hide until she's recovered." He glanced at Dominic. "He's a suitable candidate. He's shown an interest. Yes, I think that will work."

Dominic shook his head, but he could see the necessity. "I wanted to wait until your father and brother returned from the country."

"She's over twenty-one, so legally Claudia can marry who she wants." Binney had a bowl of water from his fresh supply by the washstand. "Hold her while I clean the wound." He dipped a cloth into the water.

Claudia leaned into him so sweetly, so naturally, that all his instincts told him she belonged there. If she left, she'd create a gaping hole in his life.

Valentinian gazed at the scene. "If it weren't for the blood, you'd appear charmingly domestic," he said dryly. "Several artists of my acquaintance would kill for that pose. Hogarth would make a whole series about it. As it is, the servants will have this story all around town by morning. We're done for."

He would not disgrace her. Whatever happened, his first priority would be to ensure she was cared for and safe. He could return to the army and live out his disgrace there. Even if society didn't disgrace him, his parents' transgressions would. His foster parents, he reminded himself. Their betrayal still staggered him, and he found it difficult to think past it and on the implications of their treachery.

"You may lay her down again," Binney said.

God help him, he didn't want to. He would continue holding her until he was sure she was safe. "If her sister stayed to chaperone, would that fit the proprieties?"

"It would probably help." Livia entered and closed the door, bringing a can of hot water with her. "I did what you had failed to do, by the way, and gave the footman at the door a hefty vail. You owe me five guineas. If he speaks, I told him I'd send my brothers back for him."

"That won't stop him gossiping," Darius said glumly.

"Yes it will." Dominic said. "He's a London servant. I got them all from the best registry office in London, and he is the only servant who saw us arrive."

"Unless others from the nearby houses took an interest," Val pointed out.

Livia pushed her way past her brother, removed the basin of bloody water, tipped it into the slop pail, and poured hot water. She'd also brought a stack of clean cloths. She'd make someone an excellent helpmeet one day.

"Here." She put the basin where Binney could reach it. Touching her sister's arm, she smiled. "I'm glad you're in good heart, Claudia. We'll get through this, just like we do all your tangles."

Claudia nodded and smiled faintly, but winced when Binney set to washing away the blood around her wound. It was nearly clear now.

Binney was right. The bullet had carved a considerable groove across her upper arm, but it hadn't penetrated her flesh. She would heal, barring infection, and Dominic would do everything in his power to ensure that didn't happen.

Binney continued to clean the wound with the fresh warm water. "While you are discussing philosophy and propriety, this young woman could be dying. Thank God one of you has more sense."

When Claudia held out her hand, Dominic took it and forced a smile. "It seems, my dear, that you are to be my guest for some time."

"They're marrying," Val said flatly.

Claudia shocked him by her loud cry of "No!"

At first Dominic thought Binney had hurt her, but apart from a few whimpers, she'd borne his probing and careful washing with great fortitude. He glared at Binney, who shrugged as if to say he'd done nothing.

"I mean I won't marry you like this," Claudia said.

The room erupted with male voices ordering her to do as she was told. Dominic wanted to order them all to be quiet. The noise disturbed her as, flinching, she buried her face in his shirt.

How could he deny her anything? "We'll find a way," he murmured to her.

"Oh, you idiots!" Livia waded into the fray. "All this talk of honor and disgrace, can't you see? I'll stay, too. You can send our maid with some clothes tomorrow. That takes care of the propriety. Now go and leave us alone. You know she'll be fine."

"I'm not going," Dominic said quietly. Not until he saw her properly settled.

"I want to dress the wound," Binney said. "Then we may see about settling her."

"She'll need some new clothes," said Livia. "We'll say Claudia was attacked by a footpad and sustained an injury severe enough to call a physician, who advised that she not be moved. That I'm staying with her until she is better. That's all we need do."

When he eased her back, Claudia had her eyes closed and a look of beatific peace on her face. "I will not marry someone who doesn't want me," she said. "Mama and Papa didn't let me wait all this time only to throw myself away at the first scandal."

Val and Darius glared at Dominic. They wanted their sister married to him. She'd created scandal enough. He would not let her believe that, but he needed time to talk to her. Now she knew his secret, how would she feel? How would society feel?

"We will obtain the license," Val said. "Just in case. For tonight, we'll leave you be. Take care of her."

"Of course," Livia replied. "Now go. She's not seriously hurt, and she'll be home soon."

As soon as Binney told her she was well. Dominic wouldn't risk her health for anything. If they had to marry, so be it, but Livia's solution was a good one. With one small change.

"You are welcome in my house," he told Claudia's sister. "I'm grateful someone, at least, has a practical solution."

Livia folded her arms across her chest. "If you'd thought properly instead of posturing, the idea would have come sooner. For goodness' sake."

"We'll return soon," Val said. He bent over his sister and kissed her forehead, ignoring the bloody mess she was in. "We'll bring Julius."

Claudia groaned and closed her eyes. "Can I go to sleep now?"

Chapter 10

Claudia stirred and her sore shoulder sent a shot of pain through her, waking her up.

Dominic roused from the daybed with a smile. "Is there anything you need?"

This was the second night she'd slept in his bed and the second he'd dozed on the daybed. He must be exhausted. She'd tried to get him to leave, but he'd refused. He refused to talk about anything but her getting better.

The first night she'd slept. When the bullet had initially struck her she had felt nothing. Only the wet heat of her blood had told her something was wrong. That and the expression on Dominic's face just before he leaped for her and took her down to the ground. She'd seen absolute horror, and something she'd never expected to see from him—fear. For her. Only then had fear crept into her. If he was afraid, what had happened?

Then her idiot brothers arrived and her clever sister. Livia was still here. On Dominic's refusal to leave her, Claudia's twin had taken herself off to the room next door and slept there, without fuss.

She had spent much of the next day sleeping and when she wasn't doing that she'd had her wound dressings changed or she was eating. Still nobody would discuss anything, but she feared she might not be able to concentrate.

He wasn't his parent's son? She didn't care. Whoever he was, and wherever he came from, she still wanted him. If he wanted her. She would not be a martyr or be forced into something. Or more importantly see him forced. He would come to resent her, and that would kill her.

Looking at him now, so handsome and sleepy, dark hair tousled, she just wanted him. Being Claudia, she would do her best to get him. This was by far the worst mess she'd ever found herself in, but this time it was not of her own making and nobody blamed her. That in itself felt strange. Nobody was blaming her or accusing her of anything.

"Could I have…some water?" It was the best she could do. The cook here had made her some barley water but she'd drunk it all.

"I'll get you some." He climbed wearily to his feet.

"No, no don't. I don't really want water."

He turned and gazed at her. No condemnation or complaint lay in his soft gaze.

"Come here," she said, and patted the bed next to her with her good hand.

His attention flicked from her to the bed and back again. "It's not wise."

"Why not? You're not going to pounce are you?" She wanted him to get some rest. Nobody entered the room without knocking, so he had time to move should someone try to enter. He wasn't sleeping properly, and now she was feeling better, she needed to know he was rested.

"No. I can't do that. I should let your sister in now you're feeling better."

"Why didn't you do that before?" she asked softly. Had he, or was he fooling himself with thoughts of propriety and honor?

With a groan, he sank on to the cover but didn't touch her. This was a big bed.

"Because I wanted to be the one to care for you. I wanted to ensure you were safe."

"You haven't slept well," she said. She didn't move her hand.

"I have survived on much less."

He was wearing a shirt and breeches, his feet tucked into slippers, and he appeared so much more approachable than he did when dressed up. His wig sat on a stand on his dressing-table, but he hadn't touched it in two days. He'd served her himself, with Livia around to add a tinge of respectability. For the first day, he'd insisted on carrying her to the powder room when she'd needed it.

Her wound hadn't been as bad as they'd imagined and was healing already, a scab forming over the raw flesh. It had bled a lot, and from his response he felt far more for her than he was admitting. Until her injury, she'd begun to think that he was avoiding her for reasons other than he claimed. Perhaps he'd had his fill, or her reputation was deterring him. He rarely did anything without a great deal of thought.

Now he looked at her with warmth, and she longed for more. With her sister here, she could risk a little more. Livia would support her in anything she wanted to say. They had always acted together.

She was so conflicted. She wanted him, but she needed to be sure he wanted her in the same way. "Are you still determined not to marry me?" she asked.

"I can't."

He shifted his hand so she couldn't reach it without leaning over, and that would disturb her wound. It was hellish sore.

"I'm still trying to cope with what I've learned. I'm not the son of the people who brought me up believing that I was. Did they do that to disinherit my cousins, or did they have another reason?"

"They loved you, did they not?"

The single candle they'd left burning illuminated the room so dimly she could hardly see him. Half his face was cast in shadow.

"Yes, they said they did. They should not have done this. I've already instigated enquiries to discover any other heirs. I will not disinherit anyone from what should be theirs."

She braced herself for the pain and leaned forward to touch his arm. He swallowed, but he didn't move away. Pain shot through her arm, but she was almost used to it now. "What if there are no heirs? Your parents already searched. They found nobody."

"I must be sure."

"Why are you so insistent on honor?" Her family and friends used it whenever they could, but this was going to extremes. Besides, as most of the premier families in the country, they had their practical side. "What good will it do to confess who you are, to tell the Crown that you are not the child of your parents? You're still using your title, are you not?"

He sighed heavily. "Yes. It goes against the grain, but your brothers asked me to wait for a day or two, and so I will."

"Then why so insistent on honor?"

"You ask me that?" He stared at her. "Honor is all we have. What are we without that? Animals." He spoke softly but passion reverberated through his voice. "I have served in the army, and I have seen the worst a human being is capable of. I left home because I thought my parents were traitors. I'd long dreamed of the army, but they pleaded for me to stay and so I did. When I found a letter, I couldn't stay. It didn't discuss me, but a favor my parents had done the Pretender's court. It must have been taking me off their hands."

"You stick to your honor." That explained a lot. He clung to the notion as his only mainstay, his anchor. Her heart ached for him. He'd hidden all this since he was little but a child, held it close to his chest. Now he was about to have a lot of it explained to him. What would he do then?

Claudia wished she'd paid more attention to her family's recent intrigues, especially regarding the family's newest members, her cousin Max's wife and the new wife of another cousin, Tony. Or Maximilian and Antoninus.

"Yes, I do."

He moved closer so that she could lean back, but she couldn't rest her elbow on anything to help her. That would hurt like the devil. He lifted her by her waist and laid her against the pillows so tenderly she didn't feel a twinge.

"You're well enough to go home now."

"Yes I am." She bit her lip. "I don't want to."

"You must. I'm not the man for you."

"I disagree."

In that fraught moment, so close to him, she caught a new expression in his eyes. Yearning. He wanted, so much. Please let it be her he wanted. She would have to take care not to prick that shell of honor, his creed. "In this room, here and now, can we just be a man and a woman? Please? If I swear nothing will leave the room, will you allow that?"

"You don't have to swear." His mouth flattened. "I'm not a fool. I know your family didn't get to its current exalted status by playing everything the way the law lays down. But there's a difference between that and personal honor. After what I've seen and experienced I consider the second to be more important. I know we aren't supposed to think that way, that we should consider the duty we owe to others first. But what good is that without personal integrity?"

She smiled and touched his cheek with her good hand. "I think we can promise you that."

"I wish I could say the same of my family. What I learned means I'm on shifting sands. I can't trust the word of the people I trusted most. What is left?"

Before he could answer his own question, she did it for him. "This."

Leaning forward, she kissed him. When he didn't respond, when his mouth lay unmoving beneath hers, a despair the like of which she'd never experienced before overtook her. The sense of loss devastated her.

Then he slid his arm around her shoulders, careful to angle it down so he didn't touch her injury. As he drew her closer, he kissed her back, and relief flooded through her in a great tide.

He caressed her lips with his, took care to touch them. When she opened for him, he slid his tongue into her mouth so softly that it felt more like a caress than an invasion. Yet passion lay in their kiss, banked down and more precious because of it.

For the first time, Claudia learned how dangerous suppressed desire could be. She wore nothing except a night-rail, and his shirt easily revealed the heat of his body, warming and caressing her. His chest was hard, firm with muscle, while her breasts were soft. She nestled against him, loving this new closeness. Wanting more. She whimpered into his mouth.

When she lifted her other hand to hold his arm, her wound screamed its protest into her mind, but she ignored it.

Still in the kiss, he bore her down on to the bed so she lay flat. But he didn't stop kissing her, merely changed his angle so he could lie next to her. The bedclothes still lay between them. Desire turned mindlessly voracious, overcoming the pain from her arm. When she slid her hand into his thick, dark hair she hardly felt it at all.

He ate at her, and she responded with all the passion in her heart. With a vicious tug, he stripped the covers away from her, moving so he could lie over her, surrounding her with hot, hard male. Oh, yes, at last the rigid shaft pressed against her stomach, burning through her thin night-rail and his breeches.

She wanted more. Nothing he could give her would ever be enough. She slid her good hand down and cupped his buttocks. He clenched them and gasped into her mouth.

She'd released the inner part of him, the primitive, savage man he kept locked away. She'd found the key. Glorying in her power, she would go wherever this led her, and she would never regret the consequences.

He kissed her mouth, her cheek, moved to her ear and nipped the lobe. She pulled in a sharp breath and arched her body toward him. Hungrily he kissed down her throat, resting his hot lips over the pulse at the base of her neck and teasing it with his tongue. She'd had intimations of this passion before, when he'd kissed her, but never like this.

His hot breath, his tongue, and the way he stroked her body, from breast to hip, all aroused her past anything she'd known before, anything she'd considered herself capable of. He pulled her night rail up and she helped him. Wanting only to get the thing out of the way. He lifted up, straddled her.

She used her good arm to prop herself up enough to sit and tug the offending garment over her head and toss it to the floor.

Pausing in his ministrations, he looked at her. "My God, you're lovely," he said in a voice that throbbed with passion. "Claudia, you do—" He swallowed. "I will not dishonor you, I swear, but I need this. To prove you're alive and here." He shook his head. "I don't know what this is, but I want more of it. Can you understand?"

"I want it too." At times in the past, when she'd galloped her horse on Rotten Row, or when she'd taken on some dare from her brothers, like the time she'd climbed the highest tree on the estate and nearly fell from the topmost branch, she'd felt the same reckless abandon. This beat everything.

Smiling, she reached for him, but he shook his head.

Was he about to deny her? He'd used that word again—"dishonor." She'd feared it would bring him back down to earth.

He unfastened the buttons on the cuffs of his shirt, tugged the ties free at the top, and dragged it off, revealing a chest so beautifully powerful her breath caught. Small scars here and there didn't detract from the sleek perfection of honed muscles—so masculine, so desirable.

He went up on his knees and unfastened the fall on his breeches, the six buttons taking an age to undo, and then the drawstring of his underwear. All the time he watched her, waiting, she guessed, for the minutest hesitation.

She showed him none. She wanted to touch, to kiss, to know him.

He revealed his cock, hard and long, the top mouthwateringly damp and reddened with arousal. She'd seen male members before, but never in this state, and the sight enthralled her. Were all men this big, this powerful? Not that she had any intention of finding out. This was enough. More than enough.

A flicker of doubt crossed her mind. She understood what should happen in lovemaking, but was it possible? It must be possible; otherwise the human race would not endure. A maiden's misgivings had no place in this bed.

Leaning forward, he caged her body between his arms and kicked the rest of his clothes off and away. They were both completely naked, staring at each other, spellbound in the sight.

He smelled good, of clean male with a hint of musk and sandalwood. She breathed deep, lifting her breasts to his avid gaze. With a groan of surrender, he lowered his body down to hers and took one of her nipples into his mouth.

Shards of sensation shot from her sensitive breasts to the very heart of her, linking every point of her body together in keening want.

He licked, sucked, and then touched his tongue around the colored part of her breast until it crinkled hard, the way it did in cold weather. She was anything but cold now.

"You taste of desire," he murmured.

He treated the other breast the same way, but caressed and pinched the one he'd kissed earlier. The heat of his body burned through to her now, the sprinkling of rough hair on his chest adding extra sensation to her building desire.

"Please," she said, the words bursting from her, although she was not entirely sure what she was begging for. Tension arched her back, forced her to clutch him, ignoring the pain from her arm when she did so.

"Yes, sweetheart. I won't leave you wanting." He kissed down her body, pausing to tickle her navel with the tip of his tongue, and then kissing the inside of her left hip. She yelped and jerked, but he held her firmly and carried on. "Open your legs, Claudia."

Accompanying his whisper with soft kisses on the tops of her thighs, he worked his way inside, his soft groan rewarding her when she tentatively opened them. Her desire overcame her natural shyness, for she had never revealed herself so completely to anyone.

"So lovely," he said, his hot breath increasing the sensitivity of her skin. Then he did the unbelievable.

She'd imagined he'd touch her, perhaps prepare her for what came next, but he didn't. He licked her.

"Oh my God!"

His chuckle was necessarily muffled. "You're delicious, my sweet."

How had he—could he…? But he did. He licked her, front to back and then up to the tip. Then took the knot of flesh at the front into his mouth and sucked.

Uncaring of who might hear, her mind scattered to the four winds, she screamed. Unbearable, and then it wasn't, as she concentrated on the feelings radiating from that tiny spot between her legs.

She'd known it was sensitive, but she avoided it because of that, merely ensuring she cleaned that part of herself thoroughly every morning. This—this all-encompassing, violent series of waves, building until she squirmed beneath his restraining hands. Still he did not stop. Would he, if she asked him to? The sounds he was making would normally embarrass her, but now they added to the complete experience. One she would never forget.

He touched her opening, the place he would breach when he pushed into her, and sent her into complete oblivion.

Everything—the tingles, the sensations—built to a peak. Like a volcano erupting or the sea at high tide, it washed over her, bringing burning shockingly vivid heights she had never considered possible.

Gasping, crying his name, she opened her arms when he prowled up the bed to her. Despite his resistance, she dragged him down for a kiss. His cock rested against her stomach. She tasted herself on him, and when he enclosed her in his arms, she was safe. The only danger lay in the man that had brought her such blinding ecstasy.

He pushed against her skin and cried out into her mouth as hot wetness flooded her belly. He sagged, pressing his body against hers, surrounding her with himself before lifting off her and throwing back the sheets.

"Wait there," he commanded and swung off the bed. He brought back a dampened cloth.

With great tenderness, he washed her, gently wiping the cloth over her stomach and between her legs. Then he returned to the washstand and cleaned himself.

His cock was already settling, to something more similar to the ones on the marble statues in her father's house. It had appeared completely different when erect. Darker in color and standing up, reaching almost to his navel.

She still hadn't felt it inside her. The realization shook her as she drifted slowly back down to earth.

To her relief, he came back to her and slid into bed by her side, taking her into his arms. He kissed her again before he spoke, and she threw herself into the kiss, passionately responding, even venturing to slip her tongue into his mouth.

Moaning, he sucked gently, caressed her softly, his arms around her before he drew back, and finished with a soft salute to her lips. "That should not have happened," he murmured, "But it has. I cannot be sorry for it. In you, I found peace."

"You weren't in me," she protested. "You didn't—"

His grin was the most relaxed and happy she'd ever seen him, and a sense of pride filled her that she could bring this to him.

"That will not happen until you marry me."

This time he asked her properly. This man, the one lying next to her now, the one who had brought her such joy, she could marry him.

"A betrothal," she said. "Yes."

He swung up on one elbow and leaned over her. "That will no longer do. I want it all."

Placing her hand on his chest, she savored the hot, hard flesh under her palm. "You aren't acting like a gentleman now."

"Oh, yes, I am. If I were not, you'd soon know."

That sounded intriguing. "Would you behave less like a gentleman if we married?"

"Most certainly."

He kissed her, lingering and slow, seducing her all over again. Not that she'd needed that much seducing. After two nights sharing a room with him, watching him in a state of undress, she was more than ready.

If he had been any other man, she'd have said he'd done it on purpose, but with the stalwart Lord St. Just, she wasn't so sure. Now she had him in bed with her, naked, her certainty coalesced. Not that she intended to make matters too easy for him. After all, what was a wedding without the chase? Once she'd recovered, she'd display him in the ballrooms of London, her quarry captured.

For now she found pleasure nestling close. He settled her against him, careful to keep her bandaged arm and shoulder free.

"I'll have to go soon, or I'll be asleep." He kissed her hair.

"If we marry, would we share a bed?"

"If you wished it."

"Would you wish it?" She needed to know that he wanted this as much as she did. Bringing such intimacy to her had meant more than she'd imagined. The closeness settled her restless heart, and the lovemaking had eased her tension.

"I would. Every night. Does that daunt you? Would you rather entertain your lovers?"

"You are my lover. Why would I want anyone else?"

He grinned, and just as drowsiness was overtaking her, sat up and leaned over the bed. He retrieved her night-rail.

"You'll have to put this back on, otherwise when Binney comes in to examine you, he'll find more than he planned for."

He helped her into the garment, a sleeveless night rail because that allowed Binney access to her shoulder. Tenderly, he held the opening and let her take her time inserting her arm into it. "How does it feel now?" he asked.

"Better." She bit her lip on a particularly harsh twinge. "Still, it hurts. I have to get up soon. May I do it tomorrow?"

"We'll see. If you get some sleep now and eat all your breakfast."

"Like a good girl?" she said with a smile.

"Mmm." He lifted her against him and fluffed the pillows with his other hand before laying her against them. Then he kissed her. They separated slowly, reluctantly.

"I'll call on my man of business tomorrow," he said. "Get the contracts done and the discussions under way."

There he was again, the responsible man who cared for doing matters the right way. The man of honor. She liked the man of honor, but tonight he'd given her a glimpse of the man behind the façade. That man she could love.

Chapter 11

In concluding the business of his marriage, Dominic had gone a little further than he needed to. He had meant to play with her, to show her a little of what was possible. He'd barely stopped himself entering her sweet body and riding them to a finish.

Having her in his house for three nights had meant she was compromised irrevocably. Her sister's presence helped ameliorate the problem. He had immediately turned off the talkative footman who had bruited the truth all around London by morning. But it had not been enough.

Had he allowed her out of her sickbed to discover the scandal that was taking society by storm, she'd have refused to marry him. A more perverse, awkward woman he'd never met before, but he wanted her.

Telling himself that duty played the biggest part in his campaign had worked until he'd had a taste of her. Kissing her was seductive, but tasting her, feeling her responses—that had proved his downfall. He should not have done it, but he couldn't feel sorry.

On entering White's that morning, Dominic expected responses. Cries of "You wicked dog!" from the more racy members and cold stares from those who considered themselves his superior. Normally he didn't concern himself with them.

Today he took great pleasure in their reactions. One of his future brothers-in-law hailed him. He had hoped that would be enough, that Claudia's family wasn't shunning him, but society loved a scandal, the male side as well as the female.

"You seem hale this morning," Darius said. "May I hope that means our sister is well? I'll call on her later today."

"Not only well, but finally, she has agreed to our betrothal. Consequent to the unfortunate accident, matters have moved apace."

"You're in luck then." Darius headed for a leather wing chair by the wall that held bookcases. "Join me for a celebratory glass?"

"Willingly."

Before they sat, Darius wrung his hand, man-to-man. "I think you'll prove our sister's making."

"When your father returns to London, I'll pay him a visit." He took a sip of the excellent brandy the waiter had brought over on Darius's signal.

The crystal glittered in the sunlight. Another good day. It would soon be time to repair to the country, only this time he wouldn't be going alone.

"What about your parents?"

Another hurdle he wasn't looking forward to. "Tomorrow. Believe me they'll be delighted. I could marry—" He stopped, recalling where he was. White's was a hotbed of gossip. If anyone realized his relationship with his parents was less than his usual fondness, they would start asking questions, and matters could escalate from there. He didn't want Claudia thinking she was anything but his first choice. Even though his first choice would be not to marry at all. Failing that, he'd do his best to contain the situation.

"Tell me again," Darius murmured. "Why did I allow you to talk me into having Claudia stay?"

"You could have removed her to your parents' establishment." He didn't like Darius any better for pointing that out.

"Not when she was so ill." She wasn't, only distressed. It had hurt him to see her distressed, and he had no intention of allowing her any further reason for it. If he asked himself why, he could tell himself he liked her. Only that didn't entirely explain the urge to protect her at all costs.

Marriage was a partnership, a business relationship. Love came elsewhere, if it came at all, and it was a fleeting emotion, soon past. However much he recited that to himself, he couldn't believe it. The truth didn't seem so clear-cut. Which was strange, because the truth was always clear-cut.

"Father should return tomorrow or the day after." Darius stretched his legs in front of him, fully at ease, or so it appeared. "We can formalize matters then."

He should visit his parents today and get the contract under way, before Claudia changed her mind. She was volatile, unpredictable, so he'd have to seduce her all over again.

Why did that sound so attractive? After he'd promised himself he wouldn't repeat last night's activities until he had a ring on her finger?

"I wanted to care for her," he murmured. "That's why I didn't leave." It felt good to admit that much.

Darius touched his glass to Dominic's with a small chink. "Welcome to the family. We are notorious for marrying for love. Even when we're sensible and start our marriages with an arrangement and a business agreement, somehow love rears its head again. Probably the most passionate family in the country."

A dark figure entered the room and looked around. His gaze stilled on Darius and Dominic.

"Except for the Dankworths," Darius murmured.

Someone else entered the room.

"I didn't even know he was in the building," Darius said in a louder tone.

Val was just behind the Earl of Alconbury. Dominic knew Alconbury by sight, but had never spoken to him. Alconbury was, next to his father, the Duke of Northwich, the principal member of the Dankworth family. Young, handsome in a kind of lean, dark way, and possessed of a restless energy that Dominic recognized, because he possessed it himself. It showed in the way he glanced around, taking in all the people in the room, the taut tension of his neck, and no doubt his shoulders under the fine but sober velvet coat he wore.

The earl moved with a spare economy at the same pace as Dominic. Although Dominic was dressed in his London clothes, which meant pale green and lots of lace today, his efforts to disguise his military bearing was becoming a losing challenge. He crossed one leg over the other, the cut steel on his shoe buckles catching the light merrily. He did not rise.

"Sirs," Alconbury said smoothly. He nodded rather than bowed and waited by a spare chair.

Darius and Dominic didn't invite him to sit.

"I believe I have to felicitate you." He offered Dominic a smile. Dominic offered him one back. Not a particularly fulsome one. He put down his half-full brandy glass. Tension snapped in the air, and conversation around them dulled to a murmur.

"Thank you." Dominic said and waited on events.

"I wondered if you were fully aware of certain matters," Alconbury said with a smile. "I would appreciate a private meeting to discuss it."

"What can you possibly know about me?" Dominic asked smoothly. "Sir, I have not, I believe, even been introduced to you."

"We may rectify that easily enough," Alconbury said, just as calmly.

Val stood just behind him, in a pose Dominic had seen before, but not in White's. Val had his hand on his sword hilt, a sword he should have left at the door. To say bad blood existed between the two families was an understatement, by what Dominic was witnessing here. Used to assessing situations fast, he didn't need advanced training in battle strategy to see this standoff could end at any minute.

By betrothing himself to their sister, Dominic had effectively joined the Emperors. That meant family, something he was not used to having. These two were watching for his interests.

Was Alconbury so dangerous? True, the man was big and powerful, but so was Dominic. "Sir, I have no history here. I appreciate your congratulations, but I fail to see what business it is of yours or what you would have of me."

Alconbury shifted his position and glanced at Val. No affable society gentleman, this. Val could have changed places with a St. Giles ruffian, from his pose and the fierce expression on his face, brows drawn together, mouth straight. "I have information you might find useful. That is all. My father is like to get in touch with you." He touched his fingers to his forehead and let a smile quirk the corner of his lean mouth. Val's implied threat and Darius's stillness did not concern Dominic in the least. If Alconbury wanted an open exchange, White's was far from the place to do it.

"Does it put my lady in danger?" That was all he cared about. If Claudia was imperiled, he'd meet this man anywhere he chose.

"By association." Alconbury shrugged, the shoulders of his coat shifting easily, displaying the power a lean man could conceal if he was tall enough and his tailor a good one. Clearly Dominic wasn't the only one ordering his tailor to minimize his form. "Do not complain that nobody warned you. I'm warning you now."

A threat? Dominic couldn't be sure. Perhaps Dominic would seek him out. Perhaps he'd be killed. He had no idea.

Alconbury regarded him, his dark eyes unreadable. "I will bid you good day, sir." He turned and left.

Beside Dominic, Darius let out a long breath. "Well, what was that about? By association?"

"She's already associated with us," Val said. "He must mean you, Dominic. What have you done to upset the Dankworths?"

"Absolutely nothing," Dominic said, but inside he wasn't so sure. He hadn't led a snow-white life, God knew. Did that mean he'd made an enemy of the Dankworth family without realizing it?

The Dankworths were the enemies of the Emperors primarily because of their stance on the Jacobite question. Although rumors were that the initial disputes had begun at least a generation earlier. In any case, it appeared far more personal than a political dispute. A convoluted history, and probably one nobody had all the answers to. One mystery too many for Dominic.

He wanted answers, and one person had them. He got to his feet. "I would appreciate a word with your cousin Julius," he said. "If he has a moment today, bring him to my house. I'd call on him, but I want Claudia to be present." If she wasn't, she might never forgive him. Already he knew her well enough to predict that.

She'd only make him tell her, and he would.

After bowing, he left the club and went home.

When he returned to his house, Claudia was there. She sat in the parlor at the front of the house, wearing a cream silk robe. Her hair gleamed in the afternoon sun, sparking fire where the rays caught it. He wanted to see her on his estate, sitting on the bench under the big oak by the east side of the house, enjoying the summer.

Big with his child.

No! He banished that particular notion as soon as it appeared, denying his pleasure at the momentary vision. Children were not possible, the way matters stood at present.

Until he knew the truth.

Now he could bend to her and kiss his bride-to-be with the full knowledge he was doing something totally acceptable. He kissed her. "Where is your sister?"

"She is resting. She said she didn't sleep well last night." A sweet blush rose to her cheeks. "Dominic, she came into the bedroom to see if there was anything I wanted, and she saw us asleep together." Her voice dropped. "Naked."

Dominic's cock stirred, readying for another round. The temporary satiation of his appetite was not fated to last very long. This woman had revived an urge he'd kept strictly under control for the last few years, and she'd done it unwittingly. Now it was out and unfettered. The urge offended his strong sense of self-control, but he could do nothing except endure. If she spent another night in this house, he'd do it again, because he couldn't keep away from her.

When she curled her arm around his neck and tugged him back, that was all the persuasion he needed. Instead of moving away, he took a seat on the sofa by her side and drew her into his arms, kissing her again. She tasted of all the things he'd ever wanted, and some things he hadn't known he wanted. He didn't even have words for them yet.

For now he could enjoy holding her, the silk of her gown slipping under his hands. She wore a pair of stays underneath, but light ones, so the heat of her body caressed his palms. She responded to his kiss with eagerness, caressing his tongue when he slid it into her mouth and sucking gently, the way he'd shown her last night. He guided her close to him, his arm about her shoulders, careful to avoid the bandaged part, and drew away from the kiss smiling. He hadn't smiled so much in years. Perhaps he could truly find some happiness and even better make her happy in return. He could willingly devote his life to that.

"When do you plan to return home?" he asked. "Even though this will be your home soon."

"Yes." She cuddled close. "My father is due home tomorrow. When I was hurt, my mother sent him a message. He will turn around directly, or so she said. She wrote me a note. She wants me home today, now I'm better."

Lady Strenshall had paid her an anxious visit yesterday, and it was only Claudia's obvious exhaustion and Binney's tender care that persuaded her to allow her daughter to remain. Today, Claudia was up, happy, and dressed. No further reason for her to stay.

"I went to Doctor's Commons this afternoon. We should have a special license tomorrow."

She grasped his hand. "I know we said we would do this, but you told me you intended to marry nobody. Can you tell me why?"

"Yes, I must." He caressed her hand with his thumb, stroking along the soft skin. "I invited your cousin Julius to come, since he has some answers for me, but your brothers will probably arrive first. One thing we must decide upon, sweet Claudia, is what to do with that house you inherited."

"The one in Hart Street?"

"The very same. Will you agree to sell it?"

"I would rather not. I'm warming to the idea of having a place I can call my own, even if it is a house of ill-repute."

"Witch," he said with some feeling, and kissed her again for that.

He would prefer to lose himself in her, but he was determined to have one matter at least sorted out. "If I give you one of my houses in the settlement, will you give me yours in exchange?"

"What kind of house?" Leaning against him, she traced a line along the pattern embroidered on his waistcoat, twisting vines. Down, down, she went, and since it was a long waistcoat, she would finish in his lap. "Tell me."

He swallowed and concentrated. "A small town house in London. It's near Red Square and one of my aunts used to own it. You may have it on the same terms as you have this one. As long as you promise not to allow it to become a house of ill repute or a place where traitors meet."

She smiled, dimples indenting her cheeks. "Very well, on those terms."

He breathed a sigh of relief. "It's dangerous for you to even own the house. Your name associated with it will cast all your relatives into the shadows. What possessed the woman to give it to you?"

"I don't know. I hardly spoke to her, but she said in her letter that she wanted a spirited youngster to own it. It may be a coincidence. She might not have known."

He told her with his snort what he thought of coincidences. "They sometimes happen, but not like that. Not falling into place so neatly. I will get to the bottom of it, but you need not concern yourself."

She stiffened in his arms. He loosened his hold on her, in case he was hurting her. "What is it, my sweet?"

"You will not put me to one side. You will not!"

Ah, he'd made a tactical mistake there. If he carried on explaining, he'd only dig a deeper hole for himself. He did the best thing in the circumstances. He apologized.

The door bell clanged in the middle of his apology, which had turned to something much more interesting. He barely had time to help her tuck in her fichu before a gentle knock on the door announced the entrance of his butler. The man held three cards on his tray, the corners all turned down, to indicate the owners were waiting for an answer.

"Let them in," Dominic said.

Val, Darius, and their magnificent cousin Julius entered. While Dominic wore his elaborate city clothes as a mask, Julius, Lord Winterton, wore his like a flag declaring war. He flaunted his masculinity from clothes in the most outrageous colors and wigs so snowy white they seemed made of spun silk. He was no exception today, making Dominic's green twilled silk almost ordinary.

Even Dominic would have balked at wearing that particular shade of yellow, so pale it was almost white, defying the sooty streets of London to stain it. How he kept it smut-free remained a miracle society sometimes wondered at, but he never gave the explanation to everyone. Add to that a tall, strong frame he made no attempt to conceal, a fashionable nipped-in waist and slender hips, invariably circled by a sword-belt. Julius Winterton was an unmistakable figure.

Dominic rose and bowed, and then defiantly took his seat next to Claudia.

Julius stared at her from blue eyes under hooded lids. "Do you return home soon?"

"Today," Darius said firmly. "For the last two days she's been cared for by Livia and Dominic's servant, one of the best damned surgeons I ever saw."

"I see." Julius took a seat, every movement graceful. "Any more and shocked rumor will turn into outright scandal. It's hard to overcome that, though I fancy if any family can do it, we can."

Val chuckled and took a seat on the sofa across from where Claudia sat with Dominic. She sat up straight, hands in her lap, the perfect example of a graceful society lady. Five minutes ago, she'd been in his arms, her breasts all but exposed, kissing him like a courtesan. He was proud of her.

"Where are you going from here?" Julius asked.

"I visited Doctor's Commons today. I should have a license tomorrow." His heart sinking, Dominic leaned forward, resting his arms on his knees as if ready to spring up and leave. How he wished he could. "I was hard put to know what name to put on the license. I have learned too much recently about my beginnings. I find it hard to reconcile the truth with what I have been led to believe all these years."

Julius raised a brow but didn't appear surprised. But then, little surprised Lord Winterton. "I have undertaken research of my own. So that we are not talking at cross purposes, tell me what you know."

"That my parents, who were engaged in diplomatic activity before and at the time of my birth, were not in Paris as they always said, but in Rome. That I was not born Dominic, Lord St. Just, but an unnamed baby, the child of one Maria Rubio."

Darius's curse almost drowned Val's gasp.

Julius held up a restraining hand, not taking his attention from Dominic. "Go on, if you please."

"That's it. My father was named on the certificate my parents showed me, but I don't know if it's true. She may have used his name because she was his mistress."

"Name him."

Julius's command was unequivocal. Dominic couldn't look at Claudia. "James Francis Edward Stuart, sometimes known as the Old Pretender."

The name fell like a bomb into the room. Darius leaped to his feet, his hand going to his sword belt, though what he meant to do with his weapon remained to be seen. Val went to his sister's side and put his hand on her shoulder.

Claudia's muffled sob came to Dominic through everything else. He'd hurt her. Regrets filled him, sinking his stomach. He should have told her, but he'd been too much of a coward to do it.

At least now she'd know why he couldn't marry her. "My parents bought me from Maria Rubio. They gave me a birth certificate they'd bought in France. I've known for years that they were traitors to the Crown, after I found a letter referring obliquely to the affair. They assure me they have not betrayed their country for a long time now, and I found no proof that they did."

"We will find a way around this business," Val said before anyone else could interrupt.

They accepted his word? "Don't you want to see proof?"

"We don't need it," Darius said. He went to the window in a swirl of brown cloth, sticking his hands in the capacious pockets of his coat. He leaned against the small table and glared at Dominic. "How long have you known?"

Dominic shrugged. "A week. Before that, I knew my parents were traitors, but not what they'd done. They wanted an heir so badly they bought one." He hung his head. "It's a disgrace I can never recover from."

Warmth touched his leg, just above where his elbow rested on his knee. Shocked, he faced her.

Claudia had touched him, and was gazing at him, compassion in her lovely eyes. "You're still Dominic."

"Dominic Rubio, the bastard son of an unknown Italian woman and a philandering outcast. How can you marry such a man?"

Julius cleared his throat. "Not so. I know a little more than you. As do the two men here. All the Emperors know something about the affair. We suspect the Dankworths know, also, but not how much."

Dominic whipped his head up and stared at him. Julius drew a paper from his pocket. Old, the edges curling with age, and the remains of a red seal, long gone brittle, hanging from a crimson ribbon. He laid it on his silk-clad knee. "Maria Rubio was the mistress of the Old Pretender. At least, that was what we thought until recently, until certain documents came into our possession. Now we know that she was more than that. She was his wife."

Chapter 12

Was he hearing right? What did the man mean?

Dominic dropped his head into his hands, his mind spinning. He'd all but discounted the name of the father on the birth certificate his parents had given him. Anyone could claim paternity, but only the mother knew for sure. In all the literature he'd read about the Old Pretender, he'd never come across the name Maria Rubio. It didn't make sense. None of it made sense. He lifted his head. "I thought he was married to Maria Clementina?"

"He was, but he married her after he'd married Maria Rubio."

Worse and worse. "Do you have proof?"

Julius gave him the certificate. At first Dominic couldn't focus, then he did and he read the names in old flourishing script. A marriage certificate. Something of the nature had been rumored a century before. King Charles was supposed to have married a woman when he was in exile, but it had been shown to be false. Was this the same? "Is this forged?"

"No. It's a copy. Maria Rubio married the Old Pretender in 1717. Two years before he married Clementina. His acknowledged wife gave him two sons, Charles and Henry. Then, unable to tolerate his moods, or so we are told, left him to enter a nunnery. In fact she may have discovered the earlier marriage, and instead of facing the disgrace, chosen another path.

"Maria Rubio's house burned down in 1740, and she perished in the fire. Either the documents pertaining to her marriage burned with her, or they were kept in the Vatican, where we cannot get to them. We don't know. She was aware of her perilous position and that of her children. Clementina had powerful friends. As her children were born she sent them away with a personal letter and a copy of their birth certificate and her marriage certificate."

Dominic turned the paper over and over in his hands. Julius's words didn't make sense. How could this happen? "My parents bought me from her?"

"The chances are that Maria gave you to them. They must have been a Godsend to her. They were wealthy, able to take care of you, and not under suspicion. From what we can discover, she was careful to choose families who could defend her children and ensure their safety. From that, we infer that she loved them. We could be wrong. I am still investigating, but obviously I have to be very careful who I let in to the secret."

"This is treason," Dominic murmured. "Sedition at the very least. You could be plotting to take over the throne." Wait. Facts slowly seeped into his head, resolving themselves into inescapable truth. "According to you, I'm a legitimate child of this Maria Rubio and a Stuart." He paused. "No."

"You're too good for me," Claudia said. She was the only person in the room smiling.

How could she take this lightly? Didn't she realize? Dominic rounded on her, his head pounding, his hands balled into fists, the proof of his birth falling to the floor. He was barely aware of Julius scooping it up. "How can you jest? This is—this changes everything!"

"Does it?" she said quietly. The knuckles on her clasped hands were white. "Surely it's how you feel about it—" Then her face paled. "The attack—the shooting—"

"Could have been meant for me." Yes, of course. Who would want to shoot Claudia? Who would risk the wrath of the powerful Emperors by doing so? But to kill him would be to remove a threat to the Young Pretender and possibly the British throne. The danger could have come from anywhere.

"If it was meant for you, someone else knows your secret. They're willing to kill." Julius's smooth words fell into the fraught silence.

She was in danger as long as she was with him. Dominic suffered all his dreams. They fell into dust on the pristine surface of the carpet. While he'd told himself he was marrying her to protect her, he'd be doing the exact opposite. Her vitality, her very soul would be no more. Rather than see that happen, he'd ensure she was safe.

He got to his feet, bracing himself against the inevitable bodily weakness that came with shock. "If you would escort your sister home," he said, not looking at her, but at Val. "We will contrive to get out of this scrape."

"I believe her injuries necessitate a visit to the country," Val said.

Julius interrupted them. "No. Give it a week. She must face the people who are accusing her. She must not run away. Let her appear in public with her arm in a sling. Her injuries were too severe for her to be moved. I will swear that Viscount St. Just stayed at our house. God knows the servants are due another bribe. They're getting restless. That is if you wish to take that course. Otherwise, I felicitate you both."

He rose. "I will not abandon anyone, nor will I stop in the search for the children of Maria Rubio. This attack probably means someone else knows, and they will not stop hunting them down. Maria was married to the Old Pretender for twenty-three years. We don't know if he continued to see her while he was actively married to Clementina. Even if he cut off relations, that still leaves eighteen years when he could have been begetting children. We need to find them all."

"I can't help you with that," Dominic said. "I must see my own parents. Or the people claiming to be my parents."

He turned to leave but found Julius blocking his way. The man could move swiftly when he wanted to.

"Do not tell them any more than they know already," Julius said. "Do not disown them. If you create a scandal from this, there is no going back, no helping you. I cannot tell you what to do, but think of it. You are a legitimate son of a claimant to the throne. Guess what that makes you?"

He moved out of Dominic's way. "Call on me if you need me."

* * * *

Claudia watched Dominic leave the room with a sense of helplessness that she hated. It infuriated her as it always had, the way men took control and insisted they knew what was best for her. If ever Dominic needed her, it was now. But he wouldn't claim her and would do his best to separate himself from her. But he had to stay in London.

He was a Stuart? A relative of the King? A member of a royal house?

Dear God, what a tangle!

"Do you have anything we need to collect before we leave?" Val spoke tight-lipped. He was more than angry. Val tended to cut himself off and speak coldly when he was at his most furious.

"No," she said, without really thinking. "My maid will see to it. She may come tomorrow and collect what I have forgotten."

"Then I suggest that you come home now."

Darius put his hand over hers. "He has much to think over. It would be cruel to remain."

Helplessly, she searched out her cousin, but Julius was staring into space, his teeth biting into his bottom lip. "A son," he said eventually. "Are there any more?"

Obviously his obsession had him by the tail and he was lost to them. This feud with the Dankworths and his pursuit of the children— "Are you doing this for the Crown, Julius?"

"What?" Julius blinked and stared at her as if she were a stranger. "Oh, ah. No. No, I'm not. Your betrothed is, I fear, a diehard loyalist. I'm doing it because of the people involved. Our cousin-in-law, for instance. We have only just begun. How many more are there? Eighteen years could produce ten children, maybe more. Not all will have survived. Damnation, I wish I could have just one look at the documents the Vatican has! They are probably locked away somewhere. I've seen the Vatican records, or some of 'em. Papers are shoved into boxes and put away. Different systems and different storage areas—it would take a lifetime to track them down. How many? How many of these children are there, and do any want to claim their inheritance?"

Darius lifted his head and stared at his cousin.

Julius frowned. "Don't you understand? These children are the legitimate offspring of the claimant to the British throne. They are direct descendants of the senior line. They have a right to claim the throne, but not a right to ascend. Being Stuarts, they might not understand that part, but we have changed. The people have changed."

"You mean we rule now," Val said with heavy irony. "I do not mean the common people. We will have to go a long way for that to happen, and it won't happen in my lifetime."

"Would you want it?" Claudia frowned. "Surely ruling comes with responsibilities and understanding. Doesn't a ruler have to be reasonably civilized and educated?"

Julius gave a sharp laugh. "If you think that describes the majority of the incumbents of the House of Lords, you are sadly deluded."

They were back. She'd missed that, the banter and exchanges they naturally fell into. Next to the close-lipped Dominic, they were positively loquacious. She'd had to prise everything out of him with a great deal of difficulty. Could she live with that?

The chances were that she wouldn't have to. He might never speak to her again, judging from the way he'd charged out of the house.

All this thinking was making her tired. She hated to admit it, but healing took a great deal of effort.

* * * *

Once they were back in their London home, settled in the room she shared with her sister, Claudia's recovery continued apace. Her family were being maddeningly quiet about any progress. They only allowed her out for gentle walks with her sister, a maid, and the largest footman in their employ to accompany her. No evening entertainments for a week, her mother had declared, and Claudia found herself eager to accept those edicts. At night she slept. In the afternoons she slept. In fact, sleeping was her favorite occupation for a few days.

Livia was working as her spy, but she learned very little. Their brothers were rarely at home, except for the breakfasts, which Claudia had been skipping. On the third day after her return, she felt much better. Her arm flexed when she moved it, with only a twinge of pain. She called the maid and ordered her apple-green silk sacque made ready. She loved that gown.

Dominic had called, but not to see her. He'd sent her his good wishes and he was discussing the situation with her brothers, just as if she were not a part of it. This morning he wouldn't get away without seeing her.

She waylaid him in the hall. When she heard the bell and his voice, she dumped her embroidery on the nearest chair and shot out of the morning parlor, where she'd stationed herself. "Come with me." Grabbing a startled Dominic by his sleeve, she dragged him off.

The footman, a family retainer from the country, pretended not to notice. He'd get a vail later for that. She shoved Dominic into the parlor and closed the door, standing with her back to it. If he wanted to get away, he'd have to do it through her.

"How are you?" he said. His shuttered face only displayed smooth urbanity.

"Much better. What did your parents say?"

He pursed his lips in a soundless whistle. "You don't believe in exchanging niceties, do you?"

"Not when you look as if you might leap out the window. Why leave me like this? We're still betrothed, are we not?"

He sighed heavily. "It's not a good idea."

She jutted out her chin. "Why not? You asked. You took me to bed."

Ah, the mask of urbanity dropped and he closed his eyes as if in pain. "Don't remind me."

"It was that bad?"

Whisking around, he headed for the window and stared out. "It was the best thing that has happened to me for a very long time."

He spoke so softly she had to strain to hear his words, but when she registered them, she rejoiced. She had that, and he wasn't denying it. "I'm glad to hear it." She would give him nothing, not until she knew what he intended. "Then why deny us? Why avoid me?"

He turned, but didn't come over to where she sat. His eyes were hungry, and he gazed at her as if devouring her. "I need to know for sure that I can offer you something."

So like him, so honorable. Claudia took a step toward him. Then another step. "You went to great lengths to persuade me."

"From what I'm hearing, it's unnecessary. Apparently, I was elsewhere when you were sleeping in my bed. Your cousins are adept at rewriting history."

"Not adept enough." Not as skillful as some other people. "If they were, they'd have buried those documents. What did your parents say?"

He raised his arms and then let them fall to his side with a heavy slap. "They said they knew no more than they'd told me. That they were in Rome and they were offered a child. Like me, they assumed the name on the certificate was falsified, or I was a royal bastard. Or so they said. I can persuade them to tell me no more. I was convinced they were traitors. Now I don't know what to think, but I feel I must absolve them from continued activity."

"You won't be having them sent to the Tower?"

That forced a reluctant smile from him. "No. I would never have done so, in any case. They were devoted, and they love me, I can never doubt that. They never spoke about it, never told me, even when I left home. They were distressed when I joined the army, but I couldn't stay."

Unable to resist him any longer, consumed by a need to comfort him, she stepped close and touched him. Placed her spread hands on his upper arms and pressed close. He clenched his hands into fists, and lines of strain appeared on his face.

"I'm so sorry, Dominic. You are still you. Still the man I...want." She couldn't say it. Couldn't articulate the world "love." If she was wrong that was one more way he'd be let down. She couldn't bear to do it. Couldn't hurt him that way. How did she know what love was, since she'd never experienced it before?

She could tell him what she knew. "I've missed you. Someone to talk to and laugh with, and...kiss."

A wry smile twisted one corner of his mouth. "I was going to point out that you have your sisters and brothers. I would prefer that you refrained from kissing them in that way."

"Yes." Would he kiss her now? If she stood on tiptoe, she could reach his mouth, but she didn't have the courage to initiate it. Loving and lovemaking were far too new to her. Was there an etiquette? Would she offend him? No, the reason why she could not do it was the fear of rejection. If he pushed her away. Even the idea brought a lump to her throat.

"I don't know who I am. I have nothing to offer you."

She hated how bewildered he sounded, but she could give him something at least. "If I weren't the child of my parents, my brothers and sisters would still love me because I would still be Claudia. That's the important thing, surely."

He shook his head and at last touched her, stroked her lower arms so gently as if she were made of glass. "Are you feeling better?"

"Much better," she said firmly.

He watched his fingers rather than her face. "I would have given my life for you at that moment. I still will."

"You're a soldier." She tried to still the frantic beating of her heart at that confession. "You're trained for it."

"It's so much more than that."

The admission warmed her.

She could not force herself on him as she'd planned this morning. Seduce him, get him back, her body had said, but now her mind told her different. He was deeply hurt, trying to cope with knowledge nobody should have to face. Not only that he wasn't his parents' child, but the nature of his birth.

"Dominic, I won't give up. Leave this too long and I'll come for you."

His smile when he looked up warmed her all the way through. "I know you will. That's why— Kiss me once and I'll go. I have to see your father and eldest brother. I offered for your hand, and now I have to discuss with them what is to be done."

"Will you tell them everything?"

"Of course."

She suppressed her gasp, but he must have felt something because he smiled and shook his head slightly. "Not that. Our night is ours alone." He lifted his hand and traced her cheekbone. "You have a sweet blush. Very pretty."

A small victory, then. At least she'd made him smile. "Don't tell people we didn't suit," she said. That would close the door on the matter, and she was still determined to have him, if at all possible.

Her father and oldest brother challenged that supposition as soon as Dominic had left. When they asked her into the study, their faces looked as if someone had slapped them, such was their shock. She knew how they felt.

"He told you everything?"

Marcus held a chair for her and she sat.

"Yes," her father said. "We know who fathered him, if that is what you're talking about. Unfortunately, we cannot just turn our backs. More than your affairs are at stake."

She kept her face clear at the word "affair."

Her father continued. "Our family has an interest in the person named as his father. Winterton had confirmed it to us and has undertaken to check the facts. So far, he says, they are correct, pertaining to dates. It appears the certificate told the truth." He paused. "Needless to say, you cannot remain betrothed to him."

"Father, no!" The words burst from her before she had time to stop them.

Her father gave her one of his quelling stares. "I am considerably lenient with my children, far more than many men I know, but I will not be disobeyed. Is that clear?"

"Yes, Papa." Recovering herself, she lowered her head in a submissive gesture. Not that her father's words would make any difference. If she wanted Dominic, she would have him, one way or another. And she wanted him. The only thing stopping her going after him was his doubts and his distress should she cause a breach in her family. He would feel responsible, and Heaven knew he was good at shouldering responsibility, even when he hadn't caused it.

"Very well. Then what do we do?" He sighed. "This business seems to be caught up in that house you inherited. Unfortunately, Julius has prevailed upon me to retain the property because it's a known center and he hopes to discover more from the people there. You must remain the owner for some time yet. Equally unfortunately, we cannot buy it from you from the terms in your aunt's will."

Leaning back in his chair, he sighed and laced his fingers over his stomach. "I know my children do not always tell me everything they do, but in this case, my dear, I must insist. That house is dangerous. You must not set foot over the threshold again."

"Again?"

He rolled his eyes. "Do you think I am completely blind? At the time I would have sent someone for you, but I did realize what you were up to after you returned home. You are wild to a fault, Claudia. You are Lady Claudia Shaw, the daughter of the Marquess of Strenshall, and like it or not, you owe something to that position. Please consider that more in future. You are not a child anymore. You must stop behaving like one."

Tears pricked her eyes. Such a scolding was worse than a beating, not that her father indulged in beatings often. Reproaches, he could win trophies for those. Especially hitting the mark.

Yes, recently she'd come to that realization. All her petty rebellions led to nothing. She needed something to do, a cause, a life. Something. She might have found it, but if she went off in her usual headstrong way, people would consider her a fool. Racing in the Park was all well and good for an eighteen-year-old, but at twenty-four she should show more maturity.

On the other hand, she would not allow her father to shame her into behaving exactly as he wanted. She would just re-think her strategies. She would never forget her exhilaration when she climbed that tree or urged her horse to a gallop. Even entering the house in Hart Street had given her a thrill she had rarely found anywhere else.

Only in Dominic's bed. The safest man she knew had proved a wild man in bed.

Oh, yes, she wanted that part again.

"How is your arm?"

"Much better, Papa. There will be a scar, but not a bad one, and it's too low to show over my gowns."

Her father smiled. "That of course is the important thing." His eyes smiled too, demonstrating his words were meant ironically. "When you're ready to return to society, remember what I told you. Make me proud of you."

She got to her feet and bobbed a curtsey. "Livia will do that for you, Papa, but I will undertake to do my best not to disoblige you."

Lord Strenshall sighed. "I suppose that is something."

* * * *

Dominic sipped glumly at his coffee. The Cocoa-Tree didn't serve the best coffee in London. In fact, the brew was generally either insipid or gritty. Despite that, the place was frequently crowded.

Most of the customers here were Jacobites or did not object to mixing with them. Neither applied to him, but he had come here in the hope of noticing something or hearing something. To test the air, in case his secret had slipped out.

He leaned back, holding a newspaper he'd read at his breakfast table an hour before, but it provided a reason for him to be there. A few men, for only men frequented these places, apart from the serving girls and the woman at the cash desk by the door, discussed the affairs of the day. Most leaned over the tables, muttering and discussing the only matter that interested them—the return of the Stuarts to the throne.

Dominic had avoided this place up to now, but he needed something. A thread to follow, something new. He'd have to visit Hart Street again and start his nighttime prowling, something Claudia's injury had put a temporary stop to.

He drank more coffee and tried not to grimace.

Someone sat at the table opposite him. Dominic looked up, frowning. He didn't recognize the man. Dressed respectably but not extravagantly, the man had more of the air of a Cit than one of his kind. Cits were practical and usually honorable. They did business worth thousands on the strength of a handshake.

"Lord St. Just?"

Surprised, Dominic nodded. He wasn't a prominent member of society, so to be recognized on sight by someone he was not acquainted with came as a surprise. "Do I know you, sir?"

"We have a mutual acquaintance."

"We do?" Summoning all the hauteur of which he was capable, he raised a brow. "I'm sorry but I don't recall…" A thought struck him. "Were you in the army?"

"Not yours." The man nodded. "Yes, I was in that army. Any army that opposes the current regime."

He didn't even lower his voice, damn him. Here they could gossip all they wanted, especially when government spies came in. Dominic supposed he counted as one, but not in this man's eyes. He was a messenger.

The man slid a note across the table. If he was involved in espionage, Dominic should have slapped his newspaper over it and later retrieved it. He couldn't see the point. He picked it up.

"What's this?"

"A message from our mutual acquaintance." The man regarded him with no curiosity or interest. If he was working for the Jacobites and knew Dominic's secret, he would expect more of a reaction.

"Do you require an answer?"

"No, it is in the message."

He tipped his hat and got up, stopping at the desk to pay. Then he turned back and nodded before leaving the establishment. The cracked walls of this place held many secrets, most of them useless.

Dominic opened the note.

Dear Sir,

I would appreciate a meeting at midnight tonight at the place where you saw me last. I have bespoken a room. I will take it amiss if you do not come.

Such subterfuges went hard with Dominic, but he was involved, although he would have done anything not to be. He had no choice. He looked up, caught the intent gaze of a man with startling green eyes who was sitting at another table.

Tired of the place and sick of espionage, he screwed the enigmatic note up into a tight ball and pitched it at the fire. He stood and left the establishment.

* * * *

That night, dressed in less flamboyant clothes than the ones he used in society, Dominic made his way to Hart Street. The spring was wearing on, and soon society would be leaving the city in favor of their country estates. He had none now. No doubt he'd find something to do.

He stood on the other side of the street, close to a wall, but not touching it. Heaven knew what was jettisoned from the upper windows every morning. The night-soil man was supposed to collect the more nauseating detritus. If a maid forgot a chamber pot, in a place like this she might just treat it the way they had been treated since London was built. The street certainly stank as if a lot of chamber pots had been omitted from the morning collections.

He'd known worse.

When a woman approached him, he smiled but shook his head. She was one of the lowest, the kind that toured the streets, but this close to St. Giles she was probably attached to a gang. No sense inciting the ire of someone of that nature.

The woman shrugged, not bothering to lift the sleeve of her gown when it slipped down, and moved on.

The two men who followed her did not. They stood on either side of Dominic, and nudged him. "Into the house."

This was not what he'd promised to do. He cursed himself that he'd allowed himself to fall into a trap. He should have known, should have guessed, but all his concentration was on keeping his secret. He'd hoped to come to an understanding with the Young Pretender. But what if the man had other ideas?

The hard object jabbed into his side felt enough like a pistol for him to decide not to take a chance that it was a walking stick. He walked across the street and entered the house.

Inside, the scene was much as before. Men sat or lay around, the women ministering to them. They were all in a state of undress, but none seemed to care. Dominic pulled his hat low on his forehead. The madam bustled up to greet them, only to find herself brushed away by one of the men at his side.

She nodded and gestured toward the stairs. "His honor is waitin'," she said.

Dominic went up first. One of the bullies followed, his heavy tread depressing the planks. Another heavyset man waited at the top of the stairs. This one had the kind of creased and battered face that indicated prize-fighting. Probably one of the men attached to the house, but he seemed no more friendly than the other.

As a man accustomed to assessing situations rapidly, Dominic planned his exit. He'd have to risk his bones by jumping from an upstairs window if he had to escape in a hurry. This situation was not to his liking. Especially when the bully behind him tripped him into the arms of the one in front and relieved Dominic of his sword and the two pistols he'd stowed about his person. That left a knife, which he'd tucked into the back of his waistband, a trick he'd learned from a sailor on leave in Portsmouth. That blade had saved him a time or two. It might have to save him now. That or his fists.

Anyone else might live on hope. That this meeting would be civilized, that these were normal precautions for a claimant to the throne who was here clandestinely, but Dominic knew better. The last time he'd seen the man he was to meet, that man had been drunk, cavorting downstairs and with not a bodyguard in sight. He'd been inviting the authorities to arrest him. This meeting, he definitely wasn't taking any risks.

The guard righted him and Dominic followed him to the room at the end, the one where he'd met Claudia before. At least he knew the geography of the place. These houses were older than the ones in the West End. If they were timber-based, he could break through to the house next door. His mind working rapidly, he stood and faced the other occupant of the room.

The guard shoved him, forcing him to take a step forward or fall to his knees. That was something this man would never see.

Two wall-sconces set with tarnished mirrors behind them illuminated the room, the fine beeswax candles incongruous in this untidy, dirty, stinking space. A single threadbare rug lay on the otherwise bare and dusty floor. Tawdry prints hung on the walls, no doubt of a lascivious nature. Dominic didn't bother to find out. The pictures were fronted with glass. He could use the glass as another weapon, should he need it.

Would he kill the men in this room to get away if he had to? Oh, yes, for sure he would. Except all he needed was to gain control of the man sitting in the wooden chair with the high back opposite the window. The bed was tumbled, the sheets probably the same as when he was last here.

The memory of meeting Claudia here flashed through his mind and warmed him. At least he had that.

Feeling safer, he walked forward and bowed, but only the bow he would bestow to a gentleman, no lower. The man in the chair did not rise.

"So Stuart manners are as bad as they say?" Dominic said.

The man in the throne-like chair waved a hand. "You are dismissed."

He was talking to the other man in the room, the one standing silently by the window with his arms crossed. Dominic recognized a man who could handle himself in a mêlée. Not just from the powerful build, but the air of stillness the man exuded like a scent.

"My orders are to remain here, your highness."

Dominic glanced at him. "Does he know who I am?" he asked the Young Pretender. What should he call him? "Sir."

"He knows everything. He is deep in my father's confidence."

What was that? What did the Pretender know?

Charles Stuart almost overflowed the chair. He'd made such good inroads into destroying the handsome legend of the 'forty-five that he would be unrecognizable to someone from that time. Dominic had heard tell that Flora MacDonald had come to London after she'd spirited her prince away to France. Become quite a celebrity from all accounts. They would have to get a bigger boat these days.

"I wanted to see my brother," Stuart drawled. "Until now, I thought I only had one." His pale blue eyes glinted in the soft light. He picked up a glass filled with red wine from the table at his elbow. One of the damned Jacobite glasses. He motioned to the decanter and spare glass. "You may drink."

Refusing might appear petulant or worse. Dominic poured himself a glass, sipped, and tried not to grimace at the sharpness of the inferior wine. Men addicted to drink had no idea of the quality of the beverage, but up until now he hadn't believed it. Perhaps the Pretender didn't care.

Was he addicted to drink, or was that a rumor? The bloodshot eyes and a bulbous nose proclaimed the fact, but sometimes looks could be deceptive.

"We should drink to family," the Pretender said.

"Until now, I thought my family was a different one," Dominic said, keeping his tone mild. "I still only have a piece of paper that says otherwise. I take it proofs exist somewhere else?"

The man didn't ask him to sit. Dominic strolled to the bed, and despite his distaste, perched on the edge of it, thus asserting his right to sit in this man's presence. The Pretender waved a hand and the man in the corner didn't move. "Intrigue is enough," he said. "As are other proofs. Assertions taken under oath, for example."

Ah, damn. Dominic covered his alarm by moving his head, letting the uneven light cast his face into light and shade. His parents were in danger. As long as they were alive they could attest to the fact that they were in Rome and they obtained a baby from Maria Rubio. He sucked in a breath and let it out slowly, controlling his desire to swallow. Had Stuart sent a man to kill them?

"I believe I'm your junior," Dominic said.

"When were you born?"

"Seventeen twenty-six."

"Ah. I am older. Considerably so." He said that with a smug certainty. The Pretender slurped his wine. "What did they call you?"

"Dominic."

"Is that the name on the certificate of your birth?"

"Yes. Actually it's Dominica, but my parents made it more acceptable for the child of English nobility." He kept his feet flat on the floor, the better to get to his feet quickly if he needed to. Did this man know about the other certificate, the one that detailed the marriage between their father and Dominic's mother?

"This is a damned mess." The Pretender glanced at the man in the corner as he put his empty glass down.

The man did not move. "I am here to observe proceedings, no more," he said. "I am not a servant."

Pouring a glass might mean the man could not get at his weapon in a hurry. Dominic knew as surely as he could see them that he had at least two pistols thrust into his belt, and a few other useful items. He'd sat where he could see both men, but he wasn't close enough to either of them to take them by surprise. The man met his gaze and then glanced away. "I'm here for your safety," he said.

Dominic wasn't sure which of them he meant. When he'd first entered the room, he'd assumed the man a bodyguard to the Pretender, but he'd said he was here for the King. The Pretender's father.

The Old Pretender never set foot in Britain, not since the 'fifteen had driven him out of the country for good. The chances that he was here were negligible. However, it was reasonable that he'd set someone with his son's entourage.

Grumbling, the Young Pretender poured himself a brimming glass of wine, but he didn't offer Dominic another. Dominic kept hold of his glass. Another potential weapon, though he was beginning to think he did not need one. He would not, however, rely on the faint chance provided by the watchful man in the corner.

The Old Pretender would know about his bigamous behavior. Would know that the first marriage had not been invalidated. Would know he had children, although he didn't know where they were.

"What if I refuse to accept that I am a child of your father?" Dominic said.

"Plotters still plot and people still insist on their rights. They will rally around anyone. I'm trying to assess if you are worth having as an ally. You must want our father to ascend to his rightful place on the throne."

Dominic moved around and took another sip of wine. Just as bad as the last sip. "If you say so," he said cautiously.

"You have a look of him, you know that? Of course your eyes are dark, like our father's, but you have the face and nose of a Stuart. I'm surprised nobody noticed before. You must meet him. If you have not met him already."

"I can't help the way I look." He'd have done anything at that moment to be a grey-eyed blond. He'd tied his own hair back tonight, since he hadn't any society events planned. Yes, although nobody had marked the resemblance before, nobody had any reason to. Once his secret became known, people would notice. If his secret came out. "You enjoy living like this?" He waved, his gesture encompassing the room.

"Oh, believe me, this is not normal. My lodgings are a great deal better than this." Interesting, that faint accent, the touch of his tongue on the consonants, more like his mother's language than the one his father was born into. Although the Old Pretender had been born abroad and had spent most of his life away from the country of his birth.

"You enjoy the intrigue? Do you have any time to yourself? How about a wife?"

His staccato questions had their effect. The Pretender choked on his wine. "Wife? Who have you been talking to?"

"Only the usual people. Did you not have me followed, observed? You'll know I live a fairly ordinary life."

The Young Pretender put down his glass with a force that nearly cracked it. "Except for your habit of running with the wrong people. That is one reason I called you here tonight. Break off your connection with the family that calls itself the Emperors of London."

"Why do you wish for that?"

"Isn't it obvious? They are loyal to the usurpers. I have spoken to a strong supporter of ours, Northwich. Do you know him?"

"I haven't as yet had the felicity of meeting him."

"You have now," the man in the corner said.

Chapter 13

He walked forward, his heels rapping on the uneven floorboards. Then he swept a bow, a low one. "I wanted to meet the newest member of the house of Stuart," he said. "I regret our paths have not crossed before."

Dominic returned his bow, after he'd put his glass down. The man was a duke, and Dominic gave him his due. "The head of the Dankworth family. I have briefly met your son."

"Which one?"

"Alconbury. Your heir."

The duke grimaced. Out of the shadows he appeared older than Dominic had supposed. He kept himself in good shape, but he must be at least fifty. Alconbury was in his late twenties or early thirties, so the duke was probably a few years over fifty.

"Alconbury has his own way of doing things that aren't always mine. His highness has agreed to meet you partly on my account. After all, we will be working together, will we not?"

Dominic regarded him steadily. Then he retook his seat, claiming his right to sit in the presence of a duke, as a king's son should. He hated the situation, but he would use every bit of it to his advantage. His aims remained consistent. He wanted to ensure Claudia's safety. That above all things. He wanted to discover more about this family trying to claim him as its own.

Perhaps he'd discover more about himself. He had to know more about them, and to do that he needed face-to-face meetings. "I haven't yet made up my mind."

"We have other proofs," Northwich said. "Paper, your looks, and circumstances. We can show that the people who reared you were not in Paris, but in Rome. We can show that you were born in a private house close to the Palazzo Muti, where the King has his court."

He meant the Old Pretender. Dominic refused to call him king. No one not consecrated and approved by the people could be his monarch.

"We can show any number of things that will prove you are who we say you are. You are with us. Either that, or we will condemn you to the authorities."

Charles Stuart was watching Dominic strangely, as if he would say more, but was holding his tongue. Northwich took care, as Dominic did, to keep all the occupants of the room under observation. Stuart was not appearing the confident prince of a few moments earlier. Tension filled the space between them.

"I will do as I think right, and I will take whatever consequences I have."

"What of this house?" Northwich demanded. "We know who owns it. What if it is exposed as a nest of sedition? Of a stronghold of the true King and his son? What would happen to the precious reputation of the Emperors?" He said the last word with a sneer. "One of their number, the wild daughter of the Marquess of Strenshall, has thrown her lot in with the Jacobites. I can bring enough witnesses to attest to that. She walked in here, bold as brass, displaying herself to the assembled company. Nobody could mistake that hair, that face, even though she'd tried to disguise herself."

A cold hand clutched Dominic's heart. That statement contained enough truth to prove difficult. Dangerous, even. If the power of the Emperors was reduced, that would knock one support away from the current monarchy, which was shakier than it had been since Queen Anne died.

An ailing king and his grandson, little more than a boy, or the wily grandson of an anointed King, the senior of his line?

One question hammered at Dominic's skull. Did they know that his birth parents were married? Did they realize that for want of a better, if the Stuart line prevailed, Britain could find itself with a King Dominic?

Nausea churned Dominic's stomach.

* * * *

Outside, Claudia stood in the middle of a veritable mob, consisting of her twin brothers and her cousin Max. Max had seen Dominic in The Cocoa Tree, and being of a curious nature, had collected what Dominic had discarded.

"He's in there," Claudia declared in a low whisper, although she wanted to jump up and down and shout. "Two men, one either side walked him in there. He didn't have a choice."

"Why you're here when you were told expressly to stay within bounds beats me," Val said in a disgruntled tone that barely hid his interest in the scene. "Father will rusticate you for this."

"If anyone tells him." Claudia glared at her brothers. She also viewed Max with disdain. "Why did you tell them?"

"Because they're your brothers," Max, otherwise the Marquess of Devereaux declared. "Truly, Claudia, your father should have beaten you once a week when you were little."

"By God, he should still be doing it," Val said. "I'm just glad Marcus is out of town. You were told not to come to this house again, Claudia."

"I was told not to go inside," she said. "If Max didn't want me to come, he shouldn't have told me."

They were standing at the end of the street, where Hart Street met Covent Garden. All in a form of evening dress, they looked more like people heading for the Opera House or the theater than people who had any reason to linger near a street with a raffish reputation.

"Never mind that," Claudia said hastily, seeing an argument developing. "We need to do something!"

"You mean *we* do. You don't."

Claudia snorted and stamped her foot. That hurt, since her evening slippers were not of the sturdy variety. Every cobble made its presence felt. "How do you think you'll get in? Do you want to storm the place? If you do, Dominic will get hurt, and I will never forgive any of you. Ever. I will ensure you all suffer if that happens."

Val shuddered. "I would risk even a grass snake in my bed rather than put you in danger."

Max snorted with laughter. Unlike the Shaws, Max was the only child of his parents and had never known the joys of siblings. He turned his head and his eyes glinted green in the light. "Did she really do that?" he asked Val, who was standing to one side of him.

Val nodded.

"He hates snakes," his twin added.

"Oh, tell everyone," Val mumbled. "Why don't you shout it to the heavens while you're at it?"

"Shut up!" Claudia was losing patience. "Just think about getting Dominic out of there!"

"I knew you wouldn't leave this to us. As soon as Max strode into White's, I asked him if he'd left you alone."

"He did." Max rolled his eyes.

"He said you'd promised to stay put while he came to us." Darius snorted. "He clearly doesn't know you."

"I made him go," Claudia said.

"So you, a well-born lady, get a hackney on your own to traipse over half London." Val's voice dripped with disgust. "Do you remember why that marriage act was passed two years ago? Because heiresses weren't abducted and forced into marriage with fortune hunters! Doesn't that tell you anything?"

Claudia produced a pistol from the capacious folds of her cloak. "You made sure I could use this. I have another."

"Give it to me," Val said.

"I'll need it."

"No you won't. You said you had another one."

Grumbling, Claudia handed the weapon over and pulled out the other one.

Val gave a low whistle. "These are Papa's best dueling pistols."

"They were the first I could find. He keeps them in his study and he shows them off to anyone who's interested. The box has everything you need to load them, so it was convenient."

"Beautiful," Max said. "We don't use them much in the City, but I like to have one about me in case of footpads. I should get some of these."

Claudia kept a firm grip on the one she had left. She'd also stowed her small pistol, the one that hurt her thumb when she cocked it, in her skirt pocket, but she didn't tell anyone that. The men had swords. She should have some kind of backup, too.

"We go," she said. "Now."

Before they could tell what she was about, she strode away and was half-way down the street before they caught up with her.

"Dear God, Claudia!" Max said, but of the men he had the least experience with her and he wouldn't know what she was capable of.

She would march up to the front door of the house and rap on the panels. A sliver of paint fell to the worn stone step. Somebody came and opened the door a crack.

Val shoved past Claudia and pushed the door, taking whoever answered it by surprise.

"I've come to see my house," Claudia declared.

The madam stood inside, mouth agape, ready to scream.

Claudia smiled at her. "My brothers didn't believe me when I said I owned this house, and we were at the theater so I said I'd bring them and show them. Prove to them that this is mine. You can corroborate it, can't you? You've seen the papers, and I'll wager my aunt told you too."

The madam sucked in a breath, but before she could issue more than a squeak, Darius had one hand around her waist and another over her mouth.

"We mean you no harm," he said affably. "But if you shout, I will knock you on the head and you'll wake with a lump as big as a pigeon's egg. Tell these people we're only after a good time."

Val yelled something obscene. Claudia watched him, fascinated.

"Where's the fucking whores? Come on, there's a hungry man here with a handful of guineas!"

She'd never seen her brother in this frame of mind, and she had no idea he could sound like that. Val was known for profligacy, but her experience of it was poor to nonexistent, since Val preferred to keep his debauchery away from his family. Or so he'd told her once.

He definitely had the right tone of voice, because women came flocking and the men standing by, the big powerful men, grinned.

One jerked his thumb at her. "Who's this?"

Val jerked a finger upstairs. "She's come for her gentry-mort. He's upstairs with another doxy and she's none too pleased."

"Oh, Hampstead fare, are we?" one of the girls said. She peered closer, close enough that the stink of her breath washed Claudia in nausea. "You've been here before, ain't you? I remember you. With the mort what took you upstairs. Ain't you fancy now, though?" Her sneer displayed five teeth and several gaps.

Claudia wasn't slow on the uptake. "Yes, and I've come to get him back. I'm not sharing."

Raucous female laughter followed her up the stairs.

At the top stood a huge man. Two men squashed into one, he was so big, and his face so battered.

Claudia remained three steps away and waved her pistol at him. "Like many ladies of fashion, I have taken lessons in shooting. At any rate, at this distance I can hardly miss." She smiled. "If I do, the men behind me will not."

The man stood aside. She took a chance in pushing past him, there not being much room at the top of these stairs. But one of the men behind took control of him. The muffled yelp told her he'd taken a well-situated blow from the butt of somebody's weapon. Silently she commended whoever had done it and carried on. The first room was empty, and the second, which said something for a busy brothel during opening hours. The one at the end, the one from before, had its door closed.

When Max opened the only other door off this passage, he found someone, as was evidenced by the muttered conversation and another thump. This one rocked the boards under her feet.

A shout came from the inside of the end room. They'd been discovered.

Someone shoved past her—Val, as it turned out—and struck the door, sending it swinging inwards.

Claudia breathed a thankful sigh. Dominic, seemingly at ease, half leaned on the bed, in the process of standing. He was not armed. He swept his hand around his back and came up with a wicked-looking knife. The blade was about six inches long and it gleamed in the light reflected from the candle sconces. The scent of expensive wax filled this small space. It almost but not quite drowned the other smells, the offensive stink of stale sexual activity, cheap perfume, and unwashed sheets. Deeply unpleasant smells, all of them. She was so glad to see Dominic she'd have lain with him on that bed, just to feel his body against hers, his heart beating strongly in his chest.

She didn't allow her temporary weakness to affect her. Her brothers and cousin would never allow her to forget it, if she did.

Claudia stood just inside the door, her back to the wall, not impeding access but threatening anyone who tried to leave without her permission.

Three people occupied the room. Dominic of course, was one. The other, standing in the center of the space, an amused smile quirking his lips, was the Duke of Northwich. A fat man lounged in a chair as near to a throne as cheap carving and wood allowed. The one she'd seen in this place before—Charles Stuart, sometimes called the Young Pretender.

She had absolutely no inclination to bow. Surely royalty should evoke that, but it didn't here. For all his status as deposed, or rather, never enthroned, this man was a Stuart—a member of a royal house that went back further than she could recall. Kings immemorial, one might say. When she'd been presented at court on her introduction to society and met other members of the royal family subsequently, curtseys had come naturally to her. Perhaps, stripped of all their trappings of royalty, she might feel the same about King George, but she didn't think so. This man gave her absolutely no reason to present him with an obeisance, even though he was glaring as if he expected it.

Dominic swept her brothers and Max with a level gaze, and lingered on Max before he groaned. "The man with green eyes in the Cocoa-Tree."

"Just so," Max said. "I was there on business. I don't frequent society events very often."

"Only when he wants something," Darius said. "St. Just, meet my cousin Maximilian, the Marquess of Devereaux."

Dominic only smiled and inclined his head, but in a weary tone, he added, "Is there nowhere the Emperors do not go?"

"No," Darius said shortly, and grinned.

"You must forgive me," Max said. "I am unremittingly curious. I recognized you. Part of my business is knowing people. To see you with a known Jacobite recidivist engaged my interest, particularly since you'd recently become betrothed to my cousin."

"You fished the note out of the fire."

"When you throw something into a fire, it is best to ensure the fire is actually lit," Max said.

"The note said nothing particular," Dominic said.

"It did if you knew the sender or the recipient. One visit to my cousin's house revealed the whole." He sighed. "Unfortunately, that also meant Claudia came with the note."

"How could I remain at home with Dominic in danger?" Claudia said. "In my house, too!"

"Ah, yes, we were forgetting that." Dominic tucked his knife back where it had come from.

She would have to get him to show her how he did that without cutting himself. Presumably it involved a sheath. She should really take to carrying something of the kind in her pocket.

"Has it escaped your notice that you are holding these two gentlemen at gunpoint?"

The Duke of Northwich laid his weapon carefully down on a nearby table and folded his arms. "Don't mind me. I know all about familial disputes."

Somehow she hadn't thought about Northwich in that way, as a man with a family, instead of the head of an enemy faction. He must have day-to-day business, as well as the other kind—the kind that required meeting disgraced would-be heirs to the throne in filthy rooms in Covent Garden.

"This isn't a dispute," she said. "We're all together in this."

Now they were here, what did they do?

As if to answer her, Darius left the room and returned in a second. "Unless we plan to turn this into a debating club, we should be leaving soon. The bullies out there aren't going to remain asleep too much longer."

"We came for you," she said to Dominic. Foolishness, because he was not only in this room with two traitors, he was armed. Was he with them? Was she deluded in him?

No, she was not. She understood him and his sense of justice and honor. Damned honor that had caused him to break her heart. Well, he would do so no longer.

Dominic bowed. "You have my eternal gratitude." He turned his attention to Northwich. "If I may have my weapon back, I would appreciate it. That is my favorite pistol, and I have no mind to lose it now."

Darius left the room and returned shortly with a well-worn but cared-for weapon. "This one?"

Dominic took it from him, hefted it, and smiled. "Yes. Thank you." He pocketed the pistol. It gave an odd line to his coat, but it didn't seem to burden him at all. "The next time I'll bring my gun belt. Fashionable clothing doesn't lend itself to storage."

"I have inside pockets made on all my coats," Val said, as if they were conversing at their club. "If you have the coat made to accommodate the extra size or carry a carriage pistol, you need never be without one."

Dominic saluted him. "A capital notion. Then I shall do the same."

The man in the chair sat watching them, his lowering frown ominous. She would not curtsey. She refused to give him even that much.

However she did glance at him. "Good evening."

He saluted her with his full glass, the wine slopping over the rim as a result of his expansive gesture. "You enjoyed your family outing, ma'am?" He sounded English, but with a very slight lilt. It wasn't every day she found a would-be king in a whore's bedroom.

"Tolerably, sir. I have had an experience I won't forget in a hurry." Family outing indeed! His were probably similar to this. A life of intrigue and plays for power did not appeal to her in the least. The Stuarts thrived on it. "I trust we will not meet again."

"Not until I occupy the throne." He nodded at Dominic. "However, I feel our paths will cross several more times. Or once might be enough. Who knows?"

Standing beside him, Claudia narrowed her eyes. What were they discussing before she and her brothers and cousin came in?

Her suspicions roused again, only for her to quell them. He was not the man to deceive. How he'd worked in army espionage for so long she would never know. Maybe one day she'd get to ask him.

"We need to go," Max said shortly. He'd hardly glanced at Charles Stuart, as if he didn't want to acknowledge the man existed.

"You," the duke said, "Will be hearing from me."

He was looking at Dominic, who raised a brow in a sardonic gesture. He didn't reply, but offered his arm to her, just as if they were in a fashionable drawing room.

She took it.

Val drew his watch from his pocket and flicked the lid open. "I need to go. I'm meeting Charlotte at Lady Franklin's." He rarely referred to his betrothed, and indeed she appeared to take up only a small part of his life.

Claudia glanced at Darius who shook his head slightly, warning her not to make a comment.

Val offered a stiff bow and strode from the room after tossing his pistol carelessly to his brother.

Darius snatched it out of the air one-handed and thrust it in his pocket. "At least I balance out now," he said. Although the weapons weighed his coat down more than the tailor probably planned, he didn't look as one-sided as the others.

Claudia hadn't considered fashion when she'd snatched up her father's dueling pistols and loaded them. Or when she'd rushed out of the house, only intent on getting to Dominic before he got hurt.

She was probably due a severe scolding from her father, but she'd bear it. It had been worth it.

They'd left the carriage on the Piazza and it was waiting for them when they approached it, but Max bent over her hand and wished her good evening. "I shall pay a visit to my father-in-law who lives close by. We have a particularly interesting business deal approaching."

"Do you never stop, Max? Has your wife not prevailed upon you to spend more time with her?" Claudia said.

"She is as we speak at her father's house going over the contract with him." He regarded Dominic closely, flicking his gaze over him from head to foot and back again. "I have to speak to you, but I would rather speak to my wife first. We will call on you. We have particular information you might be glad to know. She certainly will be."

Dominic tilted his head to one side, but Max refused to say any more, and turned a warning glance on to Claudia. "Keep my confidence, if you please."

"You didn't have to say anything," she replied, somewhat affronted.

Darius bowed and walked away, too, leaving the carriage to just the two of them.

Suspiciously, she narrowed her eyes at her brother's retreating back. "Should I take you to your lodgings?" she asked Dominic.

"Yes please," he said meekly.

In the carriage he sat next to her, which she viewed as a good sign. But he kept to one side of the vehicle, and she didn't have the courage to move closer. That fear of rejection again. "I suppose you will say we didn't have to rescue you?" she said coolly.

"No," he replied, surprising her. "I went armed, but they took the weapons from me. I had begun to wonder. They could have killed me, and that would have solved their problem."

"They know your secret, then?"

He glanced at her and nodded. "One of them. They know whose son I am. I don't know if they are aware of the rest, but I suspect not. Otherwise they would have killed me for sure."

Daring rejection, she took his hand. His warmth filled her with a quiet gladness she'd missed more than she realized. He let his hand remain in hers, and after a moment, curled his fingers around hers in the protective gesture that seemed so natural to him. She suspected that was the reason why he had joined the army, ton that the army had taught that to him. "There are other children."

"You know that for certain?"

She hesitated, recalling Max's warning. His wife was one of the children, but she had a different mother. She knew of one other, a full sister to Dominic. That was not her secret to tell, either. "Yes, I do. Please don't ask me who they are. I'll contact the ones I know of and ask them if they wish to meet you."

He nodded, his thumb stroking her palm in an absent gesture. "I wouldn't ask any more. Are they safe, these others?"

"They are now." They were female. Less of a threat, even though theoretically they could overset the Young Pretender's claim. If his father supported them. Considering the woeful condition of his acknowledged sons, he might consider doing so. Then— Her chest tightened. Dominic would be in real danger. They'd want him to stake his claim.

Another realization came to her, but she needed to think about it before articulating. It. She was learning. What if the present King accepted the claim? If Dominic became King? Horror filled her and she had to gasp for breath.

Immediately he turned to her. "Are you well?"

"Yes, yes, I'm fine."

"No you are not, but I won't question you now. Go home and sleep. I'll call on you tomorrow."

If he was alive. If something else hadn't happened. How on earth could she sleep?

* * * *

Livia was waiting up for her. She sat up in the big bed Claudia shared with her, a book balanced on her knees. She closed it when Claudia entered the room but didn't remove her spectacles.

Claudia went to the dressing table, removing pins from her hair as she went. "You should wear them all the time, Livia. You look enchanting in them."

Livia made a face. "Tell the society matrons. Tell Mama. In any case, I only need them for reading and close up work. I can manage perfectly well in company."

"How about gazing into your lover's face with adoration?"

Livia snorted. "As if that will ever happen. If a miracle does occur and somebody falls madly in love with me, then he'll have to live with it. The soft gazes will have to be at a distance."

Claudia laughed and sat at the dressing-table. She didn't need her maid tonight. She had dressed for an evening at home, had almost been looking forward to a quiet time with her sister, before Max had arrived in search of her brothers. "It's just as well Mama and Papa were out. Are they still out?"

"Yes, or there'd have been the devil to pay." Livia paused, giving Claudia the chance to brush out her hair. "I was worried. I'd have gone with you if I thought I would be useful."

Claudia turned around on the big backless stool they used, making no effort to hide her astonishment. "You've never wanted to go with me before."

"Tonight wasn't one of your mad adventures. It was a rescue, and it had a serious purpose. Papa might still send you to the country though, once he gets to hear."

"He might not hear." She turned back to the mirror and unlaced her bodice. She had no jewelry to take off; she'd removed that before she left the house. She shrugged. "In any case, the season will be over soon enough. I'll only be leaving a few weeks early."

"He won't ask your young man."

"My young man?" Claudia repeated in a singsong voice. "Who might that be, pray?"

"Lord St. Just is hot for you, and you know it."

Claudia stood to shed her gown. She tugged it off and laid it over a chair for the maid to deal with. Then her ruffles. She tugged at the loose stitching until she pulled it undone and laid the delicate lace on top of the gown. "I know nothing of the kind. Our betrothal was of a practical nature."

"Claudia, you're talking to me. At least do me the courtesy of looking at me when you speak."

"You sound like a governess." She spun around and faced Livia. Her sister sat in a pool of light cast by the candle set in the sconce on the bed head and one she'd set on the nightstand on her side of the bed. "Liv, there are things I can't tell you, but you can guess."

Livia grimaced. "The Dankworth business."

She nodded. "The Dankworth business. It's all to do with that. He's involved, and—oh dammit, you know!"

Livia nodded this time, and leaned forward, resting her chin on her knees. "Is it you or him?"

"What are you talking about?" She wrestled with the cord on her pocket. Somehow it had become tangled.

"Which one of you is saying no?"

Sighing, Claudia gave up and started on her hoops. "He is. I am. Papa is. All at different times."

Livia chuckled. "A proper tangle then, not one of your dares."

"How do you do it, Liv?" The hoops gave way and she left them on the floor. Her under-petticoat followed in short order but she still had her pocket and her stays to manage. She crossed the room to her sister. "Can you help with these?"

"Turn around. How do I do what? Keep out of trouble? Books, dear sister. I read, and when I'm not reading, I think. If I found something I preferred doing, I'd do it, but climbing trees and racing horses doesn't appeal to me. I can ride. I can climb. Not as well as you." With a few sharp tugs, the stays were free. Claudia breathed deeply, as she always did when she shed her stays at the end of the day. Livia tugged at the pocket. "You've knotted this." A pause, and then a snip.

She'd used her embroidery scissors to cut the tape. "The maid can sew a new one on in the morning. When the usual way doesn't work, go around and try something else. The Gordian knot."

Claudia recalled the name but not the story. If she asked her sister, Livia would forget herself recounting the tale. She was tired. She wanted to sleep.

A quick visit to the necessary in the powder room and then at the washstand and she was ready for bed. Night rail bedamned. Tonight she'd sleep in her shift.

Livia snuffed the candles and the bed rocked when she settled herself. "Claudia?"

"Yes?"

"If you really want him, go after him. You know how to create a scandal, Claudia, nobody better. It follows that you know how not to create one."

In the darkness, Claudia chuckled. "Oh, I love you, dear sister. Good night."

"Sleep well. You'll need it."

Chapter 14

Every time Claudia set foot into an establishment where he was, she knew it. Be it ballroom, theater, park or even a street, she knew it. He did too. He must. Taking her sister's oblique advice, Claudia became the pattern-card of propriety. After a severe dressing-down by her father, instead of defying him or answering back, she folded her hands and begged his forgiveness. Her actions shocked him so much, he asked her if she was her sister.

"No indeed, Papa. I suppose you might say I am growing up. Indeed I would not have gone had my brothers not sworn to take the greatest care of me."

That would put the blame in the twins' court. They could cope with it, and they had more credit with their father at the moment.

To her shock, her father's attitude softened. "Do you care for him, puss?"

She swallowed. "I believe I do, Papa."

"Then you shall have him."

"No." She made a pass with her hand in a gesture of pacification. "I mean, let me, sir. I promise you I will not do anything rash. He is an honorable man and a stubborn one. I have to——"

"Bring him to heel." Her father leaned back in his chair, the wood creaking. He should really get it changed before it broke, they all told him. But he refused to allow her mother here to arrange things elegantly, as she had the rest of the house. His study was sacrosanct. "Very well. As long as you promise to get into no more scrapes. Do not try to force his hand or compromise him. Do you understand?"

"I despise such underhand ways," she said, and she meant it. Trapping a man into marriage was not her idea of starting off well. She wanted him, but some of his honor must be rubbing off on her. No trapping him in a side room, no seducing him and then accidentally letting a maid see. That had happened, but it wasn't deliberately and they'd escaped that fate.

Now he was keeping away from her for some nonsensical sense of honor. She would not have that. If he didn't like her, that was something else, but she would not accept his sense of honor as an excuse.

She came up with another scheme. The one Ruth spoke about in the Bible. After all, what was a better example than one of the women of the Bible? Except Jezebel, perhaps.

She set her spies, and with a family as large and close as hers, that proved easy. Then set her plans accordingly.

When she insisted on attending the same milliner on Bond Street three days running, her mother demurred, until Claudia spied Lord St. Just leaving from the fencing academy across the road.

"Ah-ha. You love the yellow?" the assistant asked, bringing Claudia's attention back to the present.

The yellow bonnet was the last one Claudia would have chosen. It made her look ill. Instead of arguing, she moved on to another in emerald green that she might actually get some wear from.

Her mother accepted her change with equilibrium, but asked her daughter, "Do you have to waft it about so vigorously? It's such a bright color, Claudia. Is it entirely suitable?"

Perfect for her purposes.

Viscount St. Just stopped in his tracks and stared directly at her. A muscle in his jaw tightened, flattening the shape of his mouth. She'd ensured that he saw her yesterday with the pink straw and the day before, with the apricot hat. He must know the colors did not become her. Three days running was not a coincidence.

He crossed the road and entered the establishment. "You can't wear that," he said bluntly. "It would not do you justice. Did you buy the apricot and the pink?"

Claudia simpered. "I had not thought you noticed. No, they were not quite right, so I came back to find something that I preferred."

He picked a plain bergère from a nearby stand. "Would this not do?"

The man serving them gave him a look of pure disdain. "Far too plain for her ladyship. She deserves only the best."

"It's charming," Dominic said. "Lady Claudia looks good in anything. She just looks better in some things more than others."

Claudia caught her mother's amused glance when she looked into the mirror. Ignoring the sardonic smile, she took the hat from him and tried it on. It was plain enough to decorate as she wished. In fact, it was perfect.

She tilted it over one eye and then straightened it in the approved manner, but she considered the tilt. She could set a fashion. She set it sideways again. The angle revealed her lacy cap and the gleam of her red-gold hair. "Take the green ribbon from the other and put it on this, on the right side."

"Why not white ribbon?" someone asked from the doorway. Unknown to her someone had followed Dominic into the shop.

The Duchess of Northwich.

Tall, impossibly elegant, and gracious, the duchess usually kept clear of her husband's intrigues, but never opposed him in public. Very few people could even assess the relationship between them, and Claudia wouldn't even try.

"White does not become me."

"White becomes everyone. Powder your hair." The duchess smiled. "Of course I can understand why you are so proud of those fiery locks. They're so distinctive."

She turned and left.

Stricken, Claudia put the hat down. The message had come across clearly. A bunch of white ribbon—the White Cockade was the notorious symbol of the Jacobites. They used it to recognize each other, and to wear that particular arrangement in public was to acknowledge the connections. The duchess never wore it, but sometimes she came close. Everyone wore white ribbon. Just not in that particular way.

Her distinctive hair? Someone had seen her going into that house that she didn't know about.

By her side, Dominic clenched his jaw. "Ignore her," he said. "She knows nothing."

"You can't be sure." Recalling where she was, Claudia forced a smile to the assistant. "I'll take the bergère, with the green ribbon, if you please."

Putting up her chin, she smiled at Dominic. "Do you go to the theater tonight?"

"No, I planned to go to—"

"Lord Marks's small gathering for a few select gentlemen. Val mentioned it at breakfast this morning."

His lips twitched. "The Strenshall breakfast is a meal to be feared, or so I hear."

"You should come sometime." She touched her finger to her lips. "Oh, wait, it's family only."

"We will have to see what we can do," her mother told him, gifting him with a smile as they went to the door.

* * * *

The minx was following him. Dogging his every move would be too much of an exaggeration, but it came close. Every time he appeared in society, there she was. Talking to her friends, dancing with her admirers, greeting him with a sunny smile and a few sweet words. She'd appeared in the park wearing the "simple" hat, transformed into a riot of green ribbon, with a white rose nestled among the green. She wore it tilted to one side instead of straight on her head, and the next day half of fashionable London appeared with tilted bergère straw hats. While Claudia wasn't a fashion-setter, she'd looked so charming in the hat that society had taken notice and acted accordingly.

What they had noticed was her liveliness. Several people remarked on it, and in his hearing. Her proximity to him had started people talking. As one week went by and another started, with no unusual events occurring to mar his safety, Dominic wondered if the Young Pretender had gone home.

Perhaps the man didn't know, after all, but had been sounding him out and found him wanting. Dominic was still in turmoil. He needed someone to talk to, but the one person he could discuss things with was out of reach. Except she seemed determined not to be. She contrived to remain close to him whatever he said and however much he tried to separate himself from her.

Eventually, he got the message. He would have to do something or she'd never leave him alone, and in his heart, that was the last thing he wanted. Walking into a drawing room and not seeing her made his heart plummet. He wanted her, and as the week went by and he she danced and laughed and rode, his feelings became irrevocable.

Perhaps he could persuade her to wait until a better time, until his nemesis had returned to Italy and left him alone. Her family would keep her safe. Not as safe as he could. He wouldn't leave her side.

The night he agreed to attend the theater at Drury Lane, he'd done it at the last minute so he considered himself safe. He'd watch the play and think, take his time to consider what he truly wanted. Seeing Claudia at every turn confused him and made him no longer sure of what he wanted and why he wanted it. He planned to keep her safe, not drag her into it, but the more he saw her the worse it got to recall that.

Their betrothal had been discussed and discarded by society, when they weren't seen in public as a couple.

He sat in the box watching the play, hearing his friends exclaim at its quality. Dominic had no idea if he was watching Congreve or Shakespeare.

He tried to concentrate but his senses worsened until all he could see was a flash of red-gold hair and a pink gown.

Then there she was in that damned pink gown. Sitting in the box plumb opposite to him, fluttering her fan and chatting with her brothers. Her mother was there. Now he had no chance of knowing what the play was or why it was so good.

He got to his feet at the interval and excused himself. "A damnable headache," he said. "My military service—a knock on the head. Sometimes it comes back. The evening has been most enjoyable up to now." Muttering about old war wounds often excused him and it did now. As long as he remembered he was supposed to have a headache, he should be fine. If he could remember anything at all.

Was this an accident? Society at this level was small, but surely not that small. He had seen her everywhere he'd been this last week, apart from White's and the coffee houses. Even there he'd met some of her relatives. Surely she didn't have that many?

Deep in thought, he strode down the wide corridor leading to the exit when a movement caught his eye. There she was.

This passage was relatively free of patrons. If the play had been a bad one, they'd all be here, conversing and flirting. But apart from half a dozen people he didn't know, they were by themselves. She smiled and offered him her hand.

He had no choice but to bow over it. "Lady Claudia. If I'd known you were coming—"

"You'd have gone somewhere else?"

Her arch words didn't hide the hurt in her voice, or perhaps he'd become too sensitive to her recently. Dammit, even now he wanted to hold her, to make her his. The urge was nearly irresistible, she'd teased and taunted him so much this last week.

"Would you like a private word, sir?"

Yes, he damned well would. "Without a chaperone, Lady Claudia?"

"My mother is waiting."

He couldn't bear this any longer.

He accompanied her to the responding corridor on the other side of the theater, and then to one of the small rooms set aside for private refreshment or rest. This one was furnished with a deep, soft sofa and a chair, together with a table laid with various comestibles and a decanter of red wine. He barely gave them a glance because they were blessedly alone.

"We used this room earlier," she said, speaking fast and waving her gloved hand vaguely. "I thought we could—"

She got no further because he brought his mouth down on hers and feasted. When he touched her lips with his tongue, she opened her mouth and he was home. She tasted like…Claudia and responded sweeter than any woman he'd ever known. How they managed to reach the sofa he didn't know. But she was sitting on it, and then lying as he urged her down on to the soft cushions.

Wrapping her arms around him, she dragged him close, but moved so she could slide her hands under the heavy folds of his coat. His waistcoat still lay between them, and so did her garments, but they could do nothing about that here and now. Enough that he had her in his arms, except, like a greedy child, he wanted more.

He finished the kiss and started on her throat, groaning at the softness of her skin. Surely no woman was this soft to the touch. Only one, only one. "You're so lovely, Claudia. What have you done to me?"

"Foolish man. The same thing you've done to me. Have you wanted to talk over something with me this last week?"

He lifted up on one elbow, smiling down at her. "Many times. From the foolishness of Lady Harrison losing her gloves to a small dog to the gossip about us." He smoothed an errant curl away from her cheek, just for the pleasure of feeling all that silkiness against her flesh.

She giggled. "They are talking about us, aren't they?"

"Unfortunately yes. We need to do something about it."

"What do you suggest?"

He kissed her again. "Not this." He gazed down at her, her breasts pushed up above the décolletage of her pink gown, her hair becoming disarrayed against the green sofa cushions. She looked adorable. He touched her breasts, groaned, and bent to taste all that bounty. "I want you in my bed, naked. I want you there for a long time."

"Why?" Her expression didn't fool him for a minute.

"You know exactly why. I want to make love to you until neither of us can move. What do you do to me, Claudia?"

"I don't know, but you do the same thing to me." She slid her hand up his back to his neck and urged him down, initiating another kiss, tilting her head to seal their mouths more securely.

This time she tasted him. He loved the give and take between them. Once he'd taught her to kiss in this intimate way, she'd taken to it with enthusiasm, so much that she drove him to the brink of coming. Just with her kisses.

He lost himself in her kiss, but drew away, breathless. He nudged the gauzy folds of her fichu aside, giving him access to the upper slopes of her breasts. He licked between them, that inviting cleavage that beckoned him to do wicked things, and pressed kisses along the line between her rigid bodice and that delicious bounty beneath. "I can't stay away any more."

With an effort, he tore himself away from temptation and rested on his elbows, gazing down at her. "We can't meet like this," he said.

Her fingers caressed the back of his neck, playing havoc with his carefully tied neckcloth. Not that he cared. "Why not?"

"Because someone will catch us."

His words shocked him into a realization of where they were. He shot a glance at the door. The key was still in it.

"I turned the lock," she purred.

"Someone will miss you."

"No, they won't. Not until it's time to go home. We have hours."

He'd left after the first act of the first play. She was right. Hours. They could—not here not now. His wayward arousal pressed against his clothing. She must be able to feel it. Her skirts were light silk, and he must be crushing them. People would guess what they were up to, but he couldn't move off her. He couldn't stop himself wanting her. "Claudia, this is impossible."

"Yes it is."

He reared back, startled when she agreed with him. "I'm in danger. You know that. I can't drag you into it." He touched her hair, slid a finger along the silky mass.

"Nobody's been near you for a week." She stared at him, unusually solemn, the laughter gone from her eyes. "I worried. I wanted to be by your side to face it. Nobody approached you, nobody attacked you."

He didn't ask who "Nobody" was or how she knew. He knew the answers to both. Nobody was the Jacobites, particularly the Young Pretender and his people. She knew, because when she hadn't been watching him, her brothers had. That did not make him feel any better, except that she'd cared enough to find out. "Nobody did."

"That's why you stayed away, wasn't it?" She was too perspicacious for her own good. "I was shot, and then you were abducted. You wanted to ensure I wasn't attacked again, did you not?"

"Yes." What was the point of prevaricating? She had the truth of it. "I'd die if you were hurt. I hoped to conclude this business somehow, and then, if you were still free, come back for you."

"You are a legitimate child of the Young Pretender's father. That makes him illegitimate. It stands to reason that he'd want to eliminate you. It also stands to reason that situation isn't going to change very much. You are who you are. Julius is engaged in tracking Maria's children down. That's his real work, or has been since we discovered the secret. I cannot tell you who. Please don't ask."

He wouldn't dream of it. He didn't want her to break the confidence of other people. "I would like to meet them."

"I think we should tell Julius that." She paused. "One lives in the country. It's highly unlikely that you know her." Guiltily, she swallowed. "I'm sorry. I shouldn't even have said that."

A sister. He had a sister. Maybe more, but the prospect of meeting her made his head spin. Perhaps some good could come of this after all. "Does she know?"

Claudia nodded.

"Does she have any intention of claiming her birthright?"

Claudia shook her head. "She's violently against it. She'll be relieved now a son has turned up." She stroked his neck gently. "You. Will you claim it?"

He laughed. "I should give a direct no, should I not? I don't think it's that easy."

"That's what the Young Pretender is afraid of. You can make him illegitimate and claim the throne for yourself when the Old Pretender dies."

He shook his head. "You make it sound as if the throne is mine for the taking. You know it would be a hard fight."

For the first time her gaze faltered. She shifted under him, her silks rustling. "Yes, I do."

He pressed home his advantage. She had to understand what this poisoned chalice meant. As she pointed out, he might never be free of this inheritance. "Would you stand by my side if I announced what and who I am?"

She swallowed.

"Would you come to Rome with me and introduce yourself to my father as my wife and princess? Since his two sons have turned out such disappointments, I have no doubt the man would renounce them. He probably knows where the original certificates are. He could prove our existence, claim us, and revive the Cause. What do you think, Claudia? Would you help me with that?"

Slowly, she lifted her gaze and met his eyes. "No," she said. "I might— I couldn't help you start a war that could cause death and betrayal. My family has experience of that, don't forget. Some of our members were

Parliamentarians and others Royalists in the Civil War. That was only a hundred years ago, only just out of living memory. We won't forget the death and misery that caused. I can't aid anyone to revive that."

"What if it was a bloodless revolution?" he persisted, and this was the possibility that had kept him awake for most of the last se'enight. That and thoughts of this woman in his bed. "What if the government wished to reinstate the Stuarts? Acknowledge them as royal? Maybe some of my brothers and sisters are in abject poverty. They might be in extremis. What if they want this? Do I have the right to reject them?"

"You must," she said. "If it would lead to bloodshed, you must."

Her sentiments were so close to his, it only proved how much he needed her. "Claudia, I don't know what to do. For the first time in my life, I don't know."

"Come and see Julius with me," she said. "But only after we announce our engagement."

* * * *

Seeing her man so conflicted broke Claudia's heart. Warmed by his body for the first time in a week, her private places heated and softened. She ached for his touch, but nevertheless wanted to give him anything he needed. If only he could get rid of that lost expression.

This wasn't her strong, capable soldier. That man had an answer for any peril and could talk or fight his way out of any difficult situation. This man was lost in the myriad possibilities of what he was and who he was. Having one's childhood and youth negated in this way must be unbearable. She'd never know, but she had enough imagination to put herself in his place. Enough to want to share it with him. She'd played her game this last week knowing that whenever she could see him, something inside her eased. Although she wanted more, at least she had that, the sight of him and the knowledge that he was safe.

Proposing to him might be unusual, but she suspected she'd never get him to the point if she did not take the initiative. He wouldn't let her close. "We need to do this together," she said, smoothing her hands over either side of his face, holding him steady. "I can't stay away from you any longer. Either we are together, or we are finished."

He wet his lips. "Together," he said, his voice hoarse. "I'm a selfish bastard, but that's what I want. I need you, Claudia. Be my…viscountess."

Happiness flooded through her, and she forced herself to slow down and savor the moment. That was what she'd always done, and she wouldn't stop now. Enjoying what was happening now, instead of worrying about the past or the future was a gift, and she appreciated it and reveled in it.

"Yes." Before he could change his mind or take back his words she said it. "I will. I do!"

Dragging him down, she sealed their bargain in a kiss. He couldn't change his mind now. She'd set her brothers on him if he tried to.

When they separated, they were both breathless and laughing with happiness and shock.

"When?"

"I have the license," he said. "Whenever you like. Tomorrow, if you want to."

"My father would murder me." She couldn't stop smiling. "It's almost worth doing it for that." She kissed him again, smacking her lips against his, making him laugh. Before Dominic, she'd never imagined laughter came with passion.

"You must visit my father tomorrow and encourage him to bring the wedding forward." Because if he did not, he'd find another reason to try to keep her out of danger. Danger was everywhere. Didn't he know that yet? "Listen, Dominic." She still held his jaw, and she tightened her hold. "A family like mine faces danger of one kind or another every day. I don't take this threat lightly, but you are dividing your efforts. With me under your roof, working with you, don't you believe you will be more effective?"

At least she'd made him laugh. "You could persuade a monk to marry you." He held her close. "I've long been able to deny myself anything, but I am helpless with you. You are right, in many ways. You have an allure I don't understand. Every time you are near, I know it, and when I see you, I can't look away." He shook his head. "I don't understand it. Do you?"

She did, but she was too wise to tell him now. She might frighten him away. She shook her head, too. "Lust, perhaps?"

"More than that."

She didn't ask him how he knew. He bent and fastened his lips to hers once more, taking her in a frantic, almost desperate kiss. "Yes. I have to have you soon. Under my roof. In my bed."

When he decided on a course of action, he really committed to it, Claudia thought happily as he spent the next five minutes kissing and caressing her. Her campaign had worked better than she'd imagined. Putting herself in his way, merely being there, had done the job. She'd have to buy her sister something expensive that she really wanted. Because without Livia putting her in the way of it, Claudia would never have achieved her ambition this quickly and with so clear a conscience. If he'd ignored her or merely been polite, he wouldn't have been ready.

Either that or he didn't care enough to take the next step. Not that she cared. She was too desperate to care.

Only now could she admit that. If he'd rejected her, or worse, never approached her and left her in limbo, she might have gone to the country and meandered around the place, making a nuisance of herself. Worrying about him.

Totally happy at this moment, she kissed him and kissed him. Until finally he told her they had to go and proceeded to help her tidy herself up. Just as well one of them had a practical turn, or she'd have been there in the morning.

Chapter 15

As it was, the morning saw Dominic, hat in hand, at her door, asking formally for her hand. Of course Claudia knew, but the principal player in the scene had to stay out of the way until the menfolk called for her. The way they arranged her life infuriated her, but her mood was too sunny for her to allow it to bother her for long. She'd be at the contract signing, and she'd most certainly insist on reading the documents, even if they made no sense to her.

After the formal meeting with her father, Claudia waited with her mother in the drawing room. When he entered, her mother greeted him kindly, poured him a dish of tea, and left them alone.

Immediately he crossed the distance between them and swept her into his arms. He kissed her before he allowed her to say anything. When he lifted his lips from hers, she was nearly past words. "That was just in case you said no." He released her and took a step back.

Then dropped down on one knee. "Lady Claudia, I am not worthy to ask you this. Will you do me the greatest honor of becoming my wife?"

Oh, she liked that. She clapped her hands. "Oh, yes, please, I would like that very much." Even now, she avoided the word "Love." With him so conflicted, she didn't want to give him more to worry about. What if she was wrong, and it was lust or liking or something else? She loved her family, true, but that was different, something that was right. Her feeling for him had come out of the blue, and she was still uncertain.

He stood and took one of her hands, her left, and slid a ring on to it. A single emerald with diamonds either side.

"Oh how pretty!" The green stone was clear and unclouded, its purity only enhanced by the simple setting.

"It reminded me of you," he said. "In a few days, I'll be putting a gold band there."

She caught her breath. "A few days?"

"Saturday."

Goodness, four days, to be precise. "You persuaded my father into that?"

"He didn't take much persuading. He asked me if I was sure I understood what I was taking on."

"What did you say?" she asked, still admiring her ring.

"That I was certain. Well, I could hardly say that you'd bewitched me completely, and I couldn't wait to get you into bed!"

Gasping, she warmed. Her face would be an unbecoming shade of rose, and she wished she could get her recalcitrant complexion under control.

Dominic didn't seem to mind, but held her close and let her rest her hot cheek against his chest.

"Is that true?"

"Can you doubt it?" He kissed the top of her head, as tender as a maiden could wish for.

She wanted the other thing, too. The passion they'd shared the other night. Life, which had seemed so tedious a short while before, had suddenly become interesting and full of promise.

"I can't keep away from you when we're close."

"How long does that last?"

He laughed. "You're not supposed to ask that. You're supposed to assume that we are starting the journey fresh and new."

"Do you have a mistress?" she asked abruptly. She wouldn't apologize for asking. She didn't want to share him, but many members of society had interests elsewhere.

Although she'd be surprised if her father had someone in keeping. He appeared perfectly happy with her mother, and they shared so much of their lives that there would be little time for anyone else. She wanted that for herself, that kind of all-encompassing relationship, but did he? She should probably have asked him before.

"No," he said quietly.

"Have you had one?"

"You know you shouldn't ask me that." He stroked her hair softly, his touch soothing.

"I know. I don't care."

He laughed roughly. "I thought you might say that. I've had a mistress, yes. More than one. Not since I met you. Does that meet your expectations?"

She lifted her head and bestowed a beaming smile on him. "Yes, yes, it does. Now it's up to me, isn't it?"

He met her gaze with a frown. "How so?"

"I must strive to keep you with me, to stop you straying."

"Is that what you think?"

Her turn to frown. "Yes, isn't that the way?"

His hold on her tightened. "No, not at all. On Saturday I will make some promises to you, and I intend to keep them. If I have a problem with us, I will come to you first."

"Really? That's very enlightened of you."

He huffed a rough laugh. "I think for myself."

"You'll be an asset to the family."

He lost the smile that made the corners of his eyes crinkle and gazed down at her. "I mean to be an asset to you. We will make our own family, Claudia. I know you will wish to spend time with them, but once you marry me, we will be our own family."

She licked her lips. "That's what you want?"

"Yes."

She would not help him break away from his past, but she was willing to help him with the family he wanted. "When do we start?"

"On Saturday. Except, Claudia—" He bit his lip, but before she could urge him to continue, he spoke again. "Until I know for sure who I am, where I began, I don't want to bring anyone else into the situation."

"That's fine. I think you're right." The fewer people who knew, the better. "There's no proof, nothing except a piece of paper, and what does that mean?"

"And the word of my parents. The truth they kept back from me." He stared at the wall opposite.

That was true. "You are you, Dominic. You made your own truth. Should I look forward to becoming an army wife, moving from place to place?" She smiled, her mood lightening. "That would be interesting. A whole new world to explore! Shall we do that, Dominic? Part of your title is the one you earned. You're a major. You could go back to that. I could become a hostess in the military world. All those soldiers! Do you think they'd like me?"

"I think they'd like you too much. I think I had better keep you away from regimental dinners and the like." Smiling he dropped a quick kiss on her lips. "You would be far too popular, and I want you to myself for a while."

She tried for a mock pout. "I was hoping to have you to myself for much longer than that."

Looping his arms around her waist, he swung her off her feet and whirled her around. "You are a minx. A vixen. You make me smile, and when I look at you I forget my troubles. Nobody ever did that before."

She knew exactly how he felt, because she felt exactly the same way.

* * * *

Her mother went into her most efficient mode. Claudia had not realized how many of her possessions were scattered around the house, much less the amount she had at the country house. She would forget something, but after sending a message to the country, she would have to depend on the maids. She would be back.

Marriage meant a complete change, more profound than she'd allowed herself to think about before now. Not least she would be sharing her bed with someone else, and her sister would have the bed to herself. When she said that to Livia, her twin burst into tears.

Immediately Claudia put her arms around her sister. "It won't be bad. We're twins, but we've never lived out of each other's pockets, now have we?"

"You were always there!" Livia wailed. "You were never far away."

Shocked, Claudia rocked Livia. She hadn't realized her sister was quite so upset. They'd always known they would not spend the rest of their lives sharing a bed and living under the same roof. Neither of them wanted to remain the sad single daughters of the Marquess of Strenshall. Even though their parents had given them the time to find the mates who would form a worthwhile partnership, they were expected to marry.

"Be happy for me, Liv. I found the man I need."

"You don't even know his right name!" Of course Livia knew. How could Claudia keep anything from her?

"I know who he is and that will be enough for me."

"Not for everyone else." Dragging herself away, Livia sniffed and wiped her eyes with the back of her hand. "I shouldn't cry. It will only make my eyes red and sore. I don't cry well."

Claudia sighed. "I know." Neither of them did. They could never be too affected by a tragic opera because bawling didn't work well in the theater. They had learned to control their sadness. Perhaps that was why they tended to look on the bright side, although sometimes it had proved difficult.

Now, for instance. Claudia remained dry-eyed, but it was a close-run thing. "It's not as if you'll be completely alone. You'll have Dru, and Val and Darius. Why don't you ask Dru to share the room?"

"No, it's not that at all. I daresay I will manage." Going to the chest of drawers, Livia found a clean handkerchief and blew her nose noisily. She found another to wipe her eyes. "Forgive me. I'm happy for you, of course. I will try to find someone of my own now. Be sure I will."

"You'll take off your spectacles and close the books?" Claudia stared pointedly at the untidy pile of volumes on Livia's side of the bed.

Livia laughed shakily. "Perhaps not completely. I'll pay more attention, and I'll go out to balls more."

"Dru could do with someone to go with her sometimes. I've thought she's seemed a little lonely recently."

"Really?" Livia turned a frowning glance on her sister. "I should talk to her more. She's always been a little singular, born between two sets of twins, but I thought she preferred it that way."

"I think she's been trying to stand on her dignity. She doesn't confide in me much, but recently I've been thinking she could use someone to talk to. You and I chat every night before we go to sleep, and we're used to that. If you don't want to share with her, you could spend more time with her."

They did not ignore Drusilla exactly, but their quiet, dignified sister was easy to overlook. Occasionally, she could appear somewhat aloof. Perhaps she did that on purpose. Why Claudia had never considered that before, she didn't know, but since she'd met the man she was now betrothed to, she'd taken life a little more seriously. Not exactly that, but certainly with more consideration.

At her age, she should be married with a brood of children. Thanks to her parents, she had been given a chance to grow up, to see a little of the world. Perhaps that would make her a better wife. She would try to make it so. She would certainly try to be a better sister, even if she had to do it at more distance. "We will see each other often," she said. "I won't let Dominic separate us. He would not want to."

Even if he wasn't part of a family, or belonged to one he wanted no part of, he would appreciate her need to keep hers. Plus, the Strenshalls were part of the most influential families in society. Nobody would turn his back on that.

Dominic would become an Emperor. Was there an emperor called Dominic? When she asked Livia, she smiled and shoved her handkerchief in her pocket. "I already thought of that. There was a Domitian."

"Close enough," she said.

* * * *

Dominic had obtained a special license, which enabled them to marry in any place of their choosing, as long as the formalities were observed.

They were joined in marriage in the drawing room of the Strenshall London house. Lord and Lady Brampton appeared, and Lady Brampton shed a tear as her husband welcomed her to the family. What could have been an awkward moment was dissipated by Claudia's mother's happiness. Seeing a daughter married at last, she declared, was one of her dearest ambitions.

The ceremony itself was simple and heartfelt. Claudia recited her vows carefully, gazing at her nearly-husband's face, and he did the same as he made his promises. That part was over in ten minutes, and just as he'd promised last Wednesday, he slid a gold band on to her finger. After they were declared husband and wife, he carried her hand to his lips, watching her face, and several people sighed. They must imagine she and Dominic were in love. She still was not sure about that. Although Dominic had been most forthcoming with his kisses and smiles, he had withdrawn and confided in her less in the intervening days.

She'd read and signed the contract the day before, and that was the last time she'd seen him. That was a business meeting, when the man of business had made her aware of the disposition of her fortune. The house in Hart Street would remain hers, as the terms of her aunt's will demanded.

Not many guests attended what was, after all, a private ceremony, but afterwards, the wedding breakfast was full to bursting. The dining room held thirty guests comfortably, but fifty squeezed into the space, making what usually appeared as a gracious space seem rather small.

Used to her position in society, Claudia was nevertheless not accustomed to being the center of attention. Or of women complimenting her on her handsome husband and making jovial remarks about the night to come, in highly veiled but easily discerned remarks. Men, too, for that matter. By the end of the wedding breakfast, she was completely disarmed and blushing, disconcerted by her new position as a married woman. Now she understood why a newly married couple retired from society for a while. Because by the time they returned, they would be accepted and old news.

They could not do so, if they were to pursue the Young Pretender. She assumed they would continue, and she meant to have it out with her husband later. Her husband! Would she ever accustom herself to her new status?

Having overcome the worst of her melancholy, Livia smiled and danced and declared herself happy for her sister. The Emperors appeared en masse, as many as could come. She'd hoped to see Tony and his new bride Imogen, but they'd left for her house in the country. Since that was Lancashire, they couldn't have received the information and travelled to town in time. That would have to wait. Julius had requested an interview at their earliest convenience. He no doubt wanted news. He led her out in the impromptu dancing that followed the meal, and kissed her warmly on both cheeks. "I would have wished you well, Julius," she said. "Will you mourn Caroline forever?"

"I doubt it," he replied. Julius's hands tightened on hers. "Please don't take Caroline as your example, Claudia. Stay alive. You're starting a huge adventure, and I do not want to see it brought to a premature end."

Nobody else could have said that with more conviction. Julius's wife had died six years ago. Everyone knew how much he'd loved her, although Caroline could have outdone Claudia in madcap activities with one hand tied behind her back. In fact, she'd died from a fall from her carriage when she was racing for a bet.

Claudia nodded. "My husband won't let me."

She felt her new husband's presence behind her even though he wasn't touching her and she hadn't heard him. She just knew.

"Trust me to keep her safe," he said.

"As much as you can," Julius said. "Believe me, I tried, but Caroline was wilder and not as...sensible." That was not the word he would have chosen.

Caroline had had serious problems. Her moods swung violently, and she'd been known to shut herself away for days. She always struck Claudia as someone who was looking for something she never found. Despite being the wife of a doting husband, the mother of a lovely daughter, and wealthier than Croesus, she was restless and unhappy.

Claudia's madness was mostly as a result of rebellion and boredom. Neither of them had marked her activities in the last few weeks.

Turning, she placed her hand on her husband's velvet sleeve and bestowed a wide smile on him. Nobody seeing her expression would doubt that the reason she had married him was for love.

Except herself. Doubts filled her now she'd finally done the deed. Not unfamiliar doubts, since they had prevented her accepting some highly flattering offers in the past. But now she'd taken the final step, they crowded back to buzz in her head. He was her master now. He had jurisdiction over her. Her contract protected her as much as possible, but not from malicious gossip. While she'd courted gossip, it was on her own terms. Until recently. If he had not married her, she might have suffered more this time. Nothing she couldn't have escaped from. But she was getting older, and even for a marquess's daughter, her current state couldn't last forever.

Hence her desperation when she'd received the legacy from her aunt, unacknowledged until now. Her emotions on receiving the house had included relief, because she'd had an alternative. Something she could do, someone she could become. Did Livia and Dru have that "What's next?" feeling? They seemed so serene, but that could easily be that they hid it better.

When Dominic touched her hand, she looked up at him with a blinding smile.

"What is it?" he said gently.

The smile hadn't fooled him, then. She had no defense against him but the truth. "I nearly left it too late, didn't I?"

"No." Ignoring everyone around them, he turned her gently to face him. "You did not. Your kind of beauty will never fade, and you have a brightness and cleverness no man could fail to be enchanted by."

Tears pricked her eyes. She never cried, but that was the nearest he'd come to telling her he'd done this from choice. That he wanted to marry her because she was Claudia.

She lowered her chin, staring fixedly at their hands.

"You're finding this difficult, are you not?

She nodded. "It's the speculation and the sideways looks."

He caressed the back of her hand in a gesture so typical of him. "Shall we escape?"

They were attracting not a little attention. She dropped his hands and pasted on her society smile. "What do you mean?"

"If we leave together, people will want to see us off, with all the attendant fuss. I can arrange to have an ordinary carriage outside in ten minutes. If you step into it, I'm sure it will take you to my house. I'll stay for twenty minutes, and then I'll walk to the house. How does that sound?"

"Blissful." She could take off her new shoes, loosen her stays.

"Give me five minutes to make the arrangements and then start counting."

She didn't have to count. The clock on the mantel made very good time and it chimed every quarter-hour.

* * * *

By the time her husband arrived at the house, Claudia had called her new maid, stripped down to her shift, and donned a loose sacque. A profound sense of relief filled her as she shed her wedding finery. She laid her pearls in the jewelry box that had gone everywhere with her and had been brought here earlier in the day.

She was touching her jewels when the bedroom door opened. She didn't look around or glance in the mirror. Silk rustled as he removed his heavy coat and then he was there, and as always, she sensed his presence.

He put his hands on her shoulders, gently. "Do you like the room?"

"Yes." She did, it was relatively small but well-furnished, and it smelled familiar when she walked into it. Of citrus and male. Him.

"It's only a hired house. My parents opened up the family house when they arrived, but I chose to stay here."

"Of course." He wouldn't openly live with his parents when he wasn't sure who his parents actually were. "They were happy for you today."

"Happy for themselves, too." He spoke with finality. "Claudia, may we leave them outside? My family, your family, everything. This night is ours."

"I'll try." He meant could they not talk about them, because their presences were heavy in this room. However, she wouldn't speak of them.

"Are you afraid?"

"No. Nervous. Excited. I'm starting a new adventure." She looked up then to see his intent face reflected in the mirror. She'd had the sconces lit, and a branch of candles on the dressing table to one side of the triple mirrors. The light flared off the left side, but the others showed her face in strong relief one side, in relative shadow on the other. He was gazing at her as if he'd never seen her before.

Slowly he removed his neckcloth pin. He tossed the diamond on to the dressing table next to her jewelry box. But she only heard the tinkle as it fell, because she was concentrating on something else. Him. He unfastened his snowy white neckcloth with a few efficient tugs and tossed that down, revealing his throat and the delicious dip at the base. He looked down at her.

"Come to bed, sweetheart," he said.

Suddenly it was so simple. She'd worked herself into a frenzy wondering if she should kiss him first. If that was too forward, or if she should lie supine under him and let him do as he pleased.

She rose and stood before him, the smile curving his lips.

"I won't ask you if you're apprehensive. Just trust me this first time. Then I'll give you your head, and by God, sweetheart, I'm looking forward to that."

All the questions she wanted to ask fell away. All that she found important was the glowing look in his eyes and the promise in his touch when he took her hand and brought her to the bedside.

He positioned her by the bed and began to strip. "If you're a shy retiring maiden, you'd better look away," he said, unfastening the buttons on his waistcoat. They were gold, and glowed with a life of their own. But he stripped it off and tossed it aside as if it was of little worth.

Then he unfastened the glittering buckles at his knee and his shoes. He kicked the shoes free before unfastening the fall at his waist and stripped his lower garments off and down into an untidy bundle that he kicked aside.

She had never known him so careless with anything. This room, this house, was almost painfully neat. She was sure his influence had much to do with that, but now he seemed intent on her and nothing else. His shirt reached mid-thigh. Greedily she took in the exposed skin, hairy male legs, and the strong column of his throat. He paused to undo the buttons of his cuffs and the tie fastening his shirt at his neck.

His body appeared. Because he bent forward she saw his back first, strong and powerful. Then his shoulders as he pulled his head free and reefed the garment down his arms.

He was naked.

Chapter 16

Claudia's husband was immensely powerful, muscles roping his body. She swallowed. He could do anything he wanted, and she would not be able to do anything to stop him.

The notion filled her with a delicious passivity, that she could give herself to him and would not be responsible for anything that happened. Not to think, only to feel—she longed for it. But it gave her a delicious frisson of fear, too, that only added to the prickling tension itching her shoulder blades.

"Your turn." He smiled, but his eyes burned.

With a shaky nod, she began on her gown. At first, she fumbled, as if she hadn't unbuttoned and unhooked this garment many times before. A pretty gown, but one she liked to wear after she'd discarded her town finery because she could get out of it herself. She'd never worn it in front of anyone who wasn't family.

Dominic was family now—her closest kin.

When she glanced at him, he held his arms loosely by his sides, but the muscles in his shoulders were tense, and— Heavens! The part between his legs that she had felt before, even glimpsed once, was now blatantly on display. It stood up, a strong column of darkened flesh, the slit at the tip oozing a drop of clear liquid. She froze, fixed on it. When he said nothing, she forced her attention to his face. He raised a brow, the corner of his mouth quirked, and now, of all times, they shared a smile.

"It's not so intimidating, is it?" he said.

Swallowing her fear, she returned her fascinated attention to his... erection.

"It's a cock," he said. "Say it. I want to see your lips frame that word. I hope to hear it more than once tonight."

"Cock." That wasn't so bad, except the place between her legs heated and dampened. She fought the desire to rub her thighs together to ease the prickling sensation there.

"I want to teach you much," he said. "Ask anything, anything, Claudia, and I'll give you the answer. Here, alone, we are not bound by any rules, any people except ourselves. Nothing matters but this, and us."

"I don't know what to ask." Even to her own ears her voice sounded husky.

He made a sound—half-groan, half swallowed imprecation. "Finish what you are doing. I want to see you."

"Am I your new possession?" She'd meant it as a joke, but it sounded wrong.

A crease appeared between his brows. "Wife. Never possession. I will never—" He stopped with a rough laugh. "No, that's wrong. I will possess you, but not in the way you mean. Prove your courage now. I know you can."

Watching his muscles move so naturally with him when he smiled, when he shifted position, gave her the strength to unfasten her gown and let it fall. Underneath she usually had a petticoat or two, but she'd dispensed with them tonight, and she only wore her shift and a pair of little satin slippers. Without giving herself time to think, or her nerves to get the better of her, she stripped the shift away and kicked off her slippers.

As naked as he, she closed her eyes tightly, and then opened them again, but didn't look at his face. Desperately, she prayed she wouldn't disappoint him. This was the body she washed, tended to, and otherwise ignored, except when she visited the mantua-makers. She wasn't foolish enough to think herself ugly, but she was not an accredited beauty. What was she supposed to think? Do?

Lifting her arms, she unfastened the clasp that held her hair in place. The strands brushed her shoulders, and finally, gripping her hair clasp tightly, she looked up and met his eyes.

Hot burning need met her eyes. If she hadn't been standing against the bed, she would have taken a step back. She'd never been the recipient of passion like that. She spread her arms and hands. "See? This is all you're getting."

"So much." He breathed the words, so softly she had to read his lips. "I need to hold you now."

She shrank back as he advanced, but when he closed his arms around her, his warmth drew her, and his masculine strength surrounded her.

She'd been here before, but not skin to skin, just them with nothing between them. He overwhelmed her, and she loved it.

"Look at me, sweetheart."

She had her head buried against his chest, but at his words, she lifted her chin. Close up, that gaze was even more intense, dark eyes made darker by passion.

He kissed her. Took control of her mouth and her body, cupped the back of her head, guiding her to the position he wanted. Leaning her cheek against his chest, Claudia hummed into his mouth, moaned her need of him. Her body ripened—she actually felt it, the way her sex opened and heated, preparing itself for his possession.

He stroked her, at first like a man with a bird in his hands. Then with more purpose, moving to her breasts, to touch the sides. She pressed herself close, her nipples hardening against the rough hair on his chest.

His kiss turned hungry, open-mouthed, and voracious, eating at her and commanding her response. She gave it, uncertainly, but she opened to his demands, clutched his shoulders, the smooth muscles bunching under her palms.

In response he gave a totally masculine grunt, the sound reverberating down her throat as they kissed. One kiss followed another, until she felt drunk on them, her stance unsteady.

When he released her, she wavered. His face alight with pleasure, he bent to lift her. He swept his arm under her knees, shoved back the covers with his free hand, and helped her on to the crisp white sheets. He followed her down, straddling her body with his, and kissed her again.

This time he drew back and tenderly brushed the hair back off her forehead. "Let me know if you dislike anything. If you find something is uncomfortable, tell me. Except— You know I'll have to hurt you a little, do you not?"

She nodded. "When you—"

He chuckled softly, deep in his throat. "Yes. When I do that. Not for a while yet. Let me prepare you." He kissed her again. "Let me explore you."

She was recovering a little, looking forward to whatever came next. His obvious pleasure had emboldened her. Spreading her hands over his back, she smoothed along the powerful muscle as far as she could reach and then back again, up to his shoulders. She framed them, marveling at the width between her hands. Of course he had a soldier's body, but he bore himself so well, he didn't seem so large when dressed.

"Do you want to be a slave girl?" he murmured. "We can play games like that when we want to. Just us, in our room, with nobody to see or criticize what we do. But for tonight, let us be more conventional."

She wriggled under Dominic, his shaft pressing against the soft skin of her stomach. It left a damp mark. Intriguing. When she slid her hand between them with the intention of touching him, he hissed a breath and moved away.

"Another time you can touch me all you like but not now. I'm not made of stone."

"That's not what it feels like to me."

They both laughed. It should have been a tension reliever, but when their bodies shifted and moved against each other, Claudia only felt more restless. She moved her feet, finding a small amount of relief in rubbing against him, the rough hair of his legs abrading her calves. His attention sharpened, and he sealed their mouths in another kiss, deep and passionate but not lingering. Moving down, he kissed her neck and throat, touching his tongue to taste her, and farther down to her breasts.

This time he would not stop. He would not pull away. The notion excited her immeasurably. Trills of sensation swept through her, like a keyboard player performing elaborate arpeggios. Each one was stronger than the last, centering on that part of her where he was slowly but inevitably heading.

He lavished attention on her breasts, sucking her nipples to hard, sharp peaks. Then he licked around, moaning her name, together with endearments that scalded her soul.

"Soft and delicious, exactly the right size for my hands. You are lovely, Claudia, more than I even imagined." With one hand tucked by her side and the other caressing her breast, he looked up. He did that after he moved to her stomach. Then that place on the inside of her hips that sent fresh shocks through her. She could not remain still, but squirmed under his hands.

Down he went and farther. Every so often he glanced up at her face, and seemingly satisfied, carried on to that place between her thighs. "The clitoris is sometimes called the pearl of passion by poets." He touched the bundle of flesh, the hard bit at the front of her cleft, and she yelped, catching her breath.

He muttered something, then, "I have to taste you."

His head descended between her legs as he pushed her thighs apart and hooked his arms beneath, curling his hands up to rest them on her hips.

When he sucked, she cried out, but he took no notice of her protests. Perhaps he knew that she'd kill him if he stopped. Sensation built, peaked, and grew even more. Only when she was close to exploding did he bring one of his arms back down to touch her. He stroked her and circled her opening. Holding her breath, she kept still for him as he explored and stimulated.

Then he pushed one finger inside. It felt like a branch being shoved inside her and alarm shot through her, piercing the miasma of desire he'd carefully built. He would hurt her. The sting was anything but pleasant. But she trusted Dominic. He would ensure her safety.

Reaching out blindly, she clutched his hair and held on. He grunted again, but didn't stop that powerful suction that was slowly but inevitably driving her to a conclusion she had not yet reached. When she'd touched herself in the past, she'd sensed something like this, but not so controlled or inexorable. Or so powerful.

Her mind stopped working as the sensations built and built until, with a scream, she came. Her body throbbed, clenched, and tightened, her heart pounding as she cried out in the throes of her release.

He progressed up her body, kissing her breasts in passing, her throat, her mouth.

Just as when he'd touched her there before, she tasted her own flavor on his mouth. At first the flavor shocked her, but the blatant carnality soon encouraged a response from her. She thrust her tongue against his in a search for more. When he drew away, he gazed down at her, bright-eyed. Lifting his body, he gripped his cock in his own hand and guided it to her cleft. Her slick body accepted it. Such intimacy sent thrills through her to replace the momentary panic of a moment before. She clutched at him, grabbed his shoulders.

"Ready?"

He smiled, his teeth sharp and white when she nodded eagerly. Whatever he had to give her, she wanted it, would claim it for her own. He pushed, and then pressed against her opening.

"It's too big," she protested

"Shhh. No it's not. I've worked you open. Let it happen, sweetheart." With small kisses to her mouth he helped her ease his way. But he waited, infinitely patient, until she sighed and let her legs fall open, cradling his hips between them.

He pushed again, and then jabbed. She winced. He murmured her name, kissed her and tried again. This time he drew away farther and used his hand once more to hold himself as he drove through her maidenhead.

He didn't pause but forged a path into her body, only stopping when his groin touched hers and their stomachs pressed firmly together. His heat burned through her as she gasped, the lancing pain piercing right through her.

She shoved him, trying to get him away, but he didn't budge. "No, we can't do this. Can we start again tomorrow?" Perhaps it would be easier then, once he'd essayed her.

"It's done," he said. "I know you find patience difficult, sweetheart, but summon some now. We are committed to this act." He kissed her softly, with delicacy. "You will feel better in a moment."

Surprisingly, she did. He remained still and let her accustom herself to the feel of him inside her. She had read of the act, but she had never imagined the unutterable intimacy of it. Naked, touching from breast to toe, with part of his body actually inside hers—even in her most imaginative dreams this had never happened. Never felt so real. Indeed the world had disappeared, ephemeral and unimportant next to what they were sharing now.

He moved, and so did her world. As he pulled out of her, a new shard of sensation captured her, so close to pain but not quite, ending as absolute pleasure. She cried out in delight. "Oh, do that again!"

Growling, he pushed back in, drew out, and back in. The repetitious movement varied slightly when he rested his upper weight on his elbows and tilted his hips. "Lift your legs. Put them around me."

His voice was lower. Gasping his name, she curled her feet around his calves, lifted her knees higher. Then she dared to stretch out and cup his powerful buttocks in her hands.

A wordless cry broke from his throat as he pushed in again, and then withdrew. He pushed her up, like when he sucked her but not quite, the sensation deeper and faster. It encompassed her whole body, swept away any remnant of pain from his piercing of her, bringing new heights of passion. Wrapping her arms around him, she held on and let him take her to paradise.

Or somewhere. Hard to believe in the celestial existence of something so earthly, so very visceral, but so sublime. Words poured out of her, but they were the same two. "Don't stop, don't stop, don't stop…"

The cry of effort that erupted from his throat every time he punched deep into her seemed involuntary, drawn by something deep inside him that bypassed civilized behavior. Anything less civilized she couldn't imagine, and she loved it.

Her own peak broke and washed over her, but this time her channel pulsed around him, clenching his cock as if milking it. It had its effect on him. Sweat broke out on his skin, her hands sliding when he arched his back, thrust one more time, and buried his forehead against her shoulder.

Then he moved convulsively, dragged his body out of hers, and hot, warm pulses of his seed splashed against her belly.

* * * *

"Why did you do that?"

He'd found a damp cloth and gently cleaned her before joining her in bed again. He lifted her hand and kissed the back of it. "Do what, sweetheart?"

She snatched her hand away. "You know what. Am I not good enough for you?"

"What?" His eyes widened with shock and he went up on one elbow. Claudia drew the covers over her naked body. Now she'd had time to recover, she had thought long and hard. "A wedding night is a time to make children. How can we do that if you don't…?" She paused, groping for the right words.

"Come inside you?" His expression hardened and he sighed. "I cannot. You deserve…better."

"Better than you?" She scoffed. "I can't think of anyone better."

The sheets lay between them, channeled on her side, and solitude fell over her. After that—after they'd engaged in the most intimate activity she had ever shared with anyone else—he was cutting her out. She sensed his retreat, the way he was putting the experience behind him, placing in its rightful place in his mind.

He flopped down on to his back. "While matters are so uncertain, I do not wish to put anyone else in jeopardy. You or a child."

"You married me."

"You ensured that was inevitable."

"You could have resisted. All I did was ensure you saw me. I gave you something to think about. To decide if you really wanted to let me go."

Now she lifted up to glare at him. He didn't avoid her eyes, but met them squarely. She could no longer read his expression. "I did not force you to anything. I did not lure you into a compromising situation, and I did not make my family compel yours in any way. I didn't have my father visit your parents, for instance."

A tiny muscle next to his eye twitched when she said "parents." That was it. She waited for him to respond. She would absolutely not take the blame for his marrying her, if guilt had to be assigned.

He acknowledged her point with a small nod. "Every time I saw you, I wanted you more. I've never known an impulse like it. You enchant and infuriate me. I took to my club, but your family was there, even if you were not. They made me think of you."

That was good. She hadn't realized her family had supported her in her silent determination to get into his presence. "I just wanted to know one way or the other. Oh, yes, I wanted you, but not at all costs. I would not compel you in any way. Did I?"

He sighed and pulled his hand out of the blankets to reach for her fingers and twine them between his. "No, you did not. You merely made it impossible for me to forget you."

"Good. I could see you were determined to walk away, but if you wanted me, I wanted you too. I did. I do." Daring to take the initiative, she bent and kissed his lips.

He responded gratifyingly but drew back before their actions could turn incendiary.

"Dominic, you are you. I chose you, not your family or your connections."

"I know, and I appreciate it. That was the only reason. No, that's not true." He grinned wryly, the lines beside his mouth deepening. "I wanted you too badly to see you with anyone else. I needed to make you mine."

"You have nearly done that."

When he would have rolled out of bed she trapped him by the simple expedient of rolling over him and lying on top of him. A length of sheet remained between their bodies. They'd made a complete tangle of the bedding. "I said nearly, Dominic, and you know why. Never, ever do that again. Don't withdraw."

He cupped her cheek, his palm hot and hard. "I must. I cannot create children when I don't know what they'll inherit."

"I'll leave them the house in Hart Street," she said.

His mouth hardened. Clearly he had not found her pathetic attempt at levity funny. "I am not entitled to my parents' honors and titles. I have put a search in place to find the next in line."

Exasperated, she wanted to hit him, but clenched her fist. Her other hand remained clasped in his. "That is foolish. You know there is no heir to your father's title. Your parents set up an exhaustive search before they…went to Rome."

"And bought me."

"They did not buy you! Don't talk such nonsense, Dominic. Perhaps Maria Rubio loved you and her other children so much that she wanted them out of danger. Away from intrigue."

His mouth flattened. "If she was involved with a Stuart, it is more likely that she was using us as pawns for power. We were sent away because we might become useful to her one day, and we were better alive than dead."

She shook her head vigorously, her tousled curls bouncing against her shoulders and cheeks. "How do you know that? You don't, do you? Plenty of people fell in love with the Stuarts. Look at Nell Gwyn! She loved King Charles, all the sources say so! Queen Henrietta Maria loved the first Charles quite desperately."

Lady Claudia Shaw was in danger of doing exactly the same thing. No, she was Lady St. Just now. She left Claudia Shaw behind that morning. "Dominic, you cannot make assumption like that."

He stroked her cheek, pushing back her hair, his expression softening. "You are very good for me, Claudia. I am deeply selfish for giving in to my impulses and marrying you, but I cannot be sorry. Not completely. What will make me sorry is if all this comes to light and I am exposed for the impostor I am."

"You knew nothing of it. In any case, there are better ways of making amends than giving everything up in a massive sacrificial gesture. How will that help your father's tenants when they find themselves under someone who never expected to inherit and has no inclination to do so?"

"Now you're making assumptions."

"Not at all." She thumped her fist against his chest. "Be serious, Dominic! You were brought up to love the land and the inheritance and to do your best for it and its people. Just as my father is bringing up his sons. Responsibility and respect are vital, he always says, both for the owner and the tenants. Why, do you not believe that?"

He sighed, still stroking her hair. Catching a curl, he wound it between his fingers. "Yes, I do. But another person could be just as effective. Someone who has been cut out by my parents' actions."

"There was nobody then. It stands to reason that there is nobody now." She wouldn't let him look away, but put her hand on the side of his face and forced him to look at her. "I want your children, Dominic. I don't care what you call yourself or what society calls you. This morning you willingly joined with me in marriage, and that makes us a unit. A potential family unit, one I intend to fulfil the best way I can. I cannot do that if you will not perform your side of the bargain." If he would not accept her any other way, she'd make him stick to his side of the bargain. Honor. Let him think about that, if his precious honor was so important to him.

He sighed. "I have not yet decided what to do."

She knew, but she was wise enough to realize that she could not force everything on him at once. She would speak to him again, though, that was sure. Honor went two ways. He should honor the people who behaved honorably to him. The world was not so easy. Neither were the choices people had to make. "Then forget it. We have this time. Let's enjoy it, refresh ourselves, and go back to the lists ready to fight again." Soldier talk. She put on a bright smile. "Besides, I want to do that again. I find I enjoy making love."

His response was to burst into shocked laughter. "My sweet wife, you'll be the death of me!"

* * * *

Dominic took her advice and accepted her determination, consoling himself with the consideration that most couples didn't conceive after one night, or even two.

She might not be the death of him, but she exhausted him over the next day. Pausing only to eat the food servants brought to the room next door, sometimes reluctantly on her part, Dominic's wife proved an able— no, an eager—pupil. She would not stay a pupil for long. Dominic had intended to order a bath for her, to take care of her and pamper her until she recovered from the loss of her virginity. But not to make love to her again. His Claudia would have none of that.

Dominic woke to the sensation of delicate, exploring fingers on his already burgeoning cock. "It's a fine one, is it not?" she murmured from under the covers.

With a shouted laugh, he threw the sheets away and saw her, busily exploring, stroking him until he rapidly grew.

"I never imagined it would be so big."

"Careful, sweetheart, or my head will swell, too. I am comfortably endowed, I think I might say, although I cannot add that I have compared myself in this state to other men."

She met his gaze, a curious note in hers. "Do they do that?"

"I believe some do. I have never felt the need. I have what God has given me, and I strive to please the best I can. That is all I can do."

Her hand was still busy, dancing over his flesh. He had never felt anyone stroke the tip as delicately. The slight scrape of her nail gave him a jolt, bolts of lightning running over him. "You should take care," he warned her. "I meant to let you rest. Women are supposed to be exhausted after their first time."

"I want to ensure it will happen again. Is it just the first time it feels this way?"

"What way?"

He shifted, trying to get some measure of ease, but she followed him. Her experimentations would kill him. Circling his shaft with her fingers, as best she could, she discovered the up and down movement that would drive him to his peak if she didn't stop. As if she heard him, she did so.

As did his heart when she swept her tongue over the tip of his cock. Of course women had performed that act for him before, but they'd been practiced, the exchange purely physical. This was far more. This woman was learning the man she would spend the rest of her life with. Her curiosity was put to a better cause here than spying out houses of ill repute. Already he knew her better than to imagine she would give up any pursuits, or that he could keep her busy in bed for evermore.

Dominic accepted the inevitable. Claudia would take childbearing and motherhood in her stride. She would not be a stranger to his bed. To their bed, he imagined it would become.

Grasping her under her arms, he hauled her up the bed and settled her over him. Her eyes widened, and her sweet, reddened lips curved in a smile. "Are you still tutoring me?"

"I am. Come down on me. Put my cock in you."

"Oh!" She shivered. "Oh, yes!"

She'd like that. Being in control suited her, but it suited him, too, so she'd have to take turns. "One thing," he added, trying to keep his tones steady. "If it hurts, if you're too sore, we stop. I want you for a very long time. That doesn't include making our wedding night one that will keep you too sore to fuck me again for a week." He closed his eyes and groaned. "I should not have used that word. I'm sorry."

"No. I like it. It's honest and so down to earth. Please."

She could make him laugh even now. "Ride me, you witch, and stop drawing me to places I should not take you."

Summoning up enough control to make her ease her body on to him steadily, rather than plunging down, he watched her take him. His cock disappeared inside her hot, wet passage, enclosing and embracing him.

He'd used the word "ride" deliberately, evoking that morning when her horse had sped past him and he'd admired her seat. Oh, yes, his Claudia could ride.

She used it, too, clamping her knees against his flanks and rising up on him before coming down in the kind of plunge that turned him mindless. His head went back hard against the pillows and he yelped. Before he had time to recover, she did it again, and then she laughed. She showed him no mercy, and went from trot to canter to gallop almost without pause.

In a pathetic effort to regain some control, he gripped her hips, but only in an effort to steady her, not to control her. He adored the way she took to this, and he feared it would draw him closer to her. Every time she came down on him his arousal rose. Holding his orgasm at bay was one of the hardest things he'd ever done. He forced every particle of control into his body and held himself rigid for her, gritting his teeth until the first wave passed. Or it transmuted to something else, he couldn't be sure. He didn't care.

Her skin gleamed with exertion, but she didn't stop. The light of exhilaration brightened her eyes, and she was smiling as she rode him, pushing him inexorably toward his inevitable climax. His laughter rang around the room. He wasn't sure why he laughed, except that pure joy radiated through him. That hadn't happened to him since childhood, that pure happiness had struck him like that. He'd forgotten.

She reminded him of so much, the things that had escaped him in his relentless pursuit of independence and honor. Now they laughed together, and they were still laughing when the first wave hit him. Bucking, he sat up and held her in his arms, desperate to ensure she came too. Then the first quiver of her peak rippled over his cock, a deliciously intimate squirm from her hips. She gave a small cry, helpless in the throes of her orgasm.

The ripples increased, grew more deliberate, and she gripped him, held on. "Give way. Let it take you," he murmured. He kissed the shell of her ear, nipping it while his balls tightened. The first unmistakable twinge signaled his peak.

They came together, holding on, his control completely gone now. A still moment when everything peaked and coalesced and then he was over the top, falling through clouds with no means of safety and now way of holding on.

When it was done, there she was, his anchor and his partner. Not once had he felt alone. With others, he'd always come to that point on his own. While courteously helping his partner, this time he wouldn't have felt complete if he hadn't taken her with him.

Or had she taken him with her? Yes, that was it. His heart pounded in time with hers and breath sawed out of their throats.

"When can we do it again?" she said.

He chuckled, helplessly lost in her. "It will take me some time to recover. Unlike you, I can't immediately go again."

He was still hard within her, so he gave a few shallow thrusts, enjoying the aftermath as much as the process. That was a first time for him, too. Usually when he engaged in sexual congress with a woman, once he'd done he recalled what else he should be doing, and left. That, coupled with a faint sense of shame he'd never been able to rid himself of.

With her, he was supposed to be doing this, although not quite in this way. "You are supposed to be maidenly and reticent. You should complain after the first time and make me pamper you, or leave you alone so that you can do something else. Women are excellent at putting their lives on to a series of shelves."

"Shelves?" she mumbled. She had her head on his shoulder, and her breath heated his neck when she spoke. She didn't seem to be in the least concerned about her sweat-slicked body or her tousled, glorious mane of red-gold hair.

"Intimacy goes on the shelf labelled I, work on the shelf labelled W." He'd tried to keep his life like that for himself. Like a well-organized lawyer's office, with each case tied up with red ribbon and put in its rightful place.

"Hmm. I don't think much to that. Life should be a glorious muddle."

He shuddered.

She laughed. "Perhaps it's me who is the glorious muddle."

"Glorious certainly." He kissed her hair. "Shall I order a bath?"

"In a little while." She moved away so he could see the sweet curves of her breasts, but her nipples still grazed his chest. "Can we order some more food? I'm absolutely ravenous."

Chapter 17

Lord and Lady St. Just made their first public appearance at Drury Lane Theater. They sent a footman to bespeak a box early in the day. They set forth after an intimate dinner that nearly meant that they forgot the theater and went straight back to bed. Since they'd spent most of the last two days there, Dominic set Claudia determinedly away from him. "After tonight, we should consider going to the country."

"Oh? Are we, then, spending our summer alone?"

"If you like." He smiled down at her.

He'd smiled much more in the last few days, but then, she'd given him cause to.

"I had thought at least the first part. We are owed a honeymoon, are we not?" He paused, and then continued, "I have a house. I bought it with my own earnings, booty from my years in the army. It's modest, but private. It will be ours alone. Any visitors will be local ones, since I have not told many people of this house. Mail reaches me through trusted servants. I haven't gone so far as to go by another name, but it's not a house I speak about."

"Do your parents know?"

He paused before answering. Enough to tell her that he was still thinking about his parentage. They had discussed that part of his inheritance very little after their first discussion.

"Yes, they do."

In the country, he and Claudia would have time to discuss their future. That he was seriously considering what to do meant much to her. However, he wouldn't do anything without her. She had married him, and to her that meant she would remain by his side, whatever he said, wherever he was.

If he staked his claim to the throne, he would do it for good reasons. She trusted him to make that decision in the best interests of everyone.

He was the most honorable man she had ever met, and considering her family, that was saying a great deal.

"I like the idea. We may sleep late—"

He kissed her. "Or not at all. Claudia, I swear we will talk."

"Yes." She returned his kiss. "Do you think your parents will want you to visit?"

"Undoubtedly. I will have made my decision by then. Whether to reveal the truth or not. This is not a decision to take lightly. I cannot make it instantly, as some might, so I will take my time. Nobody will affect me."

"Not even me?"

He gazed down at her and shook his head. "I'm sorry, Claudia. I value your opinion more than any other, but I must come to a decision I can be comfortable with for the rest of my life. On one side, I would have to live a lie and perhaps dispossess someone of something that is rightfully theirs. On the other, I claim my birthright and risk starting a war. I've seen what war can do, and I would not willingly be the cause of one."

She nodded. "What if I cannot agree?"

"We may live apart. Separate." A streak of pain passed over his features, but at that moment the footman knocked at the drawing-room door to tell them the carriage was ready.

He took her out and ushered her into the carriage with great ceremony. His punctiliousness made her laugh. "You know my parents will demand a visit in the summer?"

He bowed once more before joining her and allowing the footman to fold up the steps and close the door. Then sat next to her and took her gloved hand. The carriage, pulled by two fine greys, set off smoothly, and Claudia turned to glance out of the window.

Their route took them past Julius's door. He lived on Brook Street, not the most fashionable street in the West End, but one of the most interesting. She pointed out Mr. Handel's house to her husband and he gazed at it. "We should go and see one of his operas. I enjoy listening to spectacular music done well."

"Yes we should."

They were talking like an old married couple, but under the comfortable current ran a streak of desire, always present at the moment. Would it ever dissipate? She prayed not. She was enjoying it far too much.

"We should certainly visit your parents," he said.

"They have a house party in August. Most of the month." She enjoyed Augusts at home. They celebrated the Glorious Twelfth, held dances and invited the local gentry. People spoke of the Strenshall house parties with awe and invitations were rarely refused.

"It sounds interesting." He squeezed her hand. "I will have to become accustomed to having a large family, at least on my wife's side."

As the carriage turned a tight corner, something landed with a clatter on the floor of the vehicle. It must have fallen through the window. A hiss indicated it was alive, or something was working. Clockwork, perhaps?

No. Fire. The thing was on fire. Smoke wound up in a thin stream from the——thing.

Her first impulse was to grab it, but before she could do so, her husband wrapped his arms about her. He dragged her backward, the door of the carriage crashing open, slamming against the side of the vehicle.

They hurtled through the door of the carriage, Dominic yelling. Her ears rang with the noise. That and the shouting. She landed with a sickening *thump,* and Dominic rolled over her, smothering her with the weight of his body.

When she gasped for breath, the noxious stench of the road beneath her face made her head spin. She didn't have the breath to choke. It all happened in a minute, so fast she only had time to register it dimly before a *boom* took out what was left of her hearing.

Footsteps vibrated under her body, together with rumbling wheels and clattering hooves, but she closed her eyes. She was going to die. Whatever had happened had killed her.

What was this? What had happened?

Someone shouted, so loud she detected it through the ringing in her ears. "Give her to me!" A male voice, close. Vaguely familiar.

At last, light flooded in when Dominic rolled off her. He rolled her on to her back, staring anxiously into her face. "Are you hurt?"

She sat up, but he pushed her down again. She was covered in street filth, stinking and bruised. But she wasn't hurt, not like he meant, not the way his face was twisted and creased with concern.

Lifting a hand to her face, she dashed a few tears of shock away and tried to make sense of what had just happened. They'd been in the carriage and then… Had someone attacked them? How? The thing on the floor of the carriage?

"Come with me," Julius said. Then made an noise deep in his throat that sounded like exasperation. He bent to scoop her up. "I'll take her into the house," he said.

"I didn't think you were that strong," she managed to say, bewildered at the turn of events.

She looked towards the coach. Or what was left of it. The top was shattered, and flames flickered from the windows where she'd recently been sitting. The footman who'd jumped up behind, who'd held the door for her, was lying on the ground. One leg was twisted under him and blood stained his forehead. The coachman was cutting the traces, releasing the horses who were squealing and kicking. They were bloodstained, too, but the coachman seemed unhurt, just blackened and ragged. Nothing remained of the smart equipage.

Queasiness churned her stomach and her throat tightened. She shook, unable to control her trembling limbs and unbidden, tears came to her eyes.

This was no accident.

* * * *

Julius took her up to a guest bedroom and settled her on the bed. A maid followed. Claudia watched them numbly, letting them do whatever they wanted.

Shortly after, Helena, Julius's sister burst into the room. She was a lovely capable woman. Although she was wringing her hands she was also firing off orders to the footman who followed her in. "Bring hot water, and get a robe for her."

"Brandy," Julius said grimly, and crossed to the sideboard, spilling the amber liquid into a glass.

Claudia pushed it away, her hand still shaking. "I don't like brandy."

"Take a sip," Julius said softly. The warmth of his hand on her arm soothed her.

When she took the glass, her hands shook, and the liquid trembled. "Dominic! Is he safe?"

"Yes, I'm sure he is, but I'd like to check on him." Julius glanced at his sister, who nodded. He left the room, and his steps echoed on the stairs.

Her ears still rang. She swallowed the brandy, taking it like medicine. "What happened?"

"An attack," Helena said. "It's something I have no experience with. Come, can you stand? We'll get those clothes off you. You'll feel better when you're clean."

Not better, but more like herself. Half an hour later, she had dressed in a robe borrowed from Helena. Claudia's hair was cleaned and brushed out and washed, the street filth was finally expunged and she had stopped shaking.

Helena was so patient and kind, even gave her a handkerchief unasked when Claudia shed a few more tears. Nothing like that had ever happened to her, and she was still fighting to make sense of it.

The same question was on her lips when she went down to the drawing room and someone brought her a dish of tea. Better than the brandy.

Her husband ran in and knelt at her feet just as she was putting the dish back in its saucer on the table. She nearly dropped it. Fresh tears sprang to her eyes, but she blinked them away.

Dominic was in shirtsleeves, his fine clothes begrimed, his wig gone, and his own hair roughly shoved back from his face. "They told me you were unhurt. I'm sorry, Claudia, so sorry!"

"For what?" Had he caused this—whatever it was?"

He kissed her hands and clasped them between his. "Someone tried to kill me. Did you see it?"

"What?"

"The device? The bomb?"

The word fell dully on her ears. "Who would have one of those things in the middle of a city?" No, she hadn't meant to say that, but she couldn't get closer to her real meaning while her mind was still numb.

"An assassin?" He laughed harshly, a strange sound in this elegant civilized room.

She looked up to see Julius in much the same state as her husband, but his wig was still in place. He must glue it on, she thought dully.

"You're right. Who would expect such a weapon in the city?"

"Hopefully that will help us trace the culprit," Julius said grimly. "However, don't you think you are being a little presumptuous? Claudia is an Emperor. She has her enemies, too."

Turning away, Julius grasped the glass of liquor a servant handed him, glancing at the man with a muttered word of thanks. He downed the glassful in one swallow. "Whoever did this will not stay free much longer. I can promise you that."

Heedless of the other occupants of the room—Helena, Julius and the footman—Dominic ran his hands over her, feeling for injuries. When she winced he hung his head and groaned. "What is it?"

"A bruise," she said. "That's all. I don't have many. My clothes padded me. Thank goodness for petticoats!"

At least her feeble sally raised a smile.

Julius thrust the glass at the servant. "Leave us," he said.

The man nodded and left the room, closing the door quietly behind him.

Julius walked to the window. "The authorities are likely to call soon. I'm not sure who it will be. Considering the weapon involved, it could be someone from Bow Street, or even Horse Guards. Was it a military weapon?"

"I've never seen the like outside the army," Dominic said. Finally, he got to his feet and sat next to her, curving his arm protectively around her. She leaned into him gratefully. "I suppose you're right. It might make tracking the culprit down easier."

Her mind had finally started working properly again. "Don't you think they might have wanted us to know?" she said.

Julius swung around and fixed her with a steely glare. "Explain."

Her cousin had made grown men tremble with that look. Claudia merely met his eyes and nodded. "I mean, with something that rare in civilian life, they might have wanted to send some kind of message."

"It's a possibility," her husband said. "But that was not a weapon made for a warning. If I hadn't recognized it, it would have killed us both."

Claudia repressed her shudder. If she showed signs of weakness, he'd shut her out, and then she would become a burden, the thing she hated most. She would not be a useless appendage or a pampered pet. She'd never wanted that and she wouldn't start now. "But we're alive. If not a message to us, who?"

"Me," Julius said grimly. "My enemies know they can hurt me by hurting my relatives. It's a possibility, you have to admit."

For an instant, he met Claudia's gaze, and she saw the message he was transmitting to her. He didn't believe that any more than she did. That bomb was meant to kill her husband and possibly her. Nobody would send Julius any kind of message that way.

Julius knew her well, better than most other people in the world. Even Dominic hadn't discerned that side of her. At least she prayed he hadn't. "Exactly. If they split us up, they've weakened us."

Julius pulled off his wig and tossed it on a nearby chair before running his fingers through the short fair curls that lay underneath. Without his formal wig, he appeared more approachable. More human.

"You'll be safe in my house in the country," Dominic said firmly.

She knew he was going there. She could have wagered on it. If she hadn't made her little play, he'd have determined on it, too. She snuggled closer to him. "No, I won't. Julius is right. We need to stay together. We don't know which of us that bomb was meant for. In effect, it would have taken both of us, but what if the attacker wanted me, and you sent me off alone?"

Dominic groaned. "Devils, you Emperors. I was warned, but I took no notice." Turning to her, he touched her chin. "Why would you put yourself in danger?"

"You know," she said softly.

He touched his lips to hers. "I know. If I lose you——" He shook his head. "We need to find out who did this and ensure they can't do it again."

"Already being taken care of," Julius said. "I will of course pass on any discoveries to you." He thrust his hands in his breeches' pockets, his waistcoat bunched above. "The question is——was it the Dankworths——or the Young Pretender?"

* * * *

"Either," Dominic said. "Both, most likely. Aren't the Dankworths supporters of the pretender?" His mind was exactly fixed on the problem.

Julius shrugged. Damn him, how could he remain so cool in the face of this? He'd nearly lost his lovely wife. He'd never forgive himself that he'd let his guard down enough to allow her to get hurt.

"The point is," Julius persisted, "we need to know where to target our efforts."

Dominic caught his exasperated glare, but Julius shrugged.

"No matter. If you want to take your wife away, let me know and I'll plan accordingly."

"I can't see a world in which you will be taking control of this," Dominic said softly. "This is my problem. While your help is much appreciated, I am perfectly capable of discovering certain matters for myself. I thank you for your concern and taking such good care of Claudia." He lifted his hard gaze and met Julius's equally determined eyes.

"I would appreciate you keeping me apprised of your discoveries," Julius said eventually.

Dominic nodded curtly. "You may be sure of it. I will not fall in with your plans. Understand this. What is mine, I keep. I make my own decisions."

Julius nodded. "You should know that if you decide to accept your birthright, you will become my enemy. I strive against a return to the old absolute monarchy and of further bloodshed. I fear today there has been more."

"Sometimes bloodshed is the cleanest way," Dominic said. He'd far rather meet his enemy on the battlefield than sneaking around the edges. Cleaner, more decisive, and shorter. Less damaging to all concerned, except those who gained advantage from intrigue.

Already he was making plans, deciding what to do, and he could see no harm in telling Julius. "Sometimes those more used to intrigue are confused and beaten by direct action. They have no idea what to do if confronted by someone demanding the truth."

Julius raised a brow. "Not a theory I have used very often, but it has its benefits. As long as there is a secondary plan in place."

"When possible." Once, he hadn't been averse to the idea of dying in honorable combat. But not now he had so much to live for. "The attack appears like one a man of action, a soldier or the like, would use. That might be a blind, someone trying to fool me into thinking that. Whoever did it wanted us dead. Shooting at us might result in one death, but not both. Either the attacker wanted to kill both of us, or he didn't care if others died in the indiscriminate attack."

"That sounds more like the Stuarts," Julius said. "The Dankworths live here, and they have avoided trouble for a long time, partly by careful targeting."

He glanced out of the window and then back to them. "The street will be cleared soon, but I can have a carriage brought around for you. It can go the other way." The sounds from outside had not abated, with shouting and the noise of splintering wood as they doubtless cleared the way using the fastest method possible. "The Dankworths would rather avoid a scene like this."

"If the Stuart tried to have us killed, that means he probably knows about the marriage certificate."

The one that made him legitimate, an important symbol for the Cause. The person who could oust the Young Pretender from his perch. "Since I saw them together, may we assume that Dankworth knows too?"

"He knows," Julius said briefly. "Would he have told the Young Pretender? I don't know. The man is too subtle in his thinking, and he can never be outguessed." His mouth kicked up in a half smile. "I have had to learn to match him."

"What about your father?" The Duke of Kirkburton surely should have some hand in this.

"He remains aloof," Julius said, "Deliberately. I keep him informed. He has once or twice asked me to leave off my investigations." He shrugged, a fluid, powerful motion that belied his usual dandified appearance. "Not recently, though. You are not the only child of the Stuarts who is a member of this family. I've heard from the people concerned, and I have permission to inform you that you have siblings."

Dull shock reverberated through Dominic. "I've always been an only child." What a stupid thing to say! He could think of no other way of putting it. Not only did he have half-siblings, he could have full ones. The possibility had haunted him since he'd discovered his true origins. The reality made him nervous.

Claudia squeezed his hand and he discovered it was her turn to comfort him. "Not now," she said to Julius. "Let's clear this matter up."

"Ah, but they want to be involved in the discovery," Julius said. "One is out of town, but he will be here in the next three days."

"He?" A brother?

"Ah, yes, but he's married to your sibling. Your sister."

This could be a problem, but equally it could prove a blessing. He would discover in due course. Claudia was right. He needed no distractions. "After I have concluded my business, I want to meet them," he said.

Julius bowed his head. "Of course. One is in London. The other, as you've heard, is on her way. There will likely be more."

"A family within a family," he said. "But not until I have made my decision." He got to his feet. "If I may win the position as legitimate child to the Stuart, I could dissipate the problem. I would not wish to take the crown, even if it were offered to me."

Julius gazed at him. "I had not thought of that." He gained a faraway look. "Yes, that could prove a solution. If a true heir voluntarily disclaimed any interest in the throne…"

Dominic shook his head. "Whether you like it or not, you would be the center of dissidence. People will look for excuses. They will make you their leader whether you wish it or not."

"They would find an excuse whatever I did." When he paid attention to his wife, he saw she had gone quite white. He would say no more, but they had to consider the possibility. Or he did. "It was why I wanted to defer our wedding, and why—" Why he'd withdrawn from her on their wedding night. Although she had not allowed that to continue for long.

Sometimes he wished she had. It would be one less concern. In his heart, he knew he wouldn't have wanted to remain childless.

"I will not allow this to continue," he said. "This is not acceptable." He meant it. Whoever had just tried to kill his wife had decided on his course of action. His mind worked rapidly. "Tomorrow I will put my plans into place."

Tonight he would take her home.

Chapter 18

Dominic had meant to put her to bed and leave her to sleep, but again his wife thwarted him. When he cossetted her, she slid a hand inside his shirt and stroked him.

"I won't sleep if you're not here."

"I'll just hold you," he told her.

He stripped and used the basin to give himself a thorough wash, but she distracted him. When he glanced into the mirror, he met her avid gaze. She was watching him.

"I love the way your muscles move when you're naked."

He paused and gazed down at himself. True, he had a well-formed body, but he'd needed one in his erstwhile occupation. He still lived a active life. He'd have grown bored, sitting in front of a club fire drinking brandy and discussing current affairs. "I'd never considered the artistic value of it before."

"Neither have I." She spoke quietly, but a low throb of desire colored her voice.

Inevitably, his cock reacted to her words. He closed his eyes and put the washcloth down, leaning on the washstand until the wood creaked. "You shouldn't do this."

"I have the feeling that as long as I live, I will be doing this." The sheets rustled and he turned to see her removing her night rail.

Her curves, revealed so blatantly and beautifully for him, roused him to an almost unbearable state of arousal. He would have echoed her words. She would draw him to her for the rest of his life.

He couldn't imagine breasts more perfect than hers or a waist so sweetly framed over lush, inviting hips.

When she opened her legs, she gave him a glimpse of glistening pink paradise. "Claudia, you are shameless," he croaked out of a throat gone dry. "Your beauty unnerves me."

"As does yours." She wriggled, flashing the most intimate part of her body. "I want you, Dominic. Prove to me that we're still alive."

Her hair, blazing against the dark wood of the bedhead and between her legs, gleamed with a fire of its own. But it was all her, all Claudia.

After shedding the rest of his clothes and leaving them tossed over a chair, he strode to the bed. By now his erection was blatant, and he displayed it to her with pride, like an animal performing a mating ritual. Except he felt more than that. He could not hold off from telling her any longer.

She shifted to give him room, but he climbed into bed and dragged her close. "I should never have married you, shouldn't have admitted the possibility of children."

Eyes wide, she stared at him.

"I should not have waylaid you and kissed you that first night. I shouldn't have courted you, appeared with you in public, or put you in danger. You know why I did?"

When she shook her head the gesture was tentative. "No."

"Yes, you do." Unable to maintain his strict expression any longer, he smiled down at her. "Because I love you. I've been lost since the moment I saw you. Lost in you, my love. When I first saw you I wanted to care for you, but that is my nature, and it didn't concern me. It was when I started to dream of you at night, here, in my bed."

"Did you…?"

She paused, but her wicked smile told him what she meant. Had he acted on his desire, here, in his lonely bed? Had he touched himself and thought about her?

"Yes. Since I first saw you, all my fantasies have been about you. You have no idea how inventive I can get."

"I will, though." She spoke with certainty. "I'll make you show me."

"All of it," he promised. "I will tell you how much I want you in the most inconvenient places. You'll have to go to court again, to be presented as my wife. I will not let you do that unless I have you considerably aroused."

She gasped, and then laughed. "Then I shall have to work out a way to get my revenge."

He kissed the tip of her nose. "I'll look forward to it."

She glanced down, at his chest. Then her brilliant blue eyes met his again. "I love you, too. I wanted you, and I did everything I could to get you."

"Yes, you did." He kissed her properly then, sliding his tongue into her mouth for a full lascivious exchange.

She held him, made him helpless under the caress of her small hands. As he explored the sweet cavern of her mouth, she slid her fingers down his chest and between their bodies to touch his cock. He jerked, her touch sending tongues of fire through him.

His kiss turned voracious. As she explored him, her delicate fingers playing him like a fiddle, he took her mouth, her throat, and her breasts. He adored her breasts and told her so, in between sucking and caressing them. Lost in her and in their love, he spread her legs with one less than steady sweep of his hand and ensured her readiness. The heat and wetness between her legs drew him.

"I want everything at once, like a greedy child presented with a box of candied fruit. You, my love, are the ultimate fruit."

"I don't know if to be happy or insulted," she said. "Aren't I a delicate flower, or something of that nature?"

"You're a strong, loving woman," he replied after kissing her thoroughly. "And you're mine.

"Yes, I am," she replied, wriggling to help him get their bodies into alignment.

He entered her with a deep, thrilling thrust. She surrounded him, wrapped her legs around his waist, and pulled him more securely inside her, demonstrating her state of bliss with a deep sigh.

They had all the time in the world. As if to prove it, he set a lazy rhythm, giving him time to explore her inside. The sensitive skin of his cock took stock of every part of her inner channel. His. A world for him to explore and never tire of, because he knew that he never would.

The floodgates opened. He talked to her, told her how very much he loved her, and followed with a litany of endearments, some heartfelt, some funny. When she laughed, her body moved around him in the most delightful way, so he thought up some more.

"You are my sweet apricot," he said, pleased with that one. It reflected the glory of her hair, that deep gold with rosy tinges.

"You are nothing but a bear." She arched her back, pushing against him, accepting and celebrating their love. "So big."

"Dwarfing poor little you?" He paused, grinning, and brushed the hair out of her eyes. Her hair truly had a will of its own and never stayed put. He loved that about her. Come to think of it, he couldn't think of anything he didn't love about her. "What you lack in size, my darling, you make up for in courage and beauty."

She made a scoffing sound at the back of her throat. "I've never been a beauty."

He punished her with a particularly hard thrust that made her groan low in her throat. "Does this feel as if I don't think you're beautiful? My love, you are the most beautiful woman in the world, and I'll kill any man who disagrees with me."

He put paid to any saucy response by increasing and deepening his drives into her lush body. This time he didn't relent until she cried his name and clung to him as her body trembled with the force of her orgasm.

This time when he came, he gave himself wholly to the experience, giving his body and soul into her care. She accepted him, enclosed him in her body, her arms and legs wrapped around him.

Oblivion beckoned, and he willingly gave into it.

They awoke at dawn, light filtering in through a crack in the curtains. The candles had guttered out long ago, but enough light remained for him to see her face. He traced a finger down her cheek and across her mouth, smiling when she growled and then opened her eyes, blinking owlishly at him. The sheet had made a crease down one side of her face. He kissed it.

"You slept soundly."

"So did you." She made a face. "You snore."

"It's manly."

"It's loud." She grinned. "I think I can accustom myself to it. My love."

"Sweetheart." He kissed her, playing with her tongue, but gently. "You must still be tired. It's barely dawn."

"Why are you awake, then?" Sleepily she curled her hand behind his head.

"I used to wake at this time every day. I still wake from habit. Usually I turn over and go back to sleep, but you're here, and you're a devilish distraction, wife."

"Should I use another room to sleep in?"

He loved her drowsiness. "If you do, I'll only join you." He stroked her warm body and came back to cup her breasts. "Do you need anything? We ordered supper served next door. There should be something there if you're hungry."

She shook her head. "How can an evening that started so badly end so well?"

"I don't know." Reminded of the attack, his mind sobered. "We aren't out of this yet. I want to send you to the country."

Predictably, she said, "No." She touched his face and cupped his chin, rasping her palm against the stubble. "I promise not to take risks. I can't molder in the country, Dominic, not knowing what is happening."

"Very well." He would have missed her unbearably, but it would have been worth it to keep her safe. "Then if I promise to keep you informed, please promise to stay in the house and only receive the people you know well. No levees, receptions, or anything of the kind. I'll make it up to you."

"You don't have to." She smiled softly. "All I want is you to be safe. I can promise that. I know the difference between reckless and stupid, although my family might tell you otherwise."

He grinned. "One or two expressed astonishment at my bravery, as some put it, at our wedding. They don't know the secret to controlling you."

The crease between her brows appeared right on cue. "Tell me how you control me."

"Simple. I don't. I talk to you. Love you."

The frown disappeared as he leaned over to kiss her.

* * * *

The next day, after a distressing visit to the parents of the dead footman, Dominic headed for Horse Guards. Although General Court's assistant tried very hard to keep him at bay, Dominic ended the discussion by walking past him and straight into the office.

He closed the doors quietly behind him. He detested door slammers. "Why wouldn't you let me in?"

The general looked up from the papers he was signing. "I'm busy." His thick brows drew together. "What is so important that it cannot keep? I have more than one affair of state to deal with."

"Thankfully I do not," Dominic said. Without being asked, he took a seat on the chair before the huge mahogany desk. "You asked me to do you a favor, sir. I am still doing it, and yesterday it nearly cost me my life."

"Yes, I heard." Finally the general put down his pen, placing it carefully in the brass standish. Folding his hands across his expansive stomach, he leaned back in his chair. "I take it you were getting too close?"

"You may also have heard that I married recently."

General Court nodded. "Ah, yes, congratulations."

"Thank you." The man was a complete boor. He was immaculately turned-out, red braided coat and cream waistcoat with gold buttons perfectly clean and uncreased. Underneath lay a man with the sensibilities of a pig. Although useful on the battlefield, the general was a liability in civilian life.

"Then you might be aware that my wife was in the carriage with me. In addition, the weapon used was a bomb. To my eyes, it appeared much like the explosive devices I've seen before, although I only caught a glance of it. If I had not recognized it, we would have died."

The general gazed at him, and his eyes lost their faraway look. He touched the papers on his desk. "Know what these are? We're close to war, St. Just. So close I can taste it. I have no intention of allowing it to happen, not yet. We need time. Your fracas yesterday brought the possibility a touch closer."

"I'm sorry to hear that, sir, but there was very little I could do about it. The attackers meant to create a scene, and they did. If my wife's cousin were not living nearby, we'd have created more of a scene."

"Don't you think that is odd?"

"What?" What could he be inferring?

"That the house of the Earl of Winterton was nearby." The General grunted. "Winterton is what they like to call an Emperor. Although they declare themselves loyalists, they are so powerful they rival the Pelhams. To be frank, sir, they are distrusted in some quarters."

Dominic could hardly believe what he was hearing, but he would not contradict the man directly. Why create enemies when they had perfectly good ones for the taking? "I am part of that family now," he gently pointed out.

"Yes, you are."

He tried to move on. "What about Stuart? The Young Pretender?"

"That's part of what I wished to discuss with you. I would have sent for you later today."

Dominic raised a brow, but he didn't correct Court's arrogance. The man wouldn't understand anyway. He lived in his own world with his own points of reference. "Then speak."

The general studied him, his eyes cold. An assessment. Dominic had been through worse.

"We have the affair of Stuart in hand. We're close to an arrest, and then we will bring him to trial. Another matter has come to our notice that might make the affair less important. Have you heard of a woman called Maria Rubio?"

He hated lying. Detested it. "No."

"We discovered a paper in one of the Young Pretender's haunts with her name on it and the name of the Earl of Winterton. Yes, you may wonder. It occurred to us that Winterton could be playing the game from both sides. The Jacobites love a plot, and that strategy would appeal to them."

"May I see the paper?"

The general drew out a worn sheet of plain notepaper from the stack of documents on his desk and handed it over. He found the note very easily, just as if he'd put it ready. It was merely a list of names. Notes and small designs decorated the margins. An informal list.

"These could be people the Pretender considered enemies." It meant nothing.

It would be surprising had the Young Pretender not come across Maria's name sometime in his life, as she had been close to his father. Closer than he might know. It was no proof. Except—something nagged at the back of his mind. He needed to think.

The other names meant nothing to him, but he memorized them anyway. "I have no idea what this list means, sir, but it's hardly conclusive proof. May I keep it?"

"Certainly not. It's government property."

Reluctantly, Dominic returned the note. The handwriting might have proved useful, but he had the names now. "What is your point, sir?"

"Now you are a member of the family, one of the Emperors"—the General spoke as if the word were a curse—"you may keep an eye on them for us. Report back from time to time. Tell us what they are up to. Do not forget, you are a loyal officer of the Crown, and that supersedes anything else."

"You want me to spy on them, in fact?"

Most other people would have been warned by his smooth, silky tones, but General Court ploughed on regardless. "We consider it your duty."

"Who is 'we'?"

"The people closest to the Crown. In fact, so close you could not put a breath of air between them."

Which did not mean the current administration. Dominic had his suspicions. However, he had matters of his own to pursue. "Do you have any idea who might have thrown the explosives into our carriage yesterday?"

For the first time, the general looked away. He straightened his papers, lifting them and rapping the edges against his desk. "I do not. Not for certain. It could have been anybody with a rudimentary knowledge of weaponry."

"It looked somewhat like a mine. The kind we used to fire at the enemy."

"For an officer, you have too vivid an imagination. Perhaps that is why we recruited you for the service."

From the shifty way the general refused to look at him directly and the way he shuffled his papers and shifted, Dominic knew. The general was dissimulating, and not very well. "Can you tell me who wielded that weapon?"

General Court passed his hand over his eyes, and then pinched the bridge of his nose. Suddenly he looked very weary. "We have been following someone for the last week, yes. We now have the man in custody. He was a disaffected recruit, someone who took the King's shilling and later regretted it. He took someone else's shilling, too. I very much fear that the man was a known traitor and one we were following when he committed the crime. We have arrested him and we will ensure he never sees these shores again."

And they wouldn't have told him unless he'd pressed the point. They would have allowed him to go on fruitless chases after the man. To distract him from other pursuits, probably.

Frankly, Dominic didn't care if the man was alive or dead. "Why were you following him?"

"Because he was working with Stuart."

That was all Dominic wanted to know. He got to his feet. "I bid you good day, General. I do not scruple to tell you that I will not spy on my family for the Crown or anyone else. The Crown should be ashamed of itself. I had not thought it that desperate, to ask the despicable crime of lying to people who hold you in a position of trust."

His position became clear. No one asking that of him deserved his loyalty. His only desire now was to reduce the possibility of death and destruction, the inevitable consequences of war. A civil war would be worse. A century ago, this country had faced the bloodiest conflict in its history. He would not risk that again, and he would not help anyone who was willing to risk it.

This man would call it "The greater good" and proselytize about the necessity of politics, the reality of life. Dominic had heard it all before, and it impressed him even less than it did now. He left the office, his mind made up. Perhaps he'd left it for the last time.

* * * *

He walked to Julius's house and made his plans while doing so. With his new aims firmly in mind, the rest fell into place and he would not hesitate to act now.

Julius was in and received him upstairs in the drawing room. Dominic halted at the door, transfixed by this new vision of the haughty Lord Winterton.

The elegant furniture and fine carpets seemed no bar to Julius's lively daughter. She and her father sprawled on the floor, working with chalks on a large piece of paper. Julius glanced up. "I trust you don't mind receiving me this way. After all, you're family now."

That encomium meant far more to Dominic than anything he'd received recently. Apart, of course, from Claudia's praise.

With a new sense of purpose, he smiled and pulled off his coat, adding it to the chair where Julius's was carelessly slung. He was amused to notice Julius's wig, dangling from one arm of the chair. "What is the picture?" He walked around so he could see it. "A gown."

"Caroline is considering becoming a mantua-maker when she grows up." Julius glanced up with a smile. "What do you think?"

"I think it will create a sensation in the ballrooms." Anything that was orange and lemons, with huge oranges sewn on to the garment would do that.

"They're real oranges," Caroline declared, adding a vine. "Papa says there's always a crush around the refreshment tables at balls, and this way a lady could carry her own refreshment."

"She'd still need a fruit knife," Dominic said, completely enthralled by the idea.

"She can carry one, like the ones Papa has in his pockets."

Julius rolled on to his back, grabbed his daughter by her waist, and swung her high. She kicked, her lacy petticoats frothing around her and laughed.

He rolled to the other side and carefully deposited her before getting to his feet. "Go now, puss. You have real lessons waiting for you upstairs."

Caroline's lower lip turned down in a pout. Her father raised a brow, but said nothing.

Hastily she gathered up her chalks, put them in their box and ran to the door. "You may keep the drawing," she said. "I have lots of other ideas."

Julius dug in his breeches' pocket for a handkerchief and wiped his fingers free of chalk before offering a hand for Dominic to shake. "Any developments?"

"I came to consult with you," he said carefully.

"Good, because your brothers-in-law are headed here for that very purpose." He bent and picked up the drawing, carrying it carefully to the table by the window and laying it flat. "I keep everything she does," he remarked. "I shall soon have a special library for them. However, I need to find someone to care for her, a governess. I also need a companion for Helena because the one we have is making sheep's eyes at me."

He glanced out the window. "Here they are." Downstairs, the front door banged.

Time to confess at least one thing. "I'm not used to a family like this, but I'd like to belong," Dominic said.

"That depends on your decisions. We are not unified on all fronts, but on one thing, we are determined. We will not see the country plunged back into pointless civil war."

"Then we agree."

He had no time to say more before the door opened to admit Val and Darius. They carried the apologies of their older brother. Marcus was in the country, although what was keeping him was a little mysterious.

"He gives one excuse and then another," Darius said with a shrug. "We sent a message back to say he must stay where he is. Our father has a meeting with some committee or other, but I think it might be preferable if he doesn't know everything."

"Not until we've done it," Val agreed.

"Tea?" Julius suggested.

"Brandy," Val said firmly. "I have to escort Charlotte to some damn fool Venetian breakfast later. I doubt there'll be much other than dancing and fruit cup."

"Why not marry her and have done?" Darius demanded. "Just hold your nose and jump in. Look at Dominic here, courted and married all inside one season."

On the point of asking Darius if he had anyone in mind, Dominic clamped his jaw shut. Darius preferred his own sex, but very few people knew, and he wasn't even sure he was supposed to know. It could prove a considerable weakness as far as their enemies were concerned, but he'd picked the knowledge up from a few awkward comments Claudia had made.

Dominic accepted the brandy with more than usual enthusiasm for a variety of reasons. After his meeting with the general and his change of heart, he needed a little fortification. Being Julius's brandy, it was very good indeed.

They settled themselves on the chairs, which despite being spindly in appearance proved sturdier than he'd thought. Certainly more comfortable than the set in his own drawing room.

Julius motioned to him. "I take it this is more than a social call? You were saying as much when the twins arrived." He put his half-consumed glass down on the table by his side.

"I came straight here from Horse Guards," Dominic said. When his mind went back to that interview, the anger he'd tried to quell on the walk over here surged anew. "I talked to my old commander. After some pressure, General Court admitted that he had someone in custody who might have used it. What he didn't say made many things clear to me."

Julius held up a hand, the lace at his cuffs falling back to reveal a sinewy wrist. "You have decided not to obey all his requests, then? To report back about us, the Emperors?"

Dominic didn't ask how he knew. If General Court thought he had the only spies in London, he was either naïve or incurious. "Since my marriage, my loyalties have changed. My first is to my wife. My second is to my country."

"I have always considered that the right order," Julius said calmly, although what Dominic had said was barely short of sedition.

Dominic continued, "The general knew about the attack. I believe he allowed it to happen. Otherwise, how could they have arrested the perpetrator so quickly and discreetly? They were following him, and they merely took him once he'd done the deed."

"They may have sponsored him," Julius said quietly.

Dominic considered the possibility, vaguely shocked that he wasn't more surprised. "It's possible. The man certainly used a military weapon. But I consider my service to the Crown, formal or informal, at an end. They put my wife at risk of her life. I will not forgive them for that. With that in mind, I have to decide what to do about my unexpected legacy. I was on the point of informing the general what I had discovered about my birth. No longer. If they discover it, it won't be from me. I'm a legitimate son of the Old Pretender." Saying it aloud sent cold shivers down his spine. "I had considered claiming my birthright and then officially renouncing it."

Val swore, Darius stared at him goggle-eyed, and Julius nodded, his attention concentrated on Dominic's face.

"If I did that, it might sort out the Stuart claim once and for all."

"I would not take that course," Julius said. "The factions around the Stuarts are greedy and wily."

Dominic smiled dryly. "I would not allow them to change my mind."

"In my experience, they would take action and ask you later. You might find yourself king without quite knowing how they achieved it."

Val laughed harshly. "And my sister would be queen."

"She'd make a wonderful queen," Dominic said, with all the fervency he was capable of. "However, I thought hard about the issue on the way over here, and I believe you might be right about the scheming. My coming out into the open would achieve nothing. Besides, it would draw attention to any siblings I might have, and they might not wish it. I've come to a decision. After I've settled the final thing."

"Which is?"

"The threat to my wife, or course. Nobody touches her or causes her a moment's concern. I will not accept anyone trying to hurt her any longer. Now I've spoken with the General, I think I know who is responsible."

Julius leaned forward. "Do tell."

"In due course." He recited the names on the paper. "Are the two women my sisters?"

Julius pinched the bridge of his nose. "They are. I need to contact their husbands. We were hoping to keep the information quiet, but if the government knows, there's a strong possibility others do, too." He looked up. "There will be more. So far you have one half-sister and a full-blood sister. There are probably more sons. We need to find them."

"I pray there are, because that means I would not be the oldest son." A swell of relief swept through him at the thought. "There is no doubt about this marriage?"

Julius shook his head. "I fear not. It happened. When she gave the children away, Maria sent a copy of the marriage certificate and the birth certificate with each one. Although it isn't the original, the evidence exists. From the research I've accomplished, I think the original is in the Vatican. In fact, it would be as well if it is, because it gives the Pope something to hold against the Stuarts."

"I thought they were of a mind?"

Julius shrugged and leaned back once more. "Sometimes. Maria was shrewd."

"She had to be." Darius turned the nearly empty cut-glass tumbler around in his hands so it caught the light. To all intents and purposes, he was studying it closely. "Surrounded by schemers, she had to make plans of her own to survive."

"She'll have signed affidavits and so on," Julius said briskly. "I don't think she'd have kept all of them in her house, although the general feeling is that most of the documents were destroyed when she died. I don't believe that's true. I have put a lot of effort into investigating precisely what happened that night, although I may have to pay a visit to Rome before I'm done."

"Incognito?" Val asked.

"Perhaps." He shrugged. "Not today. Now we have to put our minds to solving this problem and ensuring Claudia is safe."

"It's my problem and my operation," Dominic said. "I will put Claudia's safety in nobody else's hands. Believe me, I trust you, especially after my interview this morning, but she is my wife." He cleared his throat. "I love her." He wouldn't meet their gaze. "I need a few things put in place, and then I will act."

"How soon?" Julius asked.

"As soon as possible."

Val laughed heartily and rose from his chair to clap him on the back. "Welcome to the family."

A shout went up from the hall, and the front door opened. Swiftly, Julius got to his feet and raced to the window. "We have to turn to the practical, gentlemen."

Feet thundered up the stairs. A knock sounded loudly on the door to the room and a footman entered precipitately. "Please, sir, my lord, this just arrived. It was pushed under the door, and when we opened it, there was nobody in sight. Well, not anybody who looked like they'd just shoved something under the door."

Julius sprang to his feet and seized the note, scanning it as he crossed the room. Silently he handed it to Dominic.

We have your wife. You will do as we say or she will die. Bring all the documents you and your friends have to the house in Hart Street tomorrow night at seven.

It wasn't signed.

Dominic stared at the words numbly, as if by staring he could change them.

The footman still waited, but Julius sent him away with an impatient gesture.

Shoving his hands in his breeches' pockets, Julius took a turn around the room. He let out such a string of curses that Dominic's were almost lost in the exchange.

Val read the note and bit his lip, and Darius growled, glancing at his brother.

"Who?" he asked.

"The Young Pretender, or his agents," Dominic said.

"Or the Dankworths," Julius added.

After his first shock, Dominic found himself the calmest person in the room. His mind worked as it always had in a crisis—coolly, assessing.

"Then my plan will still work. I will just bring it forward. The first thing is to verify the truth of what's in that note. I would beg the favor of using one of your servants for that purpose."

Because if he went home and discovered it was true, he might well kill somebody.

Coolly, crisply, he outlined what he wanted.

Chapter 19

Once the information in the note was confirmed, Dominic went into action. Pushing his emotions to the back of his mind in the way he'd learned long ago, he laid his plans, and now everything was in place.

Dominic stood in a doorway a few yards down from the house in Hart Street. Something hard and circular pressed against his temple. He went still.

Right on time, Val walked up the street.

"Don't let him go in," a voice said softly next to his ear. "Call him back. It doesn't matter if someone sees you. There's nobody there."

The something hard was the barrel of a pistol. "Why should I believe you?" He used a voice so faint it was hardly there.

"Because I've been watching this house for weeks."

"So have I."

"I know," Lord Alconbury said. "I saw you."

The pressure disappeared. Dominic stepped back so he could see Alconbury and the house.

Val knocked.

"There is one person in the house," Alconbury said. "The others have gone."

"How is that possible?"

A shame this street was one of the few in London that was never deserted. People strolled along, some arm in arm, others in raucous groups. At least the madness of late night celebrations had not started yet. However, Dominic badly wanted to hit Alconbury. He'd wanted to hit someone since that note arrived.

"These houses have a single attic space. That is, the attic space is not divided off. The inhabitants walked through to the end of the street and left by the house there. I became suspicious when I saw someone very like the madam in a coffee shop this morning. I investigated."

"How did you do that?"

"Come now, you know I am welcome in the place. My father goes there regularly, and since I like to know what he's up to, I made some investigations." He sighed. "The house is mined."

Shock coursed through Dominic.

He could not take the risk that Alconbury was telling the truth, not even if Claudia was in the house. If she was, she was dead if the house was mined. They had planned to get one person in the house to get the lay of the land and then storm it. No subtleties necessary.

He stepped out and waved.

Julius and Darius raced from their hiding places to join him. Society wouldn't recognize Julius for the man in the dark, simple clothes and plain wig. Max strolled over from his place nearer to Dominic's station.

Swiftly, Dominic told them what Alconbury had said. Val joined them. Dominic's plan was in shreds, but he couldn't take the risk.

Julius confronted Alconbury, the son of his worst enemy. They stood, nose to nose, dark and fair, glaring at each other.

"You believe this man?" Julius said quietly.

"I can't risk it. If Val stepped in that house and Claudia was there, they'd set off the mines and kill her. If we storm it, they'll have us all. If Alconbury is lying, we have him."

Alconbury sneered. "You believe I'd offer myself up? No. I'd prefer that my father was not responsible for exploding half of one of London's best known streets and taking half the inhabitants with it. I can't see that is in anyone's interests." He shook his head. "I have a concern for my family, but I will not let this happen. A man is waiting by the back door," Alconbury said. "As soon as anyone enters by the front door—it's unlocked, by the way—he will set the mines and run."

Dominic glanced at Darius who nodded and raced off.

The men stood in a row, crowding Alconbury so he could not get away. They did not speak. The seconds ticked off, slowly, but Darius returned in ten minutes accompanied by Max, who was stationed at the end of the street. He grimaced. "He's right," he said, jerking his head at Alconbury. "Now what?"

"This isn't the only house." Cold fury coursing through him, Dominic shoved Julius aside and confronted Alconbury. "Where is she?"

"Where is who?" Alconbury seemed genuinely perplexed, frowning at him.

"My wife."

He was close enough to see the genuine shock in the earl's face. "Your wife?"

"Your father abducted her."

"I wondered at the increased activity." Alconbury groaned and sighed heavily. "I had no idea."

"You expect us to believe that?" Julius demanded. His jaw clenched and his eyes flashed anger in the dim light cast from the houses nearby and the soft light of early evening. Dusk had fallen, but this street was narrow and never admitted much light even on the brightest day.

"Believe what you like. If their trap fails, your wife's life is in more danger."

"You will tell us," Dominic growled. He gripped the folds of Alconbury's neckcloth and twisted, tightening the strip of linen. "There's your choice. Tell us where she is or die here, where you stand."

"No choice," Alconbury said, although his voice had tightened considerably. "I can't tell you if you strangle me."

Dominic loosened the neckcloth enough to allow him to talk.

Alconbury took a couple of deep breaths. "She's not here. I have men watching another house, deeper into the City, in Spitalfields. Yesterday a group of women went in. My man counted six going in but only five came out. They were close enough to carry someone." He growled. "Do you think I want to see this? I will not be accounted responsible. That house is unknown to my father or me. We are not involved in a scheme so crass. Yes, crass." He shot a withering glare at Julius. "He understands."

Julius nodded, but said nothing, only jerked his head for Alconbury to continue. "We heard from our sources that the government intends to bring the Prince to trial this time. Or rather, Bute does."

At the mention of the chief advisor to the Princess of Wales, rumored in some quarters to be her lover, Julius's head went back. "Unfortunately that makes sense." He spoke softly, venom infusing every syllable. It was clear how much he hated working with Alconbury or accepting that anything he said was true.

He had to. Now, Alconbury was their only hope. "Take us to the house," Dominic said.

They set off, ostensibly a group of men on the town, as so many others around them were. Although early, the great piazza of Covent Garden was already alive with people.

Dominic and Val brought up the rear. Darius and Julius walked either side of Alconbury, who carried on talking and Max followed.

"Tonight, at least we want the same things," Alconbury said. "I want to stop any bloodshed and get the Prince out of the country. I cannot see any purpose in him staying and getting himself taken."

The kidnappers wanted the papers. It had taken an hour to make copies. Since there were copies in the first place, they didn't have to work too hard. Then they'd frayed and roughened the edges, and stained them. Enough to make them look twenty or more years old.

Dominic had brought one original. His birth certificate, the one his parents had given to him. He had plans for it. He hadn't told anyone what he would do, because most likely they would not approve. Particularly Julius.

"What do you want?"

"To get the Prince out of the country. To prevent any bloodshed. My father wishes that, too. He is not yet ready." Alconbury snapped out the words, as if they hurt him.

"I want my wife back." That was the objective he would not give in.

Alconbury shot him a glance. "I will help you with that."

"I have a weapon trained on you," Val murmured from behind. "Your own, as it happens. One false move and I won't hesitate to shoot."

Alconbury gave a mock wince. "Ouch."

"I on the other hand," Dominic said smoothly, "am wondering whether to take off your right hand or gouge out your eyes. Killing you would lead to an arrest and trial. However, if you are set upon by footpads and injured, that is the nature of London, is it not? I could lead you into St. Giles rookery and dare you to find your way out."

"Now that," Alconbury said, "Is a real threat."

They had crossed the square and reached the streets beyond. On one side, the Hart Street side, the streets eventually gave way to the shopping areas. Then the residences of the well to do and the rich. On this side, it led to the legal district, and then the City, the warren of streets that contained much of the wealth that had built London. Max's kingdom. He was married to a daughter of one of the wealthiest men, and he had built his fortune on investments and insurance after his father's depredations. He knew this area better than the others. Therefore, after Alconbury had given the address, he led the way.

It wasn't far.

Just past Lincoln's Inn Fields lay a narrow street lined in respectable houses. A quiet residential area, with the occasional coffee shop, it was one of the streets rebuilt after the fire of nearly a hundred years before. The houses were built of golden stone, the windows and doors faced with white stones. Tranquil next to the bustle of Covent Garden. Deceptively so.

Alconbury halted at the end of the street. "It's at the other end. Number seven. This is one of the more private places the Prince frequents." He paused. "My father owns it."

A low rumble indicated Julius's growl. "What do you suggest?"

"They know me. If Lady St. Just is not there, they are likely to know where she has gone, although I think she's inside. I will take two of you in with me. Not you—" He glanced at Julius. "You are too well-known."

"I go," Dominic said. He would not budge on that. However, Alconbury nodded. "Without the wig and fashionable trappings, you look entirely different."

"That was the idea," Dominic said laconically. Now he was so close, his throat tightened and a familiar sensation zinged through his veins.

With the ease of long practice, he captured that feeling, used it to hone his warrior edge. He touched his sword hilt—not his dress sword but a good army weapon. This would have taken off Alconbury's hand at a single stroke. It still might.

He wore a dark green country coat without the exaggeration of the skirts and huge cuffs. Linen adorned his wrists instead of lace. As Alconbury had said, he'd left off his wig.

He did indeed appear entirely different. Northwich might recognize him, but he'd have to risk the duke being present. If he was named, he was more than ready to fight his way out.

"I'll go," Val said. He had a reputation in society for recklessness, worse than his sister, but that could make him useful. Or dangerous. It was less likely that one twin would be recognized where people were used to two.

"Yes," Alconbury said. "You two. The house has much the same pattern of rooms as any other in London. If they have her, it will be upstairs, where it's less easy to escape."

"And if they do not?"

"I'll find out."

Their only hope was in their avowed enemy. Alconbury had the ingress into this place, and he could question without resistance. After he had found her, Dominic had one more task to achieve. Far less important.

Darius, Max, and Julius disposed themselves in the street around the house.

Alconbury led Dominic and Val to the house and rapped on the door, using a series of complex knocks and taps. Dominic memorized them.

Someone opened the door cautiously and held a lamp out to illuminate Alconbury's face. He stood his ground, but frowned. "Let me in, you fool!"

That did the trick. The door opened enough for him to pass through. When he would have barred Dominic and Val, Alconbury knocked the man's arm aside. "Let them in. Is my father here?"

"No, sir." It spoke for the establishment that they didn't call Alconbury "my lord." Clandestine indeed.

Dominic breathed out in relief. The one person who would know him for sure was absent.

The door closed behind them, revealing a narrow hallway lit by the lantern the man who had let them in was holding. Without another word, he turned and led the way up an equally narrow staircase to a room at the front of the house on the first floor. It would be considered spacious by many. With the man inside and the three who entered, it was full.

Dominic gritted his teeth and followed Alconbury's example of bowing low to the man who called himself prince. He stood back, as befitted a bodyguard or lesser companion. All the better to shoot the man, if he made a false move.

This room was much better furnished than the one in Hart Street. Fine furnishings and delicate china adorned the place, as well as the cut glass from which the prince drank deeply. The ruby liquid glistened in the light of the expensive beeswax candles that festooned the sconces and holders.

"You are come for a reason, Alconbury?" he asked.

He didn't even asked to be introduced to Dominic and Val. They kept their heads down, but of necessity they had taken off their hats. The prince spared them barely a glance. He had pale blue protuberant eyes, most unlike Dominic's. Meeting his half-brother in these circumstances unnerved him more than he had thought. Did this man know who was legitimate and who the bastard?

"The house?" the Pretender asked.

"Is still standing, sir. At least it was when I left."

Max had sent a message to some people he knew. If they were successful, the house would be standing for some time to come.

"A pity. I grow bored, Alconbury. Something had better happen soon."

Alconbury glanced away. Dominic had positioned himself so he could see the side of his face and gauge his expression. Trained to observe every little detail, he put all his expertise to use now. "Sir, you have initiated action. At least, I assume you have done so. I heard this afternoon that the wife of Lord St. Just is missing. Abducted, some say."

"What does his lordship say?" He glanced toward Dominic.

"You can guess."

The men exchanged a long, grave look, but neither of them said anything.

A shuffling sound came from above. More inhabitants. Dominic tried hard not to get his hopes up. After all, this house would contain a number of people, set here to protect and provide cover for the Young Pretender. He would probably move in a few days. At least, if Dominic had charge of him, that was what he'd do. How many more houses were there? How long before he found her?

"How did you take her?" he asked smoothly.

"We got her out of the back gate."

"We?" Alconbury raised a brow.

The Pretender shrugged. "My men." He glanced at Dominic. "I want some things you would probably not give me without a little... persuasion."

"Sir, you should have waited for us to act on your behalf," Alconbury said, his dark eyes glinting. "You cannot kill her."

"Can I not? I have heard rumors I have to confirm before I give myself up."

"You are determined on that course, then, sir?"

Stuart shrugged. "I am."

Alconbury sighed. "I cannot help but think it is a dangerous gesture."

Stuart's jowls quivered and his color rose. "What do I care for danger? A public trial will put my claims at the forefront of people's minds. They will not kill me. They will not dare. At present, Europe is balanced on a knife-edge and my father holds considerable influence. My case will be heard."

"Sir, they will arrest you and lock you up. Remember the case of Mary, Queen of Scots. She was an honorable guest of the Crown for over twenty years."

Stuart snorted. "She was betrayed by France."

"As you were, sir."

King Louis of France had left Stuart on the quayside at Calais. Although the Old Pretender had ordered his son to retreat, since he had lost France's support, the Young Pretender had left anyway. He'd come far too damned close. He was finished, and desperate. Also, considering Dominic had seen him three times before, he appeared permanently drunk.

A feminine voice called out once. Too brief for him to identify, but a woman.

"You brought a her here?" Alconbury asked smoothly.

The Young Pretender glanced up. "She will not settle, however much we tell her she will come to no harm," he said viciously.

Dominic suppressed his smile.

"You have men guarding her, I presume?" Alconbury smiled and relaxed his hands by his sides.

If Stuart didn't know the signs of imminent attack, Dominic did. Alconbury was preparing to strike.

"Naturally."

Enough. Dominic stepped forward, drew his gun, and held it to the side of the Young Pretender's head. The man's arrogance was stupendous. "You will have her brought here."

"I beg your pardon, sir! Pray step back!"

Val drew his weapon—one of them at any rate—and held it to Alconbury. "I'm afraid he cannot. Have her brought down."

Despite the weapon, Stuart turned his head and confronted Dominic. He smiled, a stretching of full lips that revealed dingy teeth. "Another brother," he said. "I am right, am I not?"

"That depends. Get my wife. If you do not, I will not hesitate. You will die. Think on this—the authorities will thank me if I kill you."

"They will not. You will make so many enemies that you and your wife will never be safe." The smile broadened.

"On the contrary. You're here incognito. That means I killed a man in a brawl in the City. In self-defense." He let that sink in. "If the authorities find you dead on British soil, do you think they will admit to it? Don't you think they'd send you quietly back to Italy, or bury you somewhere and you would merely disappear? Even your father doesn't know where you are, does he?"

"Our father," the Young Pretender said softly. "Don't you want this? If you kill me, you are heir." He glanced around the room. "Royalty may legitimize children, if it suits them."

"Just as well for you, then." Dominic glanced at Alconbury while still keeping his attention on his brother. The earl showed no surprise. It could be a good straight face, though. Telling his enemy anything more than he knew already went hard with him. Already he was getting Alconbury's measure. As far as Dominic could see, Alconbury was far more dangerous an opponent than Charles Stuart. "Get my wife," he said.

Alconbury's mouth twitched in a smile. "Very well."

He and Val left the room.

Dominic had his moment. He moved away, still holding the gun, but far enough to get the document out of his pocket. He tossed it at the man. "Have you seen this before?"

The Pretender took it between finger and thumb. "I have not. Not this copy, at any rate." He glanced at the two men guarding him. "One word and you die." They must be trusted indeed for them to remain here, because Dominic intended to leave nothing hidden.

Stuart flourished the paper. "You know what this means? You could be King. Fight by my side. With this we may defy the world and reclaim what was stolen from us."

Dominic beckoned, and his brother returned the paper to him. "Do you truly think I want that? I will tell you now that if my wife is hurt, if you ever do anything again to harm either of us, I will stake my claim. I'll declare you a bastard in the process."

Stuart picked up his glass and drained it in two gulps. Dominic ignored the thumps and scuffles from above. "This document is my guarantee of safety. You know there are more, and you know what they mean. Does the Duke of Kirkburton?"

The Young Pretender's mouth turned up at one corner. "Unfortunately, yes. He acquired a copy of the certificate. He will try to force you into the open."

"He doesn't know it's me, though, does he? There is no record of what happened. The baby could have died, could it not?" His smile was more genuine as relief flooded through him, making him weak in the aftermath. "Tell him, and he will become my supporter, not yours."

"Kirkburton is after the main chance," Stuart said. "His son is cut from the same cloth. Take care who you trust."

"I do. Shall I tell you what will happen? You will return to the Palazzo Muti, and I will take my wife to my house in the country. I will accept the Earl and Countess of Brampton as my parents, and in the fullness of time I will inherit the title. You will go back on your travels. You will never find peace or happiness. You're a broken man, are you not? Sick of fighting and getting nowhere."

"I'm still fighting."

Never had Charles Stuart appeared more regal to Dominic. He sat still in his chair, his head tilted at an arrogant angle and his eyes shrewd. Dominic was afforded a glimpse of the bonny prince who had captivated all who met him instead of the wreck of a man who grasped at straws to gain what he thought he still wanted.

"I would retire. After you die, and your brother, if you leave no issue, the cause dies with you. Your brother is not likely to leave issue, is he?"

"No." Charles's lip twisted. "Even if he were not a Cardinal. He preaches constantly on virtue and purity. One would imagine he was afraid of simple human pleasures." He nodded to the weapon. "Put that away and have a drink. You won't use it."

"I have yet to see my wife." He still would, if he needed to.

Stuart shrugged and picked up the decanter, which glittered like a huge ruby in the light. He poured the liquid into his glass and toasted Dominic. "To you, brother. May you live happily."

"Thank you."

"A good prince knows when he is defeated," the Pretender went on, after taking a sip. "But not for long. Take your wife. If you accept your foster father's title, that is an end of it. Your progeny are of no interest to me. Is that clear enough?"

"It is." So clear, he wanted to weep. He'd won. "If you renege on this, so will I." Because of his insistence on honor, sometimes people thought he was incapable of thinking deviously, or getting his way in less than perfect conditions. The men under him had soon learned differently. As did this man tonight. "I will still make my claim."

The Pretender took another drink, more substantial this time. "I'll be glad to get back to good wine. I have a woman waiting for me. Yes, I will leave, this time. I will return, you may count on it." He sighed. "Another campaign over. I should have been a soldier, but my father would not allow it. Only leading troops, not being part of them."

"I was a soldier."

He sighed again. "I know."

The door opened to admit the most beautiful sight Dominic had clapped eyes on for more than a day. His wife. She appeared disheveled. Her red-gold hair stood out like a halo around her head, the shadows under her eyes pronounced. But she was alive, and as far as he could see, unharmed.

She saw him and took off. It would have taken more than Val and Alconbury to stop her flying across the room into his arms. Dominic held her tight, and when Val came closer, handed him his pistol. An accidental discharge would not do at this stage.

The Pretender stayed in his chair.

Alconbury stood by the mantelpiece, leaned against the wall, and folded his arms. "We are excused, then?" he said. "You may safely leave matters to me. I have a ship waiting at the Pool of London. I fear we may have to leave tonight."

"My men?" Stuart asked.

"Asleep, sir. They will remain so for a while. They were my father's men. He was joining you in this attempt?" He didn't sound pleased. Clearly, he and his father were in disagreement over this strategy.

The Pretender merely met his gaze and said, "They are loyalists. To the true King and his family." He didn't look at Dominic, who was cradling his wife close, uncaring about any other matters.

"We are leaving for the country in the morning," he said. "I'll have no arguments."

"Yes, my lord," she said meekly.

Chapter 20

It had taken two days for Lord St. Just and his bride to reach the private house he owned, set like a jewel in the lush countryside of Leicestershire. Dominic had not allowed Claudia to lift a finger for herself, despite her assuring him that she had come to no harm. She had been kept captive in a comfortable, if small bedroom, fed adequately, and they had not threatened her. They had not needed to. She didn't tell him that part, where Charles Stuart had calmly told her that he meant to kill her if her husband didn't appear soon. That he meant to kill her husband when he arrived.

That had terrified her. She'd rather they beat and starved her. The man had told her with such detached calmness that she had to believe him. She had no idea how Dominic had changed the mind of the Young Pretender, but somehow he had, and they had come away free and clear. Only to find London thinning of company and the weather decidedly sunnier.

Dominic had pampered her. At first, realizing that he needed to spoil her, to reassure himself that she was not hurt, she let him. She recognized that he needed to take care of her. He'd exclaimed over the very small bruise on the back of her head where the abductor had struck her, tucked her into bed, and refused to join her.

She wanted him badly, at least to hold her, but after the first day she wanted more. He had driven her screaming mad by his refusal to listen. He made calm arrangements and lifted her into the carriage as if she were a damned invalid. She had allowed him his way, her savior.

Besides, two inns they stopped at, while perfectly adequate, offered little in the way of privacy. She could hear every snore of the man in the bed next to their room on the first night. She had no mind to try to seduce him with an audience nearby.

When they arrived at the house, she'd insisted on seeing it. Then Dominic had kindly suggested that she might like to retire to bed for a while. At first ready to protest, Claudia had another thought. "Yes, I would," she said. "I'd like to wash the grime of the road off first. Could I order a bath?"

"This is your house as much as it is mine, my love. You must order whatever you wish."

She went up to the charming bedroom with the wide bay window that looked out over the neat park attached to the house. The servants brought up a French enameled bath and poured the contents of numerous water cans into it. With the water steaming and the towels laid ready, she allowed her maid to undress her and stepped into the tub.

When her maid would have picked up the big sponge to wash her, she stopped her. "No, let me relax for a few moments." She met the woman's gaze directly. "If my husband asks for me, tell him I am ready to receive him. I wish him to think I am in bed."

If her maid had not been so well trained, she would probably have smiled. Claudia caught the ghost of her amusement in her grey eyes.

She bobbed a curtsey. "Very well, my lady." The maid quietly left the room.

Claudia waited for ten minutes and was just making up her mind that Dominic wasn't coming, when the door opened and he entered. After a muffled exclamation, he backed up, but she was too fast for him.

"No, come here. I need someone to wash my back for me."

With a winsome smile, she held out the sponge. He swore, and then he swore again, but very low, under his breath, as if he thought she wouldn't hear. "You will be the death of me."

"I sincerely pray I will not. Who will catch me when I fall from my horse?"

He snorted. "You have the best seat of any woman I've ever seen."

"Who will stop me getting into appalling scrapes at balls and making indiscreet comments?"

"People love you for it." He came forward and took the sponge. "Those who do not?" He snapped his fingers. "That for them."

Then he proceeded to get his revenge. He washed her very, very thoroughly. He rubbed the soap on the sponge and passed it over her back with such a gentle touch he barely roused her senses. Only just, but with a thoroughness that made her gasp. Then he gently urged her back against the towels draped over the tub to soften and warm her and treated her front with the same kind of detailed attention. He lifted her left breast and ensured the fold beneath was clean, making her gasp with longing. He cupped the curve of it and held it steady while he washed and rinsed it. Then he did the same to her right breast. He took care over her navel was clean, moving close to study it. Then he skimmed past her cleft to wash her legs, calves, ankles, between each toe to come back up and finally wash her thighs.

By then she was shuddering with need.

He abandoned the sponge and leaned over to kiss her. Not one of the sweet, loving kisses of the last few days, but a ravaging, conquering kiss, the kind that laid waste to her senses.

Curling her hand around his neck, she tried to drag him closer, into the water if necessary, but he resisted her easily. He stroked down her stomach and between her legs. He eased her inner lips apart to reach the sensitive skin inside and gave it to the same thorough treatment. "Dominic please…" Her voice trailed off in a shivering gasp.

"Let me do this. Let me touch you." His voice was deep and not entirely steady. Dominic probed her skin, slid his fingers just inside her opening and then up to her pearl, to pinch and tease her into hardness. At the same time, he marauded her mouth, claiming it for his own with slick glides of his tongue.

Neither cared when, as he lifted her, a sheet of water landed on the carpet. He grabbed one of the towels lying on a chair nearby, tucked it around her, and carried her to the bed. For once she didn't care if he wouldn't allow her to walk. Once there, he kept his burning gaze fixed on her while he undressed. To think this man had once been the neatest she had ever met.

Dominic tossed his clothes to the carpet, and climbed into bed with her, his shaft satisfactorily hard. She grabbed it when he was with her, glorying at its erect potency and the softness of the skin that covered it.

"Claudia, I meant to let you rest for a week. I want you, my love. Every way I can have you. I want you like this." Instead of climbing over her, he sat cross-legged on the sheets. "Come to me."

Arousal rising in her like a living thing, Claudia went. She sat as he instructed her, her legs over his, their bodies meeting. They both watched as he entered her body.

"A miracle," she said, but wasn't aware of saying it out loud until he agreed.

They moved together, and she understood why he wanted her this way. This was equality, togetherness, both exerting the same effort to bring joy to the other. His happiness was more important to her than hers was, and she knew without him telling her that he felt the same way.

His shaft lay deep in her, and when he touched her, he sent her up and up until she flew. Her body turned into living flame as she moved on him.

She took him as deeply as she could. His voice sounded increasingly hoarse as he cried her name. Then with one rough cry, he came in jagged, uncontrolled jerks, taking him with her, triggering her peak.

Panting, laughing, they lay down, and he drew a sheet over them, for the evening was warm and they needed no more than that.

"I love you," she said, totally unnecessarily.

But he seemed to take pleasure from her saying it and repeated the sentiment before kissing her with tender lasciviousness.

"You are and always will be the love of my life," he said. "Also the thorn in my side and my exasperation. I will never know what you plan next, will I?"

"Probably not. May we go riding tomorrow? I want to see the estate."

"I thought we already went riding. I may not let you out of this bed for a week." He laughed and kissed her. "You are adorable, you know that? I love that you never hide your expression from me. Sweetheart, you may have anything you choose. Ask me for anything."

"How about the throne?" she said, secure in the knowledge that he would take the statement as frivolously as she made it. Few people understood her sometimes rash statements, but this man did. He always would.

He kissed her once more. "I'd rather be an emperor than a king."

That was the perfect answer.

Meet the Author

Lynne Connolly was born in Leicester, England, and lived in her family's cobbler's shop with her parents and sister. She loves all periods of history, but her favorites are the Tudor and Georgian eras. She loves doing research and creating a credible story with people who lived in past ages. In addition to her Emperors of London series she writes several historical, contemporary and paranormal romance series. Visit her on the web at lynneconnolly.com, read her blog: lynneconnolly.blogspot.co.uk, find her on Facebook, and follow her on Twitter @lynneconnolly.

Keep reading for a special sneak peek of the first Emperors of London novel

Temptation Has Green Eyes

There's more to love than meets the eye...

The daughter of a wealthy merchant, Sophia Russell has no interest in marriage, especially after a recent humiliation—and especially not to Maximilian, Marquess of Devereaux. But it's the only way to save herself from fortune hunters—and those who wish to seize a powerful connection she prefers to keep secret—even from her future husband...

Marrying Sophia is the only way Max can regain the wealth his father squandered on an extravagant country palace. And while Max and his bride are civil, theirs is clearly a marriage of convenience—until a family enemy takes a questionable interest in Sophia—one that may lead all the way to the throne. Forced to become allies in a battle they hadn't foreseen, the newlyweds soon grow closer—and discover a love, and a passion, they never expected...

A Lyrical e-book on sale now!

Learn more about Lynne at
http://www.kensingtonbooks.com/book.aspx/31122

Chapter 1

Maximilian Wallace, Marquess of Devereaux, strode through London's crowded streets, feeling completely at home. With the dexterity of a seasoned Londoner, Max dodged past an urchin who appeared determined to collide with him—and probably relieve him of his purse at the same time. That boy's Wednesday haul would be absent one fine linen kerchief and a purse heavy with guineas.

Max reached his destination and flattened his palm over the weathered paint of the door to Lloyd's coffee house. As he shoved it open, he breathed in the intoxicating fragrance of coffee and tobacco.

A group of men sat in the worn leather-upholstered chairs by the fire, puffing on long-stemmed churchwarden pipes. More sat at the long, plain tables, making deals that would cause even a duke to gulp. Max had made many in his time.

This place had been part of Max's life since he'd attained the age of sixteen and discovered the state of the family's finances.

Spotting the man he'd come to meet, Max made his way past the tables and cubicles to the one Thomas Russell occupied, in the corner, where they wouldn't be overheard. Men nodded to him and he returned the acknowledgement. He was well known here, despite his title, not because of it. Men of the City had little time for aristocrats. He liked the busy hum of people doing business. Lloyd's was the center for insurance and shipping matters and as such could get very noisy at times. Not today. Obviously, no large ships or cargoes were in dispute.

Russell stood as Max approached. He was smiling broadly, his round, apparently guileless face displaying nothing but bonhomie and pleasure. That was part of his danger. Max had been trying to work with Russell for years but had never before gathered the capital to make an investment of this size and importance. With this deal, Max would become an insurer in his own right. His fortune would expand beyond anything he'd achieved, his future secure. So much was balanced on this transaction that he was keyed up beyond the level he considered possible. Not that he allowed any of it to show.

Max went on guard at Russell's words. When Russell showed that untroubled, smiling face, he had something on his mind. A twist in the deal?

Mentally, Max went through the complicated contract he knew by heart. They'd made a few tiny amendments, none of which threatened to wreck this agreement, and that was all. Nothing. But this man was planning something. Russell hadn't climbed the tree to become one of the wealthiest men in the precious square mile known as the City of London by being pleasant to everyone.

Russell was in many ways the epitome of the City businessman. Dressed in sober, though excellent, clothes, today of russet brown with spotlessly clean linen and a simple bob-wig, he was neither this nor that, neither ostentatious nor puritanical. Keeping a steady course between all factions had gone a long way to his success. His shining face spoke both of his attention to cleanliness and the heat in this place. Whatever the temperature outside, it was never cold in Lloyd's, due to the huge fire kept burning well into April and the hot air rising from the discussions.

A waiting-woman approached him. Max gave her a friendly smile and asked for tea. No women were allowed here except for the serving girls and the lady sitting behind the desk by the door, where the customers paid before they left. Knowing the caliber of some of the women in the City, Max wondered that none of them had stormed the citadel before. Perhaps they disliked tobacco smoke. Or preferred to use agents, as many of the City's other investments did.

Max had always conducted his business for himself. Just as well, since he couldn't afford an agent when he first started to make deals at the tender age of seventeen. He'd had to use the estate trustees to commission the actual business and sign the documents until he came of age. Now, partly due to the man who took a seat at the table across from him, he could afford much more. He was as wealthy as anyone in this room, and that was saying something.

He waited on events. One thing Max had learned over the years was the value of silence.

"You were concerned about the quantity of barrels on the lower deck?" Russell queried.

Right to business. Max settled into the final discussions. "I thought we could get more in if we stacked them deeper into the hull."

Russell nodded. "It's possible, but not advisable, although when you brought the matter up, I did speak to the captain of the fleet. Apparently it would unbalance the disposition of the cargo."

Max agreed to let that part of the contract stay as it was. He dug in the inside pocket of his olive-green coat for his account book and flipped through the well-worn pages until he reached the one he needed.

The coffee house kept a bottle of ink and pens on every table for that purpose, the ink invariably gritty and the pens often blunt. It made a mark, and that was all Max required.

The girl delivered his tea. He picked it up and took a sip.

They worked through the other matters swiftly. This contract would involve a fleet of six ships with varied cargo. They'd insure them all, and Max had some investment in the cargo, too.

A failure at this stage wouldn't ruin him as it might have at the beginning of his City career, but it meant a great deal. Success would finally boost him to the heights he'd been aiming for right from the beginning.

Light at heart, he finished his tea and prepared to leave to sign the contracts. Probably in triplicate, at least.

"A moment," Russell murmured.

Max's mood plummeted to his well-shod feet. He hadn't been wrong then. Russell had suggested Lloyd's because he wanted to discuss something else. "You have another caveat?"

Russell shook his head. "Not precisely. Hear me out, if you please."

"I'm very happy with the business as it stands, sir." Would be happier after they'd signed. "Is this a fresh agreement?" His heart lifted at the prospect. More business would only prove better, especially with this man.

"This is, I hope, the first of many contracts between us. Our methods suit and our processes are similar. We work well together."

Max said nothing, but nodded. He agreed completely. Russell was so wealthy Max suspected even the man himself didn't know how much he was worth. Max had the prestige and the contacts to find new opportunities, which benefited everyone. The burgeoning wealth of the men in the City with the new worlds they were opening could only be good for the country. This association with Thomas Russell was the start of many such contracts. He didn't doubt that for a minute.

Was the man suggesting a more formal association? A jointly owned company? Despite his determination to remain focused, Max breathed deeply to quell his excitement at the prospect. His fingertips tingled.

Under the table, he pressed them together. He forced a slight smile to his lips. "I, too, look forward to the day when we may work together again."

"I'm gratified that you would think so." Russell waved, flicking his hand in a gesture of dismissal.

Max turned his head. The serving girl retreated. A private matter, then. His heart in his mouth, he waited to hear what Russell had in mind.

The wily man bent nearer, speaking lower. "I have worked hard to build a business my descendants can be proud of."

Russell was a widower with one child, a girl. Max had met Sophia Russell a time or two but taken little notice of the self-effacing, cool woman.

So Russell wanted a more permanent association. Perhaps a company that would give his daughter a good amount of money. Enough to net herself a husband.

Max needed Russell to speak clearer, but he didn't know the man well enough to demand clarification straight out. "You've done much. You have a great deal to be proud of."

"So do you." Russell fixed him with a clear gaze. "I've worked hard to make the business my father entrusted to my care even greater. When it became obvious I would have no more children of my own, I expected to find a youth I could train, who would take over when I was gone. I found one and set matters in place. I was also considering marrying him to Sophia. She liked him well enough. He was an intelligent young man, presentable and bright who would continue the business after I'm gone."

His face changed to heavy-jowled depression, his mouth turning hard and his eyes to chips of flint. "Unfortunately, the man I chose did not prove suitable after all." He paused. "He was—untrustworthy."

Had this person endangered Russell's business? Was it safe to invest with him any longer?

"He attempted to…seduce my daughter before I'd given him permission to approach her."

"*Seduce*?" Max snapped. Had the man offered violence to Sophia? Violence to any woman was anathema to any decent man. He glanced around. Nobody sat within listening distance, but still… "Why meet here to discuss such a personal matter?"

Russell rubbed his forehead. "Sophia is at home to visitors today. The house is full of her guests. Today at least, I have considerably more privacy here than at home. I need my daughter married, and soon."

No, oh no. Not that. Surely Russell wouldn't want that.

Russell spread his hands, indicating the company. Men chatted, busy about their own concerns, uninterested in the doings of two of the regular customers. Whereas, if he visited Russell's home during an at home day, gossip would spread.

If Russell took him to his office, showed him favor, he would be bound to go through with it to save face. However, if either of them walked away here, in the coffee house, nobody would consider it amiss. Gossip was the very devil.

If he wanted this business—and he did, so badly he could taste it—he'd have to take the daughter. His head whirled. He needed time to think this over. Time he didn't have, because this wily old fox had arranged it that way.

He could always ask more about the situation. "So tell me," he said, careful to keep his voice low. "What did you do with this man?"

"I sent him away." The older man's pale eyes sharpened. He lifted his coffee cup to his lips and then put it down, the rim rattling against the table. It was already empty. "Unfortunately he spread a rumor that Sophia had seduced *him.* And succeeded in persuading some. It has besmirched her reputation in certain circles."

So he was being asked to take on soiled goods. As long as the chit wasn't pregnant, he would at least consider the possibility. But for Russell, marrying his daughter to a peer of the realm was a leap up the social scale.

"I haven't heard it." But then, Max didn't move in the social milieu of the City. He attended dinners and other functions at the Guildhall, but no more than that.

"Good. I had considered leaving my business solely to Sophia when I die. She's a clever woman, and it's not unknown for women to run businesses."

The worm on the end of the hook. Take Sophia, take the business. A very juicy worm. Max would be an idiot if the prospect didn't tempt him.

Max quirked his lips. "I'm not unaware of that, sir. The company that provides much of my silverware is run by a woman." He had no objection to a female running a business. Max never denied the truth when it presented itself as such.

Russell heaved a sigh. "I could provide her with the structure she needs. A woman cannot come to a place like this, but her prestige would mean that they would go to her. My man of business is solidly reliable, as is my chief clerk, my shipping agent, and so on." He leaned back, touched his cup, glanced up, and leaned forward again. "The recent incident has convinced me that I'm placing her in a dangerous position. She will be a woman of considerable substance. Fortune hunters will abound. They do now, but she doesn't encourage them. Already, rumors are spreading, thanks to the despicable youth whose name I will not mention."

He sighed and spread his hands in a gesture of helplessness. "Despite the recent marriage laws, wealthy young women are still abducted and forcibly wed. The rumors have weakened Sophia's position, and the vultures are gathering. I need her married to a man I can trust, and it must happen quickly."

Max didn't like the way this conversation was going, but at least Russell seemed to be putting his cards on the table. But did he have an ace shoved up his sleeve? "Could you not find a good man for your daughter? One she could rely on to stay out of the way of the business?"

"A cipher you mean?" Russell shook his head. "Sophia would never stand for that. Neither would I. Once she marries, what is hers belongs to her husband, and what I have will come to her in the fullness of time. There are few men who would resist the challenge to take control."

Max breathed more easily. This was a business proposition like any other. "So who do you have in mind?" A notion occurred to him. "Do you wish Sophia introduced into society so she can find a husband of her own?"

Russell shook his head. "She did that once. She didn't take. You may not be aware of this, but my late wife was Lady Mary Howard of Lancashire. She had a certain cachet in several circles. But there was some dispute, and my wife preferred not to acknowledge her family."

Some dispute? What on earth did that mean? Sophia was still a cit, and some members of society were unreasonably prejudiced against men of the City of London. However Sophia could enter society, and her mother's connections would satisfy all but the highest sticklers. "I can certainly help you there. My mother, my sister, could introduce her."

"No need." Russell clamped his mouth shut and stared at Max.

How the hell did he get out of this? He ached to continue the association with Russell, but enough to marry his daughter? Marriage didn't figure in his plans, not for years yet. Or hadn't until just now.

A pair of crease lines appeared between Russell's brows. "While I appreciate your offer, the recent incident has disturbed me more than I'd like. Introducing her to society, finding her a husband would all take too long. In any case, I know my Sophia. Her charms aren't obvious to many, and she may not have the skills to shine." His lips tightened. "She tried. She had her come-out, her mother made sure of that, but Sophia doesn't have the… She's not accomplished."

"You told me that she was." What was Russell was trying to say? She wanted a teacher? Perhaps his cousin Helena could help. She had taken Alex Ripley's beloved under her wing, so successfully that the lady was now Lady Ripley. Or maybe his mother and his sister Poppea, known in the family as Poppy, would agree to take Sophia in hand. "You mean she needs some town bronze?"

The frown disappeared and Russell laughed outright. He glanced around as someone approached them, but their combined stares saw him off. The man quickly turned tail and turned around.

"No." Russell turned back to Max. "She's been on the town all her life. Here's my proposition, and it's as businesslike as any other we've undertaken or are likely to make. You're young, you're wealthy, and you're as honest as any businessman I've ever met. I observed you for some time before I agreed to work with you, and I've been very pleased with our dealings together so far. I want you for Sophia. Wait—"

As Max would have spoken, Russell held up his gnarled hand. Max remained silent.

"My Sophia deserves the best. You could take my company and make it the biggest in the City of London, which means in the world."

Staggered, Max was lost for words. He closed his mouth with a snap. Russell continued with his proposal.

"If you agree to do this, I'll make you my heir. It will be part of the marriage settlement." He leaned back, his attention fixed on Max. "It's a good offer."

Just as if he was offering another business deal, which, to all intents and purposes, he was. Except it involved far more personal relations than any other business deal would. Was Max ready to let a woman into his well-ordered life?

The sound of the coffee house continued as if Max's world hadn't spun on its axis. The buzz of conversation went on around them, punctuated by occasional shout or laugh. Normal life revolved around him as he fought to get his thoughts into some kind of order.

"Sophia will make you an excellent marchioness."

About to refuse outright, Max paused, staring at the man who had made such an outrageous offer. A cit to a marquess. But an extremely wealthy cit to a previously impoverished marquess. His title hadn't put food on the table; his business acumen had done that.

If he wanted a wife, Sophia was the kind of woman he'd be looking for, rather than a society maiden fresh out of the schoolroom. She had business acumen, and she was attractive enough, from what he'd seen of her.

And the inducement—mouthwatering. He could give his mother her life back and continue with his own. After all, he knew hardly anyone whose marriage hadn't been arranged. What was this but another one?

What was he thinking? Max had always sworn to avoid the arranged marriage. He wanted to choose his wife for himself. But if he agreed to this, he'd have everything he ever wanted, not just for himself, but for his mother and his sister, Poppy. Not such a sacrifice. And many married couples lived completely separate lives. His heart sank and his stomach hollowed. Above all things he wanted a harmonious home, someone he could build a life with. But love—he didn't want that. Bile rose to his throat. Not for him, never.

Russell tapped one finger on the table, bringing Max back to attention. "Walk back some of the way with me."

Max accompanied Russell to the offices of his man of business, where his own would be waiting in a very different frame of mind to the one he'd expected. Not happy with a job well done, but in complete turmoil. Marry? He tipped back his head, sucking down as much fresh air as this crowded part of London afforded, trying to shake some sense into it.

Russell remained mainly silent during the short journey, giving Max a chance to settle his whirling thoughts.

Without a husband and with the gossips busy circulating the stories spread by her erstwhile suitor, Sophia would be a target for every unscrupulous fortune-hunter in the country. But no respectable men. Her reputation would be wrecked by the man she'd refused.

Russell's wealth ensured that she'd find *someone*. Max could induce his mother to introduce her. But the kind of society his family moved in contained more fortune hunters than anywhere else, because it also contained some of the wealthiest and best connected people in the country. Mercenary and vicious, they'd quell Sophia, mistreat her, and waste her fortune. Several of that breed had attached themselves to Poppy, or tried to, before Max or another of his male relatives had seen them off. Without that protection, Sophia would be achingly vulnerable.

Max wasn't the only man left with little fortune and a huge monstrosity of a house to care for. Many men would be glad of Sophia's wealth to shore up their ailing finances. They'd care for her, too. Not all fortune hunters were heartless.

But that wouldn't help his business. Max could help Sophia find someone suitable, but that would distance him from the business he'd worked so hard to connect with.

They walked past other coffee houses with businesses as thriving as Lloyd's—Tom's with its clutch of men looking for women to pass the time with. A house that infuriated the magistrates at Bow Street because no actual illegal acts ever took place on the premises.

Then they passed the theater at Drury Lane, its doors currently closed pending the evening's performances, and turned the corner, away from Seven Dials. Nobody went that way unless they had some criminal business to pursue. They passed several tall buildings lining the narrow streets with columns of brass plaques outside, indicating the concerns based there.

Normally Max would be reveling in the place, in the variety and the exhibition of life in all its variations, but this time he only noted the familiar landmarks without thought. His mind was occupied with one thing. Sophia. A pretty girl, and one who answered sensibly when addressed, but not someone who quickened his heart or had attracted much of his attention. No sense of excitement or anticipation when he'd seen her, which was rarely.

Was she avoiding him? He didn't think so. Perhaps she was as reticent with everyone she met. That didn't augur well for Sophia as a society lady. Reticence would be considered bad breeding, nothing more.

Children of Max's station were bred to expect people to stare at them and single them out. They should not avoid that task. Otherwise it could be regarded as bad manners. Would Sophia make a good marchioness? The reticence didn't indicate that.

Before they reached their destination, Max recommenced discussing the problem with Russell. They were moving too fast and with too much purpose for anyone to catch more than a few words in passing, so they were as private here as at the discreet corner table at Lloyd's. "Do you intend Sophia to continue the business after she marries, or will you expect her to withdraw from commercial life?"

Russell laughed as he dodged a dark pool of something unpleasantly liquid. Since it hadn't rained for a day or so, it was unlikely to be water. "I'd consider any man who chose not to consult her an idiot. She knows the various enterprises as well as I do. It's sheer madness to ignore expertise in whatever guise it appears, male or female."

Relief flooded him. She was an intelligent woman, then. "Why the hurry to hand over your business? You, sir, are in your prime." He assumed Russell to be around fifty. His vigor and mental acuity pointed to a lack of extreme age.

Russell raised a brow. "Thank you for that. It's time I took life at a more leisurely pace."

Did he have a health problem? The lines of his face and the gnarled hands were probably from Russell's early years on board ship, where he made his first fortune. But perhaps the lines were deeper, the eyes a little less clear.

"My daughter is twenty-four. She needs a husband, one who will care for her and ensure she comes to no harm. And you are the best candidate. My lord," he added as if an afterthought.

In fact, Max's colleague was reminding him of his exalted title and station. True, he could enhance Russell's business merely by being a peer of the realm.

He could finally restore the house. His parents had spent all their money and lavished their love on the house in the country. Devereaux House had been a large establishment, suitable for a marquess's main residence, and his parents had enlarged it still further. Now it was packed with treasures, beautified, and redesigned.

His land steward had loftily informed Max that the house contained as many rooms as there were days in the year. The news appalled Max. How could anyone live in a monstrosity that size? Now the place belonged to him, or more precisely, had devolved to him with the entail on the land. He couldn't sell it. He never went there.

After his father's death, Max had closed and shuttered the place, retaining a skeleton staff to keep the house clear of the pests that might damage the treasures. Even that had cost him more than he could afford.

His mother had adored her husband, and therefore she adored the house, too. Not that she lived there. That was a constant needle in Max's side. His mother should have her house back.

With Russell's fortune, starting with the no doubt generous settlement that would come with Sophia, he could do it. Restore the parts that had suffered during his time as owner and give it back to her.

And he wanted to give his sister something more than she had now. Poppy deserved better. Because she was a single female, she had to live with her mother, which meant sharing the peripatetic life the dowager Lady Devereaux led these days.

Poppy should have a proper London season with the clothes to match. But when a lace petticoat cost more than a ship's captain could earn in half a year, that was difficult. Had been difficult.

Now Max could afford it, but he still needed a chaperone for Poppy. Somebody like—a wife.

He kept coming back to the inevitable topic. The walk only served to firm his resolve, which Russell probably knew since he kept quiet for most of it. A good businessman knew when to keep his tongue between his teeth.

They halted outside the office. Did he go in or not? Would he accept this agreement?

He had no choice.

Russell had dropped his daughter on Max like a woodcutter felling an oak tree.

"In principle, I agree to both your propositions," he said as calmly as he could. "Shall we?" Courteously he let the older man enter the building first and followed up the narrow stairway leading to the busy solicitor's office, the clerk with half a dozen quills stuck in his hair waving them on with only a small bow of acknowledgement.

All through the discussion of the various documents that put the agreement in place, Max's mind kept drifting elsewhere. Every time he hit upon an objection to the marriage, a reasonable solution popped into his mind.

Now he'd regained his fortune, women would start chasing him. He'd seen it happen to other men. Now his turn had arrived. Some mysterious scent, like trailing a corpse for the hounds affected men of title, wealth, and enough youth not to repel. No, forget the last one, Max had seen eighty-year-old dukes fall for the wiles of a twenty-year-old woman.

Hell and damnation, he'd never had this difficulty making up his mind.

Yes, damn it, he'd do it. He nodded when Mr. Fisk hesitated. "Go on. I daresay the marriage settlement is here?"

His own man of business shot him a startled look. Max gave him a beatific smile in return. The original contract agreed upon, they settled to discussing the marriage contract and its ramifications.

So Sophia was four-and-twenty? He had thought her younger. That changed his perspective on his colleague's proposal because he'd never been in favor of marrying chits straight out of the schoolroom. He'd never had the luxury of a childhood or the customary Grand Tour that young men of his status generally undertook before settling into what passed for ordinary life. Max had little in common with the brats he'd been introduced to and found more conducive conversation with older women, who'd seen a little more and expected a lot less.

He had to force himself to concentrate on the signing. He never signed a contract without reading it through just before he signed, in case the other party had tried to slip something in, hoping he wouldn't notice. He *always* noticed.

Today he could have been signing his soul away to the devil. He tried, but couldn't concentrate.

He hovered his pen over the other contract, the one binding him for life to a woman he hardly knew. And had a brainwave. "I cannot sign this without the other party present."

"Of course," Russell said smoothly. "But we can have it ready for Sophia to sign. You can sign your part now."

Max tested the proposal, considered the aspects of tying himself to someone for life. If the personal association didn't work, they would always have the business one.

When Max made a decision, he didn't delay. He preferred to see the matter through swiftly and efficiently. As far as he was concerned, the matter was set aside to be filed with a blue ribbon, his office code for "Done."

He signed the document in the requisite places with a few sure slashes of the pen. Then, with a smile, he returned them to their men of business to arrange the copies and the filing.

He'd leave telling his mother until tomorrow.

CPSIA information can be obtained
at www.ICGtesting.com
Printed in the USA
FSOW02n1323070816
23521FS